I0656729

Frances Ridley Havergal

Swiss Letters and Alpine Poems

Frances Ridley Havergal

Swiss Letters and Alpine Poems

ISBN/EAN: 9783743320109

Manufactured in Europe, USA, Canada, Australia, Japa

Cover: Foto ©Andreas Hilbeck / pixelio.de

Manufactured and distributed by brebook publishing software
(www.brebook.com)

Frances Ridley Havergal

Swiss Letters and Alpine Poems

PREFATORY NOTE.

THE world-wide interest excited by the writings and "Memorials" of my lamented sister, FRANCES RIDLEY HAVERGAL, has led her family to think that such of her letters as I have been able to collect, written to her home circle from Switzerland, will be acceptable to her many admirers.

Some will feel pleasure in mentally revisiting the sublime scenery she describes with such vigour and simplicity; and others will be interested in observing how unconsciously these letters illustrate her enthusiastic nature, her practical ability, and her ardent desire that every one should share her earthly pleasures and her heavenly aspirations.

JANE MIRIAM CRANE.

OAKHAMPTON, NEAR STOURPORT,
October 20, 1881.

CONTENTS.

SWISS LETTERS.

I.

ENCYCLICAL LETTER,

Specially for the Benefit of Maria, Ellen, and Frank.

May 31, 1869.

AFTER raining and roaring all Friday, and nearly all Saturday, the weather smiled out on Sunday, and promised for a beautiful passage on Monday, so we started from Dover this morning in good spirits. I have no notion of waiting till I am too ill to stir before making myself comfortable; so I made a regular nest in the lee of a deck cabin with a shawl for a mattress, carpet-bag for pillow, pile of tarpaulin for back rest, hat off, and cape of waterproof over my head and pinned under my chin in sister-of-mercy-looking style. Then I lay down, and as rain seemed imminent was covered with a tarpaulin all but my nose.

"You will be walked over, Fanny," says M. L. C.; "you don't look like a human being!" H. C. did not look much more like one I opined, for he was cased in a tarpaulin coat down to his heels, with a hood which stuck up in two stiff points, leaving little of his physiognomy visible but his venerable beard.

So we joked each other for the first half hour, which was in all senses smooth sailing; then sleep was suggested; then kind inquiries were exchanged; after that, silence; after that, well, we won't talk about it, as it does not belong to the pleasures of memory.

Poor J. M. C.! "Is that lady going to die?" asks H. C. of the steward.

"Oh dear no, sir; not yet awhile," says he; "but you'd much better have all sat still up here."

"In ten minutes, sir," says the steward. That keeps up our spirits; sea trials can be borne that long. But a quarter of an hour passes, and we ask again. "Not much longer now, sir; ten minutes or so will take us in." So we get unbelieving and give up asking. At last we *are* in, and happier in mind and body, rather!

A most uninteresting rail ride, leaving Calais 1.15, arriving at Brussels 6.30. Hotel de l'Europe, in Place Royale. Table d'hôte speedily, at which we chattered with a Swiss gentleman, who "could afford to be generous," as M. said, and praised the Rhine astonishingly, far more than I could, who have only Scotland to compare it with.

After this, the lady who was "going to die" in the morning proposed going out to see what could be seen in the lovely evening light; so the three went, and I stayed to rest. For this piece of prudence I had a reward. Very soon a pleasant Belgian maid came in, with her white frilled cap tied under her chin. She asked if I was not well, seeing me on the sofa. I explained that I had had a long journey from England. She asked how it was that England was all surrounded by water ; she had heard so, but could never understand it. My explanation led on to more talk, and she told me of a fearful illness she had last year when "la maladie" was raging in Brussels. This was a nice opportunity to speak of Him who "healeth all our diseases." She seemed thoughtful, and so interested that she stayed talking half an hour. She told me how near death she had been ; she did not know it at the time, but when she had since thought of it, "that one must die, and all alone,—" and she finished the sentence with a most expressive shuddering gesture. Evidently she felt the ceremonies of her church were not enough to give peace in death, nor in life either ; for when I appealed to the feeling, certain to exist even if denied, that the heart is not filled, that it has a craving for *something* that is always at the bottom *unsatisfied*, even when things are smoothest and brightest, she looked almost startled at hearing her feeling put into words, and said most sadly and earnestly : "*Mais oui, mais oui, mademoiselle, mais c'est vrai, cela!*" She promised me that she would pray for the Holy Spirit. Poor girl! she will have no earthly teacher. After she was gone I marked all I most wanted her to notice in a French St. John's Gospel, and gave it her next morning. She seemed pleased, and promised to read it. In marking it I was struck with what I have so often felt, viz, that when one reads any part of the Bible with anything special in view, it is wonderful how much seems to bear on the particular subject, as if written on purpose. So it was that every chapter seemed full of just the very teaching poor Victorine needed, the satisfied thirst, the promise of eternal life, the teaching of the Holy Spirit, and all through "Jesus only," all pointing to Him and to none other for peace and salvation.

June 1. FROM BRUSSELS TO OBERCASSEL.

We had no sunshine for the lovely Verdre valley, but the evening was exquisite. H. C. and the others stayed to see Aix and Cologne, while I went on to see Fraulein Krämer, at Bonn, where papa stayed the winter. They were heartily delighted to see any one who could bring news of him, "the best man in the whole world, so through and through good, who had left a blessing which had rested on their house ever since." Then I walked down to the Rhine ; the stream was very full and strong, and the colouring vivid as we left Bonn ; the Rhine a delicate silver blue, the east bank golden green, houses and walls almost scarlet in the evening glow ; then beyond the low sunny shore rose the Seven Mountains in deep cloud shadow, soft dark blue sharply outlined against the pale clear sky. As we neared Obercassel, the red rocks of the Rabenlei caught the last of the sunshine.

The pastor was waiting for me, and in a few minutes I was besieged by eight of his olive branches (by way of mixing up peace and war !). I went to bed at ten ; but we had talk enough to fill a book, so as I cannot record all, I shall record none.

June 2. OBERCASSEL.

Of course I have had the whole history of the war from a Prussian point of view.* The gist of it is that

---

* This was the Austro-Prussian war of 1866, which terminated at Sadowa.

Prussia had no alternative but to allow itself to *be put upon* and *sink*, or to *put upon others* and *rise*, and that it was only natural to choose the latter. Denmark was a naughty, obstinate child, which must be punished ; Hanover, ditto. Pastor S. says that all the strength and patriotism of Prussia lies in its Protestantism ; that the Catholics are an absolute drag upon both, sympathizing openly when they dare, but secretly always and everywhere, with Austria.

In the afternoon we drove to Heisterbach, a lovely ruined apse of a monastery in a little glen on the south side of the Seven Mountains. It was quite warm enough for the usual German plan of taking coffee under the trees. Here we had a talk over church matters. The pastor's impression is that the great rationalistic vein is being rapidly worked through in Germany, and that the ferment is nearly over; that in this respect the English are a few years behind, and are now giving more weight to German theology than the Germans themselves are doing. Then we had a stroll through the beech woods, poor Theodor keeping up with us on his crutches. He has had a year of terrible suffering, ending in amputation ; he is expecting his new leg this week, and hopes to return to the university in the autumn. He is a first rate *student-specimen*, full of fun, and no end of snatches of all sorts of songs *apropos* of everything, yet with abundance of talent and sense and feeling beneath it. His father read me a touchingly beautiful little poem which he had written on his last birthday in the midst of his suffering.*

The girls sing all day long, with various fraternal ac-

---

* Dear Theodor fell asleep in Jesus after several weeks' great suffering, in January, 1870.

companiments. I heard Agnes singing simply magnificently, and on going to her found her preparing some young potatoes in a basin on her lap all the time, while Theodor was playing for her! It was characteristic. She sings very like Sarah Conolly, and with great spirit and expression. My godchild, Adelheid, has not yet had lessons, but sings numbers of duets and trios very nicely.

After supper the pastor read us " Otto von Schütz," a Rhine poem by Kinkel. We worked, and Theodor, Paul, and Franz sat in great delight, listening to their favourite poet. These young Schulzeberges all follow their father's tastes, and enter into everything poetical, musical, and intellectual, most eagerly. They are exceedingly attached to each other and to home; in this respect they are a perfectly ideal family. Agnes told me that Hermann's distress at spending his first Christmas away from home was something grievous, and Paul is already dreading his own possible absence next Christmas.

June 3. OBERCASSEL TO BINGEN.

Coffee at 7.30, then the household assembled for prayers. First we sang my favourite chorale of years ago, "Ach, bleib mit deiner Gnade"; then all sit with folded hands and slightly bent heads while the pastor reads a verse or two and a short comment, something like Bogatzky. This is generally all, only on special occasions, birthdays or festivals, is it followed by prayer. But this morning the pastor closed the book and folded his hands and prayed; we all remain sitting, only the head is bent a little lower and the eyes closed. Such a sweet, loving, earnest prayer it was, specially asking abundant blessing both for the present journey and for the whole journey of life, "for her who has again filled our house with grateful joy": these dear Schulzeberges are one and all most loving and kind. Then we all went down to the Rhine to meet the boat coming up from Bonn. The pastor, Agnes, and Adelheid came with us to Königswinter, to make acquaintance with the rest of our party.

It promised well for a fine day, the sun shining through a soft mist that suggested more beauty than it hid. But that only lasted till we had passed the Seven Mountains, and the rest of the day was grey, so that we had only form and not colour; the difference between this and my last view of the Rhine was just that between an engraving and a painting.

There were very few people on board, the season has been late and cold. We got into talk with a most queer-looking, keen-eyed, elderly man, who spoke English with a strong strange accent. He was German, but had lived many years in London, and was going for a holiday to Frankfort. He seemed to know "all about everything," and was an odd mixture of shabbiness and gentlemanliness. Presently he brought his daughter, and introduced her, I think with a little pride. Oh such eyes! neither English nor German, dark, soft, beautiful, a perfect picture. She was very quiet and retiring, all the more fascinating on that account, with a gentle, sad expression, lighting up when she spoke into a very sweet smile. We decided they must be Jews; and later in the day, when better acquainted, I asked

her if it were so, and was almost sorry I did, for she
coloured deeply and answered "Yes!" in a shy, reluc-
tant tone.   So I made haste to tell her what an interest
it was to me to find that she was of that noble race, and
said I could wish that I too were of Jewish blood!
That seemed not only to relieve, but to astonish both
her and her father; and he said, in a bitter tone, "You
stand alone; other Christians feel very differently
towards us."   Then we had a long talk in German.
He said he honoured Jesus of Nazareth: "He was a
wonderful man, and a very beautiful character, and had
wrought a wonderful work in the world through His
marvellous insight into human nature and adaptation of
His teaching to the times.   But as for His being God!"
and he finished the sentence with just a look, which
spoke more contempt for the idea than words could
have done.   I replied that I saw no alternative between
His being all that He claimed to be, that is *God*, and
being a liar and impostor.   We argued frankly for some
time, and not at all unpleasantly; he was quite willing to
listen fairly, and never replied captiously.   The girl was
listening with her soft, sad eyes, so I broke away from
argument and spoke to the hard old Jew what I wanted
her to hear, just about the love, and tenderness, and
sympathy, and all-sufficiency of Jesus; tried simply to
carry out:

> " Tell them what you know is true,
>   Tell them what He is to you!"

Afterwards the old fellow was very anxious that I
should come to Frankfort.   I was "a friend of Jews,"
and as such would be heartily welcomed by himself and

his friends, and he would like to show us all he could, especially of the Jews' quarter. As we were not going there, he gave me his London address, and a most cordial invitation to call if I possibly could.

We also made acquaintance with a German-American, "travelling scientifically," and a Prussian soldier with a Königgrätz medal, overflowing with national pride.

The vineyards rather spoil than improve the scenery at this season, they are in the potato garden stage. Still the Rhine is the Rhine, and it is very lovely even under a dull sky. As we came on shore at Bingen, about forty schoolgirls went on board and instantly formed on deck and struck up "Am Rhein," the very pretty Rhine song, singing it right well in three parts.

Oh the luxury of sitting out in the hotel garden to write! We are close to the river, and the garden is full of roses, and has a long terrace entirely arched over with green; it is so delicious to sit here and rest, and not be in a town! I have (with permission) gathered splendid roses and white syringa, just for the pleasure of gathering them. H. C. and the M.'s are gone to the vineyards.

June 4. BINGEN TO HEIDELBERG.

We have come into full summer at once, a hazy heat, just relieved by an occasional light river breeze. After breakfast we went up to the Burg Klopp, a scrap of a ruined castle commanding a grand view of the Rhine valley. M. sketched, and we loitered about and enjoyed ourselves. Then we came down into the town, and hearing music went into a church. It was the Feast of the Heart of Jesus, and there had been high mass early, and now service again at 10.30. A fine solemn chorale was being sung, the congregation joining lustily. Oleander trees were set down each side of the church, and the whole altar end was decorated with flowers, both growing and gathered. While we stood just inside, relays of children, led by uncommonly pleasant-looking sisters of mercy, came in, dipping in the holy water and crossing themselves as they passed. One lot of toddling wee things could hardly reach the holy water, so the *sœur* made a dash at it and sprinkled it over them all, and hurried them in, cutting the ceremony short.

We left Bingen at 12.20. The rail to Mayence is not striking, but one gets some nice peeps of the river. At Darmstadt we had half an hour to wait, so ran into the town, which is cheerful and pretty, with wide streets and wonderfully long avenues. We passed a guard-house, so H. C. walked up to the soldiers and began making signs and talking English to them to their great amusement, till I came up to interpret. We asked if their helmets were not very hot and heavy, so one instantly took his off and handed it to him with great politeness, and another or two had medals to show. We had just time to see the Grand Ducal Palace, which looks like a great hotel, and then got back to the train. The rail to Heidelberg is extremely pretty, running under the range of hills which bound the Odenwald. To-day the sun added all its charm to the green and gold and shadow on the wooded heights and tempting ravines which broke the range at intervals. At the entrance of these valleys a picturesque village generally lay, with gardens and gable and a church tower all complete.

At Heidelberg we put up at the Prince Charles. Being much too late for table d'hôte we had to dine separately. M. left dinner ordering to us. H. C. would not say what he would like, so I told the waiter we wanted "*dinner*," and to bring anything, whatever they happened to have. So in about three-quarters of an hour we sat down and *dinner* began. When it would have ended I don't know; but after having soup, salmon, roast beef, tongue, cutlets, and a queer preparation of duck and olives, we thought we had had enough, and declined with thanks the couple of fowls we were to have eaten, and the salad and stewed cherries, and ditto three remaining courses. The waiter was afraid we were not pleased, but we explained to him that our capabilities were not unlimited; he said some English were not satisfied when they had gone through the whole menu! I shall not hear the last of this dinner; when they want to do it in style "F. shall order,"—they will say.

We had an evening stroll over the bridge and along the Neckar, not far, for we were tired, and M. L. and I go upstairs at 8.30, and potter about and write our journals.

June 5. HEIDELBERG.

A most delightful morning, spent at the castle. The way up is steep enough, but all overhung with green, which would beguile any ascent for me. The castle has a rich sunny look, being built of red stone, which is warm and full of colour without the least brickish effect. It was altogether beyond my expectations, whether as to extent, beauty of detail or of whole, or as to the lovely situation. It is a perfect combination of far and near, the splendid ruins and luxuriant foliage close at hand, the quaint town below with river and bridge, the vineyards and wooded heights opposite, the Neckar valley with its sharp turns soon closing the view to the east, and then the wide reach of plain to the west, green softening into blue distance and bounded by the dimmest grey outline where the mountains of France are *hinted.*

We sauntered about *ad libitum,* and simply enjoyed ourselves; tonics and salvolatile are nothing to lying under a tree with nothing to disturb one but birds and pretty beetles, and knowing that there is absolutely nothing to do for the next two hours but look at the green and the blue around and above. In the afternoon M. was done for and decided not to stir; so H. C. took M. L. and myself in a carriage up the valley of the Neckar among lovely wooded hills, reaches of cornfields, steep red rocks quarried here and there, and the river constantly winding and forming new pictures. We went past Neckargemünd to Neckarsteinach, where, while the horses were watered, we did the correct thing, and took coffee in the garden overlooking the river, for which we paid twopence each! I asked the driver many questions, and he was civil and communicative, and recommended an excursion to Schönan to-morrow. I said "No, not to-morrow!" "Ah, yes," he said, "I had forgotten, you are English, and the English do not go excursions on Sundays." I was glad to hear that this is an understood thing.

. Of all the noisy places I ever was in, this is the worst. Certainly till two A.M. the natives kept up chattering, whistling, shouting, and singing, and when I looked out

at five A.M. the market place was all in a buzz, and buy-
ing and selling had begun again. "Do the Germans
ever go to bed at all?" I said. "*Some* of them do, I
think," said H. C. very gravely and rather doubtfully.

June 6. SUNDAY AT HEIDELBERG.

At nine A.M. I went to German service in the large
church close by the Prince Charles. The Catholics
have the choir, and the Protestants the nave ; but there
is a division between the two, so that it is almost the
same as separate churches. The sermon was from the
gospel for the day, "And they all with one consent began to make excuse"; it was not remarkable. But the
singing ! When after a short prelude the first chorale
burst out, it went through me, and I only wished all my
Leamington friends could have been there to hear : dig-
nified, solemn, grand, massive, the very antipodes of
some of the flimsy rattling church music at home. It
was just the difference between a cheap ball dress and
coronation robes, or better, a musical embodiment of
the mighty world-upheaving Reformation as compared
with the offervescence of a revival in its least hopeful
form. The organ is played full, and all sing, so it is
very slow, and a gallop would be impossible ; but then
each chord is so rich and perfect that the ear requires
time to enjoy it, and the general effect is most elevating,
the very majesty of praise. I can hardly imagine what
my German friends would say if they heard the Te
Deum raced through, presto, to the tune of "The heavens are telling," the utter barbarians they would think
us, and the profanity it would appear to them !

It was very hot in the afternoon, and M. L. and I

found a quiet corner in the castle grounds, where we
rested a long while and enjoyed being away from the
clatter of Heidelberg, where we shall never recommend
any one to take a *rest.*

We went to the one o'clock table d'hôte, and speculated as to what Maria would have done! For had we
dined apart it would have made extra work, and yet the
table d'hôte was as un-Sunday an affair as possible,
with a band playing most of the time in very good style,
beginning with the overture to "Tancredi"! A little
girl came round with flowers, a young gentleman sitting
next M. L. took a tiny bouquet of roses and pinks and
laid it by her plate. He did not speak English, and we
had quite a talk in German. He was of Italian parentage
(though of German abode), and had all the proper ac-
companiments of dark handsome eyes, musical voice,
and courteous manners. He wanted to arrange some
excursion for us in the evening, but yielded politely at
once when we declined. Presently he offered me his
card, "Romeo Ghezzi"; I had not mine at hand, but
what did much better, my Leaflets. So I chose out
"To whom, O Saviour, shall we go!" and gave it him,
saying that was my card, having ascertained that he
could read, though not speak, English. He read it
slowly all through, asking me the German of two or
three words he did not know, and then put it in his
pocket book. He seemed a little taken aback at the
style of thing I fancy, but was too polite to make himself less agreeable for it, and for the few words with
which it was followed up.

June 7. HEIDELBERG TO FREIBURG.

Oh, we were so glad to get out of Heidelberg in spite of its surrounding beauties ; it seems to possess some peculiar acoustic properties whereby all sound is magnified. Every footstep reverberates, every voice echoes, and a passing carriage might be a pack of artillery or a fire engine at the least. We started by the Baden railway, our route being south with a wide plain to the west, and wooded ranges on the east, all day. Finding we could get three· hours at Baden-Baden, we turned off the main line at Oos. The heat was intense, and we took a carriage at once to the Trinkhalle. In front is a splendid open saloon, the inner wall covered with paintings on large panels. Within is a superb hall exquisitely decorated, in the centre a fine column with a base of flowering plants, from among which the waters hot and cold come out in little fountains. We passed on through shady gardens to the maison de conversation ; the tastefully decorated ballroom has the most superb chandeliers I ever imagined, their masses of crystal festoonery glittering with prismatic hues even in this subdued light. Through an opening in the mirrored wall we came upon a novel scene, a large green table surrounded by perhaps sixteen silent players. The banker or leader rapidly laid down cards, flung coins to various parts of the table, swept them in with a little money rake, now and then saying, "Le jeu est fait," which was followed by a sweep of the money ; there seemed no play in it. In another room we saw the roulette table ; only men were there, no ladies.

After a lunch of chicken and ices we ran up a little

height above the Trinkhalle, and got a good general view of the place, which is pretty enough, lying among these wooded hills. At three P.M. we left for Freiburg, and the country became more beautiful as we neared it; but the dust neutralized the enjoyment. Surely there could have been no dust in Eden! it must be part of the curse.

After our arrival at the Zähringer Hof, we sauntered out, and thought Freiburg charming. Half way round the town are forest-clad hills, broken by lovely valleys, stretching away into the Black Forest. On the other side the soft purple outlines of the French mountains told grandly under the sunset. A rapid mountain stream, alternately flooded and dried up (as we heard), crossed our path, making white noisy dashes over little rocky barriers. It comes from three sources in the hills above, and so is named the Dreisam.

It is an additional interest to this tour that H. C. travels agriculturally; I shall get quite up in comparative crops and so forth. We stopped to talk to a pleasant honest-faced man working on his own ground, and he gave information about lucerne, and fodder, and Indian corn with apparent pleasure, especially when I told him that Mr. C. had an English country estate and liked to know how a German one was managed. He had vines too, and we noticed the difference in foliage; some vines, having large plain leaves with only three divisions and hardly serrated at all, bore the Johannisberger grape. They were in blossom. "Smell it," he said, and verily "the vines with the tender grape give a good smell."

H. C. is very amusing to travel with, he throws himself so thoroughly into everything. It is great fun interpreting for him, not that he always waits for an interpreter; he talks English to the natives quite complacently, and they make very good guesses as to what he wants, and signs go a long way.

June 8. FREIBURG TO BASLE.

Soon after breakfast we went to Freiberg cathedral or münster, in 12th and 13th century architecture. The spire is 380 feet high, of most delicately beautiful open-work, the airiest tracery imaginable. The variety of gothic pattern in the parapet work is quite a study in itself. We had intended going to Steiz, a splendid drive through the Höllenthal (Valley of Hell), issuing in the Himmelreich (Kingdom of Heaven), so I wonder it was not called Valley of Purgatory instead; it is a sort of circumstantial evidence that the aborigines were not Papists. From Steiz we were to drive next day to Schaffhausen, but as thunderstorms blew up we went on by train to Basle instead. Our window in La Croix Blanche at Basle looks on the Rhine, which is here a beautiful blue green, inclining to silver in the light and emerald in the shade; it is flowing swiftly, and breaking white against the piers of the bridge. Opposite are quaint, many-windowed, steeple-roofed houses, the cathedral and other towers, and gardens and trees overhanging the river; above these, grey and purple folds of cloud-curtain, within which lightnings are playing and thunder is growling. But, once for all, let me remind you that I do not intend to write what Murray gives much better; and that my journal is only a prattle of individual reminiscences, of no interest to any but amiable and affectionate friends.

June 9. BASLE TO NEUHAUSEN.

I had just time to stroll over the bridge and set foot on Swiss soil for the first time, and then off by rail. For two hours it was the prettiest line we have yet seen, constantly close to the Rhine, and the valley was wide enough to allow of a fair view on both sides. The river grew gradually narrower, and at Rothenburg it was compressed into a narrow gorge, down which it thundered dark, and white, and mighty. Actually the station was placed exactly where we had apparently the best possible view of the cataract, with some old towers on the opposite bank, a quaint bridge just above, and a background of lovely wooded hills. From Waldshut the scenery was tame, and one could rest one's eyes without compunction.

At Neuhausen, three miles from Schaffhausen, we went to the Schweizer Hof, and asked for rooms fronting the Rhine, but hardly expected the *vision* when the waiter opened the glass doors and ushered us on to our tiny balcony. It was a full front view of the falls of the Rhine, 380 feet wide by 50 or 60 feet high, the hotel grounds alone intervening between us and the river. The falls are a mass of sparkling white, broken by two or three tree-covered rocks ; about four we set out to see them, by winding, shady paths to the railway bridge above the falls, which has a footway. It was fascinating to look down at the wild rapids, sheets of glasslike transparency flowing swiftly over rock tables, then a sudden precipice below. water which might go down to any depth, only that you are not looking down into darkness, but into emerald and snow, mingled and transfused marvellously, and full of motion and power and almost life. Then we went up to the castle of Laufen, and saw some fine Swiss paintings by Jenny, a pupil of Calame of Geneva (now dead), the greatest Swiss landscape painter. But the view from outside was unapproachable by any artist ; and we descended from point to point, getting new impressions of what a waterfall *can* be, at each. At one we had a rainbow in the highest spray, arching the whole fall ; at another a new rainbow hung over the lower part, seeming to rest upon the utter restlessness behind it. I felt it was perfectly impossible for any words to convey a tolerable idea of the falls, as seen from the rocks close beside them. The rocks beneath them are not a smooth ledge, but broken and varied, and thus the water is thrown into a chaos of magnificent curves and leaps infinitely more beautiful than any single chute could be, water against water, foam against foam. You look up and see masses, mountains of white, bright water hurled everlastingly and irresistibly down, down, down, with a sort of exuberance of the joy of utter strength. You look across and see shattered diamonds by millions, leaping and glittering in the sunshine. You look down, and it is a tremendous wrestling and sinking and overcoming of flood upon flood, all the more weirdly grand that it is half hidden in the clouds of spray. Only one cannot look long, it is so dazzling, so intensely white, every drop so full of light, that the eye soon wearies and memory has to begin her work. Oh, if one were only all spirit ! We came across the Rhine in a little boat just below the falls, and were thankful to rest in our charming hotel.

June 10.   NEUHAUSEN TO ZURICH.

After breakfast I could not resist a fling upon the piano, and among other things played the Wedding March.   Presently after we were told there was a wedding breakfast in the hotel that morning, the last unmarried lady in Neuhausen, said our informant; there were sixty not long ago, but the fifty-nine were already married and done for.   We saw the wedding party come in, from church I suppose; the bride, a handsome dark-eyed girl, looked radiant, and beamed out smiles with the kisses she was bestowing most graciously on a bevy of lady friends.   It was great luxury to sit on the terrace overlooking the falls, and scribble my journal under a shady tree; and, when that was done, I jotted some verses which have been haunting me.   The text was sent me lately; I never noticed it before.   How strange it is what treasures we miss every time we read!

DARKNESS AND LIGHT.

"What I tell you in darkness, that speak ye in light."—MATT. x. 27.

He hath spoken in the darkness,
   In the silence of the night,
Spoken sweetly of the Father,
   Words of life and love and light.
Floating through the sombre stillness
   Came the loved and loving Voice,
Speaking peace and solemn gladness,
   That His children might rejoice.
What He tells thee in the darkness,
   Songs He giveth in the night—

Rise and speak it in the morning,
  Rise and sing them in the light !

He hath spoken in the darkness,
  In the silence of thy grief,
Sympathy so deep and tender,
  Mighty for thy heart relief.
Speaking in thy night of sorrow
  Words of comfort and of calm,
Gently on thy wounded spirit
  Pouring true and healing balm.
What He tells thee in the darkness,
  Weary watcher for the day,
Grateful lip and life should utter
  When the shadows flee away.

He is speaking in the darkness,
  Though thou canst not see His face ;
More than angels ever needed,
  Mercy, pardon, love, and grace ;
Speaking of the many mansions,
  Where in safe and holy rest
Thou shalt be with Him for ever,
  Perfectly and always blest.
What He tells thee in the darkness,
  Whispers through time's lonely night,
Thou shalt speak in glorious praises,
  In the everlasting light !

We left at 1.15, and came on to Schaffhausen and
had a run into the town ; the cathedral is the plainest
barn that ever bore the name. "A Methodist meeting !"
opined H. C. The rail from thence to Zurich was very
pretty, giving glimpses of the Rhine, which seemed to
get greener and greener. We drove through Zurich in
an open carriage, and H. C. remarked on its very

prosperous appearance. I reminded him that it is Protestant. Presently we passed a private carriage with some very sleek well-to-do looking steeds. "Protestant horses, I suppose!" said he.

Not wishing for the dawdle of five o'clock table d'hôte, we dined alone in a side saloon tastefully decorated, and set off with a few paintings of Swiss scenery. As we sat in peace and silence, a band commenced in the large saloon, to my intense delight, the effect softened by the closed doors which barred the table d'hôte clatter, and only let sweet sounds through. It was very superior to the Heidelberg band ; I never heard better light and shade, or more gradual and delicate diminuendos, except at the festivals, and to have it all to ourselves in such quiet was something delicious.

Then we walked in the garden, which stretches down to the lake, our first Swiss lake! It was too hazy for the distant mountains, but the nearer scenery was soft and lovely, the lake very still, and delicately tinted with green and purple, while the dipping sun caught the scarlet oars and *really* snowy sails of numbers of bright little boats. I intend systematically to let the towns alone and reserve myself for the beauties of nature ; one gets knocked up if one tries to do everything ; so I shall always rest (as now) while the others are gone into any town. I am always better for a rest, and enjoy the views all the more for sacrificing the architecture.

June 11. ZURICH TO BERNE.

M. L. and her father went for a walk at 6.30 A.M. The whole day was cool and hazy. We left at ten and reached Berne at two by a still more beautiful line than

the last; and though we have seen no snow yet, we
passed near a group of sharply-peaked mountains unlike
any we have yet seen in our lives. I had a talk with an
old Swiss gentleman from Winterthür, chiefly on music.
He had been in England several times, and knew a very
musical set personally, Joachim, Piatti, Benedict, and
others. He was evidently really musical. He had been
to some of the English festivals; but catch any one
speaking the German tongue giving a good word to any
English music! "Yes, they were pretty fair, but the
English were all infatuated for large orchestras," which
he considered a great mistake; "it was impossible to get
perfect light and shade from five hundred performers."
And the Handel Festival itself had made no other impression on him. I am glad I have not arrived at that
pitch of musical cultivation! We went to see the bears
in the afternoon, and had great fun with them; the
largest literally laid himself out for our amusement,
catching the cakes lazily as he rolled about on his back.

Berne is quite the most novel and utterly foreign town
I have seen, the streets arcaded like Chester, with bright
red or orange cushions in every window seat, which
touch up the grey stone effectively and complement the
bright green venetian shutters. We ought to see the
Alps from our windows at the Berner Hof, which command a fine view even without them; but it is hope-
lessly misty.

June 12. BERNE TO THUN.

At last! About five A.M. M. L. crept quietly to the
window, and I woke as she passed. "Anything to see?"
"Oh yes, I really do believe I see them," she said quite

solemnly. Of course I was up in a second. The sun
had risen above the thick mist, and away in the south-
east were giant outlines bending towards him as if they
had been our mighty guardian spirits all night, and
were resigning their charge ere they flew away into
farther light. Anything less ethereal and less holy they
could scarcely be ; the very mist was a folding of wings
about their feet, and a veiling of what might be angel
brows, grand and serene. It is no use laughing at "fancies"; wait till you have seen what we did from the roof
of the Berner Hof! The effect was the more striking as
we had scanned the southern horizon the evening before with glasses, and not a vestige of mountains could
be seen ; and now these lofty, shadowy sentinels stood
where our senses had told us there was nothing but sky,
not even cloud, tall and majestic, far out-topping the
green hills in front. The vision did not last long ; it
seemed to melt into light rather than into mist.

We took a morning train to Thun, and got letters and
luggage, and rooms with the very perfection of a view,
at the Belle Vue, rightly named. It was the pleasantest
hour I ever spent in a train, for the Alps were visible
soon after leaving Berne, and every minute we were seeing more and more of them, and of the marvellous
glisten of the glaciers. In the afternoon we took a boat
for a two hours' sail on the lake, and saw the Jungfrau
and Mönch and Eiger in delicious restful leisure ; and
the mountains looked at leisure too, so still and mighty
and unapproachable by any human bustle and hurry
and ferment. So now the dream of all my life is realized, and I have seen snow mountains! When I was
quite a little child the idea of them took possession of

me ; at eight or nine years old I used to reverie about them, and when I heard the name of the snow-covered Sierra de la Summa Paz (perfect peace), the idea was completed, and I thenceforth always thought of eternal snow and perfect peace together, and longed to see the one and drink in the other. And I am not disappointed, not in the very least ; they are just as pure and bright and peace-suggestive as ever I dreamt them. It may be rather in the style of the old women who invariably say "it's just like heaven" whenever they get a comfortable tea meeting ; but really I never saw anything material and earthly which so suggested the ethereal and heavenly, which so seemed to lead up to the unseen, to be the very steps of the Throne ; and one could better fancy them to be the visible foundations of the invisible celestial city, bearing some wonderful relation to its transparent gold and crystal sea, than only snow and granite rising out of this same every-day earth we are treading, dusty and stony.

June 13. SUNDAY AT THUN.

And rather an ideal Sunday too, calm and bright and quiet, and with "beauty all around our path." I went to the German, or rather Swiss, service, guided by the "sweet bells jangled," though not "out of tune," only out of all order and rhythm, as continental bells always are.

The Swiss punctuality, which so far we have found perfect, extended to the service, for though I was in full two minutes before the organ began, not half a dozen came in after me, and the church was full. More than half the feminine part were in costume ; I looked over

the hymn with a velvet-bodiced, white-sleeved maiden.
It was an old favourite of mine : " Praise ye the Lord,
the mighty King of glory." Then the preacher read
the eighth Psalm, which was his text. The first part
was on God's glory in creation ; he worked up a rather
eloquent rhapsody into the climax : " And who of all on
the face of the earth should so praise God for the splendour which He has poured out upon His works as we
Swiss, in this our blessed and beautiful fatherland ! "
The old man said it with a patriotic emphasis worthy of
a son of Tell. After service the whole congregation
lingered for quite half an hour in the churchyard, which
commanded a magnificent view on all sides up and
down the valley, for the church crowns a little round
hill standing alone. Many went to different graves and
gathered a flower or adjusted a creeper. The inscriptions were chiefly on little brass plates, brightly polished,
on neat iron standards three or four feet high ; the
greater part were verses of affectionate remembrance, or
passages of well-known chorales, but there were many
Scripture ones too. On one side were several English
graves : one was to Frances Hatfield, aged 15 ; it had
been beautifully arranged, but now the little railing was
rusty, and the rosebush was straggling, and the weeds
were rank at its foot. Perhaps there are sorrowful
hearts in England, to whom that little foreign grave is
very dear.

The English service in the evening was very pleasant
and quiet, a nice little sermon on " When ye pray, say,
Our Father," etc., from the chaplain, Rev. E. Venables,
son-in-law of Frank's godfather, to whom M. introduced
herself next day.

June 14. THUN TO INTERLACHEN.

A day of considerable variation as to plans, the morning being stormy ; but as the sun came out in the afternoon we took the three o'clock steamer to Interlachen. But before we were two miles down the lake it commenced pouring, and soon the steamer seemed to be charging a rampart of fog, any view being hopeless, and we continued rushing through the wild storm till we landed at Interlachen, and were safely omnibused to the Jungfraublick, the highest hotel in Interlachen (which has the reputation of being hot and close and sleepless). Here we are perched on a terrace looking down into the valley, with the Jungfrau looking down upon us between two steep wooded hills, shining out of grey clouds every now and then like a sudden smile, with that wonderful intensity of whiteness which to me gives a totally new force to "whiter than snow." And I see too how perfectly the evangelists complete each other's description of our Lord's transfiguration raiment (St. Matthew says it was "white as the light," St. Mark "exceeding white as snow "), for this Alpine snow is light materialized and snow etherealized, it is a combination of the impressions of each. I came across "solidified hydrogen" the other day, which rather astonished me; but now I seem to have seen solidified light.

June 15. INTERLACHEN TO LAUTERBRUNNEN.

We looked out upon a morning view of grey driving cloud, where mountain summits ought to have been, with glimpses of snow on heights which were certainly bare the evening before. But a wet morning enables one to pay off arrears of scribbles and stitches, so we wrote letters and sang duets and chatted with an agreeable English lady who was pedestrianizing with her brother. Table d'hôte in a superb saloon, every chair carved, and all else in proportion. We sat next four Germans. Foreigners call the English unsociable, but not once as yet (except the Italian at Heidelberg) has a single foreigner addressed us for the sake of sociability ; we have always spoken first, and so to-day. One gentleman was evidently superior and cultivated, with a positively brilliant flow of language ; he was discussing the various construction of different languages, and then varieties of German construction, and gave fluent and clever illustrations of each. After rain, sunshine ; so we set off at four in an open carriage to Lauterbrunnen in a perfectly transparent atmosphere. Fancy nine miles' drive up a deep valley, hills six or seven thousand feet high on each side, wooded wherever trees could get root, and where not, rocky and precipitous, between them at each opening views of snow mountains glittering in brilliant light ; below, a wild stream, the Lütschine, rushing in one perpetual downhill of rapids and little falls ; every now and then a silver thread of a waterfall gleaming out on the farther side of the valley, or a broad riband of one dashing down the nearer side to our very feet, to be crossed by a little bridge, then the whole picture "grounded" with all shades of the freshest, brightest green, still wet with the morning's rain and canopied with vivid blue. And at every turn coming nearer to the Jungfrau, "Queen of the Alps," which fills up the valley in front, and only hides herself

again when we get too close under her silver throne!
Was not this "something like"?

It struck me again here, as in Scotland last summer,
what marvellous lavishment of beauty God has poured
upon the details of His works. For here, in the presence of these culminations of earthly magnificence,
scenes beyond what we ever saw before, if the eye
dropped and rested on the very ground it was just as
beautiful in its proportion as if there were no other
loveliness for us far or near; ferns, and flowers, and
grasses, and mossy boulders, and tiny streams, every
square foot being a little world of beauty. One item in
these minor charms was the luxuriant way in which the
firs had sown themselves, thousands of wee fir trees
springing up on banks and among rocks, some standing
alone in green tiny gracefulness, others growing in the
prettiest little miniature groves you can imagine. I
never saw firs growing this way anywhere else; they
were like kittens to cats, so very pretty and petable.

Near Lauterbrunnen we passed under tremendous
bastions of rock as the gorge narrowed in; and then
saw the long waving veil of delicate white mist, and
needed no telling that it was the Staubbach. We walked
on to its foot, and H. C. irreverently suggested what a
first-rate shower bath it would be! I should not mind
trying, it comes down so temptingly and fairily, not
nearly so substantially as in its picture. We walked a
mile or more up the valley, enjoying the evening sunshine on the Jungfrau, and its shining and most·pure
Silberhorn and other white peaks before us. And just
as we returned, and the valley was darkening, lo "the
afterglow," which I so much wished to see. Rosy gold,

or golden rosiness, comes as near as I can give it; but words of any sort are not much use. One more effect was still in reserve : when we came up to our room, the crescent moon was shedding a pale holy glimmer over the snow, and the sky behind it was no invisible purple or neutral tint, but a most ethereal blue, which I never saw *at night* before and do not understand.

June 16. Lauterbrunnen to Mürren.

To open our eyes upon the Jungfrau itself before one even raised one's head from the pillow was very like a dream! At nine we started, all on horses; the creatures had lively heads, and were very knowing and cautious in picking their way. "Mine is a most stupid beast," says H. C., "and a great deal more afraid of breaking his knees than I am." We did not consider this conclusive as to his stupidity, and think it must be rather advantageous to ride such "stupid beasts" up and down such break-neck places. The road to Mürren was to take us over the *top* of the Staubbach, which was rather incomprehensible, as the sides of the valley look nearly perpendicular, and a good part is *absolutely* so. But a path developed itself by degrees up an unnoticed ravine, a series of tremendously sharp steep zigzags and shelves over precipices, and crossings of wild little burns, about one-fourth torrent and three-fourths waterfall. When we got to the Staubbach we dismounted, and scrambled to the very edge from which it takes the one leap of 925 feet sheer down into the valley! The guide was a little anxious, and kept warning us to hold fast by the small trees; a slip on that "mossy bank" would have been too awful to think of.

After this, though still very steep, the path was easier, lying chiefly through fir woods, the slope being so great one wondered how they could grow at all, and the *tops* of tall trees were close below us. At every turn, as we rose higher and higher directly opposite the Jungfrau, she seemed to grow grander and grander, and we began to realize her stature. Tremendous precipices rise like Titan walls out of the valley, then rock and snow struggle for predominance, then snow prevails, and the Silberhorn rises in one smooth curved cone of pure unbroken white, and the real summit towers still higher behind, dazzling even against the dazzling sky. "It will be finer yet," said our guide, Perther. "How can that be?" "You will see!" It was true; when we finally came out of the forest the Jungfrau was still the centre, but only the centre point of the grandest of even Alpine amphitheatres. On her right the white Monk and the Eiger with its perpendicular side in full view, on the left the Rothhorn, Breithorn, and Sparrenhorn, in stately range; glaciers, avalanche tracks, snow-fields, snow-walls, and everything Alpine that ever one heard of, all in one view. And all the while "the grass of the field" was as lovely as ever at our feet, sheets of flowers around us, all delicate and tiny and exquisite, just the other pole of the world of the Beautiful.

M. seemed to know them all, though there was an immense variety. We gathered gentianellas large and small, and it is heresy to have no raptures for them; but for a perfect eye-delight of blue, commend me to the Alpine forget-me-not, I never saw anything prettier in shape and colour; and they grew as buttercups do with us, by millions, like turquoises, only alive and positively smiling.

We reached Mürren at eleven. It is a little village to which there is no nearer or easier way than that by which we came, and all the people want has to be carried on mules. "But they don't want much," said the guide; "they have wood and cows, and they don't need anything else except coffee and flour and a little cloth." There are too few for a church, so they come all the way to Lauterbrunnen on Sunday, except in the winter, when they are entirely snowed up for weeks together, and even Lauterbrunnen is in pretty much the same predicament.

We set off on foot to get as much higher as we could by goat paths, and soon came to little patches of snow which did not seem in the least to interfere with the flowers, but glittered on in a "happy family" sort of way among the forget-me-nots and saxifrage. But clouds were gathering on the heights and coming lower rather suddenly, so we were all in very good time for the table d'hôte at one o'clock; we thought we ought only to have feasted on goat's milk and such like, at 5,465 feet above sea level! Before we rose it was sleeting fast, and beyond ten yards nothing was visible. The next hour or two was decidedly lively; there was difference of opinion as to weather, so some started and others waited, but everybody had taken atmospheric champagne, and was in the best possible spirits, and all crowded to the door to see each departure and get as much fun as possible out of it. Two good-tempered and most plucky English ladies actually set off to the Stachelberg, some miles farther and a good deal higher, and did not care whether they saw anything at all, so that they went. Our German acquaintances from Interlachen were there, and rattled away most amusingly. One of them, a sweet-looking girl, reminding us a little of Emily B., took H. C.'s fancy greatly and made herself most agreeable in pretty broken English. One of the gentlemen said both his ladies had fallen in love with him, and he must have shared in the fascination, for he offered H. C. two tickets, freeing a great deal of Italian travel, including fare from hence, to use, if he would do him the honour to accept them! In the midst of it two Liverpool gentlemen came down from the Schilthorn, for which they had started at three A.M., leaving their wives to amuse themselves with watching them through a telescope, and it was rather fresh and interesting to hear them talk of being dug out of the snow only two hours before, and other small adventures of the kind. We waited longer than most, and at last set off in heavy rain and sleet. We looked down on formless cloud and fog, with no outline and no colour, filling an indefinite abyss, now and then shapeless openings disclosing darker cloud. We intended walking down all the worst places, but it was so wet and dirty, and the guides were so re-assuring, that we stuck valiantly on till we reached the Staubbach again. Here we dismounted and raced down the hill. The guides having pronounced H. C. "a right good rider," he had been allowed to go forward alone, and we found him comfortably settled at the hotel. "Why, papa!" said M., "did you ride down all those staircases?" "Why not?" said he; "the horse had got to come down, and he might as well take me on his back as not!"

June 17. LAUTERBRUNNEN TO GRINDELWALD.

A very lovely but uncertain-looking morning, which finally cleared up radiantly. We got photographs from Yakob Huggler, a clever peasant carver, at his stall of alpenstocks and knicknacks close by. The drive to Grindelwald was much such another as that to Lauterbrunnen, with the Wetterhorn instead of the Jungfrau before us and the valley rather wider. The twin Lütschinen streams meet at its entrance, and we followed the black instead of the white Lütschine. On nearing Grindelwald, the driver told us we should see the lower glacier round the next corner, so we looked eagerly and saw—a dirty mass of stones and grey mud, among which peered out dirty ice and snow, worthy of the Black Country itself. So we concluded it to be a delusion and a snare, and went to the upper glacier instead, which is much purer. We had a lovely walk and ride to its foot, which is like a very wild and wide sea beach all barren and desolate. We scrambled a little way up the sloping ice, but the man in charge urged us not to go on, for the edge of the glacier itself, high above us, was constantly breaking away and it was very dangerous, so we came down after inspecting a snowball big enough to have killed half a dozen people, which had fallen only a few hours before ; we attacked it and ate avalanche, and found it very refreshing. We went into an ice grotto, blue and glistening and transparent, but too evidently neatly hollowed out and not natural, so I did not feel frantic about it.

It is immense fun meeting all sorts of people over and over again. Already we have so many acquaintances that we meet some everywhere whom we had met before. To-day the amusing heroines of the Stachelberg came to our inn, and on our way to the glacier we saw our German friends coming down a bank upon us; one instantly hoisted his cap on his alpenstock and waved a merry welcome. Last night some Thun friends walked in to Lauterbrunnen, and we improved the acquaintance. The chambermaids are a specialty of mine, and interest me; they are always pleasant and obliging, and generally very intelligent girls. They all say they can never go to church, as Sunday is usually the busiest day; they always seem extremely pleased to be chatted with.

June 18. GRINDELWALD TO INTERLACHEN.

Thick and threatening all day, and we drove to Interlachen early. On the way we passed an alpenhorn played by a small boy not nearly so tall as the horn was long. It is fastened on a pivot, so as to command different echoes. The alpenhorns are best at a little distance, which softens the tone and assimilates it more nearly to the flute-like sweetness of the echo, which seems a sort of fairy answer coming out of some magical hall in the rock. The strain oftenest repeated, and perhaps the most telling, was this:

The tone is very powerful, and the middle notes extremely mellow.

We had aspiring ideas as to the Scheinige Platte, the

nearest height to our hotel, 6,000 feet; but clouds hung heavy all round, so we came down to a walk across the valley to Hohbühl. The afternoon also was not fine enough to be worth an excursion, so M. and I rested, and M. L. and her papa had a walk.

June 19. INTERLACHEN.

The weather settled our plans for us, as it rained nearly all day. In the morning, curious long soft white clouds went slowly creeping along the Scheinige Platte, "like great white Persian cats," said M.; and in the evening they assembled in force on the top, and came down in a heavy snow-storm. So we had a quiet day. Before settling to letters and work I wrote

EVENING TEARS AND MORNING SONGS.

"Weeping may endure in the evening, but singing cometh in the morning."—
Marginal reading of PSALM xxx. 5.

IN the evening there is weeping,
　Lengthening shadows, failing sight,
Silent darkness, slowly creeping
　Over all things dear and bright.

In the evening there is weeping,
　Lasting all the twilight through;
Phantom sorrows, never sleeping,
　Wakening slumbers of the true.

In the morning cometh singing,
　Cometh joy, and cometh sight,
When the sun ariseth, bringing
　Healing on his wings of light.

In the evening cometh singing,
　　Songs that ne'er in silence end,
Angel minstrels ever bringing
　　Praises new with thine to blend.

Are the twilight shadows casting
　　Heavy glooms upon thy heart?
Soon in radiance everlasting
　　Night for ever shall depart.

Art thou weeping, sad and lonely,
　　Through the evening of thy days?
All thy sighing shall be only
　　Prelude of more perfect praise.

Darkest hour is nearest dawning,
　　Solemn herald of the day;
Singing cometh in the morning,
　　God shall wipe thy tears away.

June 20.　Sunday at Interlachen.

The service for the Queen's accession was used at the
English church with the Communion service. Text,
Matt. xxii. 21, "Render unto Cæsar," etc. All was
orderly and nice; moreover we had reasonable chants
and no galloping. The evening service was at six; text
from the first lesson. A showery day ended in a splendid evening, and when we came out of church the Jungfrau was glowing with that indescribable tint, golden
snow with a touch of rose, shining out between two dark
heights magnificent in purple and green and bronze,
with a coronet of the fresh snow lingering on their summits, and the shadows of the western mountains darkening the fir woods of their base and sides. I overheard

a little girl say, "Mamma, I think the Jungfrau would do to form the great white throne of God." *That* expresses it. Later we had quite a treat: an American lady, one of two couples who have sat next us at dinner, came down at my entreaty to sing. She gave Mendelssohn's "Oh that I had wings of a dove" very beautifully, and "But Thou didst not leave," and "Come unto Him." I was positively thankful for her music, as the news had just reached us of that horrid wicked bill having passed the Lords, and one needed a little soothing after that.*

Mutual acquaintances always do turn up; so though I only know two people in all America, she knew one of them, Dr. Lowell Mason, and was distantly connected with him by marriage, and had been in his singing classes. She had greatly enjoyed English cathedral services, but thought it a great mistake to introduce anything of the sort into parish churches, or indeed into America at all; they belonged to the real old cathedrals, and should never be separated from them.

June 21. WEATHERBOUND AT INTERLACHEN.

Certainly the shortest longest day I ever spent! It poured from morning till night, but we resigned ourselves to it, and had a very pleasant day. A German gentleman asked H. C. to play chess, which he did; and I had two games also, and found him the best player I had ever met, and the most rapid; it was quite a treat to see his instantaneous pounce on the right man, and his unhesitating setting of it in the right place. He

---

* The bill for the Disestablishment of the Irish Church.

played again in the evening with H. C., and then with M. L. He also plays the flute, and I accompanied him for an hour or more. We had a good deal of music and talk in the evening. Mr. and Mrs. Fane, whom we met at Thun and Lauterbrunnen, make themselves very agreeable. Some German ladies, including a nice little girl, seemed delighted with the music and thanked me warmly. After I had sung "O rest in the Lord," a Scotch lady came and talked to me most refreshingly. She had just met Dr. Guthrie at Lucerne, and talked about the *Sunday Magazine ;* and we got on so well that after a while I introduced "F. R. H." to her, whom she knew perfectly well, and gave me a hearty invitation to visit her at Falkirk.

The "portier" at the Jungfraublick is quite a character ; he superintends arrivals, letters, and money matters, and sits in an office in uniform. I left my "Ministry of Song" downstairs one night, and in the morning I found the portier reading it. When we came again M. had put a "*pro bono publico*" copy in the reading room, and this he carried off likewise, and asked me if he might keep it till we left, as he could read English, and was so fond of poetry, and thought mine "most beautiful!" He said his wife had a pension near Geneva, at which Russians stayed ; also he knew Longfellow personally and poetically, and admired him extremely in both respects, and knew many of his poems by heart, and quoted part of the "Psalm of Life," to prove his words, I suppose.

June 22. INTERLACHEN TO GIESSBACH.

A bright though threatening morning, so a general exodus seemed to take place. We steamed down the lake of Brienz to Giessbach, and as my Scotch friend was on board we had another talk. She gave me a pretty thought : we spoke of cloud-shadows : "Yes," she said, "but they are the shadow of His chariot, for 'He maketh the clouds His chariot.'" We went to see the falls, which are very lovely, a whole series one above another, at least a dozen, and each a picture in itself ; but just as we passed on a little wooden path *underneath* a splendid curved leap of water, I became faint and had to turn back and go to bed. The others went to see them illuminated at 9.30, and seemed to think the effect very fine.

June 23.   GIESSBACH TO MEYRINGEN.

A lovely morning, and I was able to get up in time for the eleven o'clock steamer to cross the lake to Brienz, and then we had a nine miles' drive along the valley to Meyringen. Although M. and I had both been invalids, curiosity and excitement seemed to do us good, for we ventured down a horrible and wonderful place, the " Finsteraar Schlucht," or " Black gorge of the Aar," which strangely enough none of our guidebooks mention, though we thought it worth going miles to see. It is a sharp descent, mostly by little wooden steps, into what at first looks like a lofty cavern, very narrow, the rock on each side hollowed out in most curious round or oval sweeps, with sharp jagged edges all bending over, and quite or nearly meeting overhead. It is full of the sound of rushing water, but we saw none till near the bottom, and then the witch-hole opens out upon the Aar, tearing along apparently from nowhere to nowhere, shut in by two awful walls of rock five hundred feet high, with just room enough below for the narrow strong river and a beach like the sea, three or four yards wide on one side, and the rocks overhanging so much that there is the merest little slit of sky. Said M., "We have got into Dante!" How we ever got up the stones and steps again I don't know ; but we revivified with some red wine at a little auberge close by, and so got home ; and I had a delicious sleep of nearly ten hours.

June 24. MEYRINGEN TO ROSENLAUI.

At last M. yielded to a chaise à porteur, inasmuch as the guidebook describes the first of the ascent to Rosen-laui as a "ruined stair two thousand feet long." We rode, and these Swiss horses would go up St. Paul's or the Pyramids apparently. After some time the ascent was less stiff, the path leading along the side of an upland valley, with the Reichenbach roaring below, and fine precipices rising straight from its edge on the other side ; the last part of the way was level, and might have been any English valley with a brook at the bottom, but for the sight of the Wellhorn rising in front, with a glimpse of glacier through a cloud at its side. The Rosenlaui glacier is diminishing so rapidly that an immense basin of rock, which took us nearly half an hour to skirt, was full of ice only twelve years ago. As we returned we thought we should like a canter, and told the guide we would wait for him before the descent began ; but he scorned the idea of being waited for, he liked a run as well as we, any pace was all the same to him. Whatever H. C. rides is *cure* to *go,* and my pretty grey four-year-old pony was quite of our mind as to a canter ; but our guide was equal to anything, and raced and laughed and leaped

4

the boggy bits with his alpenstock without regard for his limbs or lungs. We went round by the Reichenbach falls ; and now for a piece of unmitigated heresy. I am inclined to class waterfalls among the good things of which one can have too much ! I calculated on silence among these mountains ; and instead of it, one has to shout to be heard above the noise. Every valley has its roar and rush of water, with a cataract every two or three hundred yards, leaping to join the chorus of torrents below, from the chorus of torrents above, and making one appreciate Wordsworth's line, which I used to think far-fetched :

" The cataracts blow their trumpets from the steep."

All night long you hear it, and clearer and louder than by day. From our window at Meyringen five separate waterfalls were within sight and sound. It is a sad case of nerves versus poetry, and will go far to prove the truth with which a chaplain hereabout took my measure, his conclusion being that I was " very matter of fact, and had no poetry in me ! "

June 25. MEYRINGEN TO LUCERNE.

We chartered a return carriage from Meyringen to Lucerne with four horses, and built to carry ten persons, so we had room enough ! This was again a fine morning, though hazy, and the passing magnificence of that drive over the Brünig, with the valley of Meyringen at our feet and the Oberland giants beyond, is one of the scenes least likely to be forgotten. Our mid-day halt at Sarnen and the glimpse up the Melchthal took one back into the old days, or rather into Schiller's revivification of them. The last ten miles lay along the lake of Lucerne, round the base of Pilatus ; but it was not a clear evening, and my first impression was one of extreme disappointment. It was lovely, no doubt, but on such a small scale compared to the Alps behind us, and I had given my allegiance so utterly to them, that I could not instantly transfer it to anything so different. Snow mountains are not less to me now than in my child dreams, and Lucerne is a town ! so I did not take kindly to it.

June 26. AT THE SCHWEIZERHOF HOTEL, LUCERNE.

The weather seems settling at last, and it is fine and even hot. We were to do nothing to-day, and unhappily it occurred to me to go and assist at the practice in the English church, so we utterly wasted an hour and a half's sunshine in trying over tunes and listening to remarks of the usual calibre of amateur choirs. Somebody tried over a "new tune," melody meagre and entirely secular, running chiefly in thirds, and spiced up with absurd and unnecessary accidentals ; and this was pronounced "simply exquisite"! And the rest to match.

Our table d'hôte was accompanied by a very charming string quartett. I subjoin the "Menu Musicale."

Soupe royale : to potpourri from Donizetti.

Salmon trout with Dutch sauce and potatoes : to a lively and pretty waltz.

Roast beef and lettuce : to a fine solid thing of Mendelssohn's.

Calf's head *en tortue :* to a set of rubbishy quadrilles.

Mutton and green peas mashed : to—silence.

Spinach and eggs *à la crème :* to Gounod's Berceuse.

Chicken and salad : to a plaintive and sweet violin air.

Lemon pudding : to Soldier's March in Faust.

Gateau Pithiviers and *compôte de pommes :* to a waltz by Strauss.

Dessert : to another waltz by Strauss.

We had a hot walk above the town, and a lovely soft view of the lake. Then we went to find the Lion of Lucerne, and when we came upon it I stood fascinated ; not merely with the wonderful sculpture, but with the perfect effect of the whole thing. You come suddenly from the glare above, or the clatter of the road below, into a deep quiet nook, shut in by large shady trees with a wide opening in their foliage through which the afternoon sun falls upon the lion cut in the living rock. Close below is a dark pool in which it is reflected beautifully. The grey rock rises perpendicularly some little height above, and ends in a crown of acacias and drooping bushes and creepers.

A photograph of the lion gives no idea at all of the sentiment of the place, which is sacred and still, and almost solemnly beautiful. It is a memorial of Swiss fidelity, and a worthy one.

June 27. SUNDAY AT LUCERNE.

The English chaplain proved a great stick, or rather a *little* stick, so in the evening we went to the Scotch service in a Roman Catholic church. We had a nice sermon on John xiv. 27, and the simple, full evangelical truth we heard contrasted strangely with a great gold-lettered shield above the altar ("*Hilf, Maria, hilf!*") (Help, Mary, help!)

The cathedral bells here are grand, filling the air with confused thundering resonance, massive and almost awful, yet magnificently beautiful; a fit accompaniment to the majesty of snow mountains, in presence of which any other sounds of human production would be puny and impertinent.

One part of the Lucerne cemetery was most touching, it was set aside for the little children. Row after row of tiny graves, with loving sorrowing inscriptions, some with little white marble crosses simply twined with ivy, all with carefully tended flowers and shrubs proportioned to the size of the little graves.

June 28. LUCERNE TO THE RIGI.

What could promise better? All the natives prophesying settled fine weather and a regular sunrise glow over mountains and lake, moreover the little cloud upon Pilatus which is supposed to make all safe!

We had a pleasant hour's sail to Küssnacht, and struck up with a clever and amusing man, a friend of Prof. Tyndall's, who travels with his eyes open as to physical science, and gave us a good deal of desultory but interesting information and observation in that line. The ride up was very pleasant, with a grandly widening horizon with occasional fine views of the picturesque outline of Pilatus. On this (north) side of the Rigi, we see several lakes, especially Zug, blue as a harebell. For the last twenty minutes we change sides, and have the south view. The panorama from the very top is immense, but I do not count it among the impressions of my life; however, our afternoon was delightful, strolling at leisure all about the top, gathering flowers and enjoying the views and the air. Heavy clouds hung over the distant mountains, but the sun was bright, and the general haze hardly made it less beautiful. Towards seven P.M. every one began to move towards the top, probably about two hundred people. Then came an excitement of hopes and fears for the sunset; would it clear, would the clouds rise, should we see the afterglow? No! The sun went down into a bank of clouds, and the Bernese Oberland did not reveal itself. I stayed a long while after, part of the time alone. Suddenly a cloud rushed up from nowhere and hid everything; in a few minutes it was gone again like a grey spirit, leaving no trace or trail, gone nowhere! Tremulous lightning was playing in a far-off low cloud towards Zurich, and once a quiver of light over the Alps gave hopes of a display; but all gradually calmed and darkened away.

June 29. RIGI KULM TO LUCERNE.

At 3.30 A.M. a queer horn, woefully out of tune, played up and down the stairs and passages. We had arranged everything overnight, to save every possible minute in the morning, and so were almost the first on the top, looking down upon an arctic sea, white downy undulations of cloud about two hundred feet below us, covering hills and lakes and plains in one billowy sea, out of which rose a few rocky islands, of which the Rigi itself was one, and Pilatus the most noticeable. The Alps bounded it like a shore, but hazy and clouded. The sun rose from a cloud, and was far too late in appearing to effect anything in the rose-tint line upon the mountain coast, but it did cast a stream of faint pink for a few moments upon the silent polar sea at our feet. In the bedrooms was a notice to " Messieurs les voyageurs," praying them not to take out blankets and bedclothes for the sunrise, which was not unlikely to put it into their heads. In spite of this there were three or four bare-faced blankets, one worn by a lady. All the wearers, as I expected, spoke the German tongue.

The beds were not luxurious, notwithstanding spring mattresses and down quilts, for the sheets were cold and clammy, and horrid to a degree. " No wonder," said M. L., " when they dry them in the clouds ; I saw them at it ! " And when we passed the neat little hotel, Rigi-Staffel, at eight A.M. in a dense cloud, they were hanging out sheets on lines for the benefit of the next comers. We had a three hours' walk down to Weggis entirely through cloud, with a chaise à porteur between us. Yet there was the lake below and mountains before us, and all sorts of beauty around us. Only we could not see !

June 30. LUCERNE TO ALTDORF.

A very threatening morning, which gradually devel-oped into a tolerable day, with pretty gleams on the shores of the lake ; the higher summits were invisible. We walked through the two covered bridges, which have paintings in the roof of scenes from Swiss history, and then took the 9.40 steamer.

It is a very lovely three hours' sail by Brunnen, the

Grütli meadow, and Tell's Chapel to Fluellen ; then we drove two miles to Altdorf, and saw the fountains where Tell and his child stood, and went to the entrance of the St. Gotthard pass, returning to Lucerne by the same route ; but I have not time for detailed description. I had my little " Wilhelm Tell," and read a few scenes, especially the Grütli one ; but actually found it too exciting, and was obliged to give it up. I had no idea before what power that sort of poetry possesses.

July 1.   LUCERNE TO LANGNAU.

A little sunshine early in the morning and evening, but otherwise gloomy and grey. We drove nearly forty miles through the Emmenthal, said to be the most fertile part of Switzerland, a very pretty country, but nothing distinctively Swiss except the houses with their enormously overhanging roofs and curious wooden coat-of-mail walls, little bits of wood nailed over each other with rounded ends. This is an unusual cross country route, and the Hotel Emmenthal was in striking contrast to the palace we left at Lucerne. The waitress looked amazed when we asked for extra spoons to attack our cupless eggs, and returned with one spoon for all of us ! I like an out-of-the-way place, and specially rejoice in not having to dress up for the evening. The Schweitzer Hof was too grand for me, and where there are so very many people one is far more isolated ; moreover there was a tantalizingly good piano in a splendid saloon with just the right resonance, but it was too much even for my audacity to sit down to it, before fifty people at least.

July 2. LANGNAU TO FRIBOURG.

A journey by rail, not specially interesting; and being cloudy, we could not see the Oberland as we ought to have done.

A very enthusiastic Swiss lady (an acquaintance of the Malans) raved about her Swiss mountains most charmingly. I like to find the Swiss appreciating their privileges. Our guard from Langnau to Berne appeared also quite alive to the beauties of nature. He came into the carriage on the way, and held up an awfully cut thumb, appealing to me for the chance of getting doctored. He had just had an accident with the brake; luckily I had a sponge and rag at hand, and made a tidy job of it for him. He was very grateful, and kept coming to us all the rest of the way to point out views and any places of interest. At Fribourg we had a fine evening, and a curious view of the deep gorge containing the old town, spanned by two long suspension bridges. These vibrate even to the tread, and a passing vehicle makes them almost swing.

A little before eight P.M. we went to the cathedral. M. had brought papa's "Forty Specimens of the Grand Chant," to give to the organist. Two years ago, when papa was here, he sent up his "Morning and Evening Hymn" (the one which is played backwards *or* forwards, and turns upside down) to M. Vogt, who introduced it forthwith into his extemporizations, and rendered it very appreciatively. So having received the little book which M. gave the verger for him, he very politely came to us and thanked M. for it. He looks about sixty, is short and stout, with a remarkable forehead and keen and full dark eyes. I asked him what he was going to play. He said: "First something from Mendelssohn, then a toccata of Bach's; after that," he added, with a look of scorn and wave of his hand, "something, more for the public" (*Etwas, mehr für das Publikum!*) Mendelssohn was a strange plaintive minor piece, a wailing of voices far and near, very striking. Bach did not come next, but a soft piece, I think extempore. Then came the Bach, unmistakably grand and masterly; and Vogt played it as if he revelled in it, as if he mastered it and it mastered him, which is a necessary paradox in true musical rendering. Then came the sop to the "Publikum," first Rossini's "Prayer of Moses" and then extemporization, introducing some astonishing thunder and showing off the ninety-seven stops, including a good deal of singing from the vox humana. The *power* of the organ is astonishing, and the pianissimo contrasts hardly less so. Still on the whole the Lucerne organ performance does not seem so very far behind, especially in the more perfect illusion of the vox humana, and in its more complete and natural thunderstorm. On these points we gave the palm unhesitatingly to Lucerne. There the thunderstorm was almost real, first the far-off growl among the mountains, then the gradual approach, the moaning gusts of wind, the nearer rumble, the distant echo, then the sudden awful crash overhead, and the burst of rain, suddenly ceasing again; then, as the peals receded, a most perfect quartett was heard singing "Hanover," beautifully harmonized and in perfect chorale time, one could hardly divest oneself of the idea that it was really a vocal quartett, only just too far off to catch the words,

which *must* be Psalm civ., " My soul praise the Lord."
As one listened the voices came a little nearer, the thunder died away into the faintest peals, seeming to come
from behind the mountains, the wail of the wind ceased
altogether, the voices died into a sweet lovely close, and
then a most exquisite flute stop predominated in a concluding symphony of perfectly enchanting sweetness.
We had nothing to compare with this at Fribourg ;. but,
on the other hand, we had nothing at Lucerne to compare with the Bach toccata, either as to organ or organist.

One never gets perfection, or if one approaches it, it
vanishes ; and so here : we were rejoicing in the dream-
like, ideal effect of darkness falling upon the cathedral
while the music was going on, shadows growing deeper,
roof and aisle darkening into mysterious grand gloom,
no light but a faint paleness through the tracery of the
windows, one tiny lamp like a star near the altar, and a
sort of veiled glimmer from the organ-loft just quivering up to the great pipes and suggesting a hidden source
of life and power somewhere among them ; it was precisely what one imagined as the right scene for such
sounds — when up stalks an odious old verger, with
creaking shoes and a horrid flaring lamp, and lights two
vile great candles, one on the pillar just over our heads
and the other just opposite, right in our eyes ! Such is
life.*

---

* This was poor old Vogt's very last thunderstorm. A few
days after we heard of a grand musical funeral service for the
organist of Fribourg. We heard him on Friday evening, July
2 ; on Saturdays there is not any performance ; on Sunday he
played the usual services in his usual health ; on Monday he
died suddenly.

July 3.   FRIBOURG TO VEVEY.

Heavy rain and fog all day, through which we went
by rail to Lausanne, imagining the Jura to the north,
and Alps to the south, and the Lake of Geneva where
the fog hung thickest, excellent practice for the imagi-
native faculty! At Lausanne we drove to the cathedral,
a plain, awkward affair, but said to be the finest in
Switzerland. (The Swiss have natural temples, and
have troubled themselves little 'about architectural
beauty in contrast with the Belgians, who have cathedrals instead of mountains). It is fitted up with plain
wooden benches, and must accommodate a large congregation. The sacristan said the attendance entirely
depended on the preacher. There are five pasteurs,
who preach in turn at this and the other churches, but
there is only one service, and that at nine A.M. We
came on to Vevey to the Hotel Monnet, which seems
to combine the attractions of our previous favourites;
and, as it left off raining for an hour, we had a little
walk by the lake, and concluded it must be a perfectly
delicious place in anything like ordinary weather.

July 4.   SUNDAY AT VEVEY.

To Swiss (French) service at 9.30 with M. The
church commands a splendid view. The service commenced with the commandments read by a deacon or
elder from the pulpit, followed by the gospel epitome
of the two tables, Matthew xxii. 27-40. Then the
pasteur went up and read a long string of banns, each
written on a separate sheet, which he deliberately unfolded and folded again into envelopes, with all their

family history on each side. No more Scripture was read except the text, "Thou art the man!" and the sermon was like most foreign ones, rather an oration than on exposition. The singing was in the old Scotch fashion, a precentor standing up in a little box under the pulpit, and roaring the tune just half a note ahead of the congregation. The tunes themselves were probably good old Genevan ones, very old church psalmody in style. The afternoon English service was quick and quiet; not remarkable.

Though a lovely day, the mountains were clouded, and the Dent du Midi never appeared till nearly sunset, and then the St. Bernard and Sugar Loaf appeared and vanished. Hotel Monnet has a flat roof with seats; it is five stories high, so no one seems to think it worth while to mount. *Tant mieux pour moi!* It is delightful, and I spent most of my Sunday evening alone on it.

July 5. Vevey to Montreux and Glion.

A splendid morning, and the white clouds so bright and soft that one would hardly quarrel with them for veiling the mountains, though as H. C. said, "they *were* obstinate." We took a boat to Clarens, three-quarters of an hour over the *pearly* blue water, then walked up to the cemetery for the view. Here we remarked, as at Lucerne and other places, the very large proportion of comparatively young persons, more than fifty years being quite exceptional. Among the English and Russian graves the ages were still lower, and told of consumption; so many between 17 and 25, who probably came here for the mild winter and never saw another summer. From Clarens a lovely road took us to Montreux, where we again made for the fine view from the churchyard. After a rest and some cherries, we mounted the hill to Glion, a little village three-quarters of an hour higher, and the view proportionally finer. We walked down and returned to Vevey by steamer. At the 5.30 table d'hôte I had a long conversation in French with a Swedish countess, handsome, polished, and very agreeable. She talked of Jenny Lind and her retirement from the stage; and said it was thought that Christine Nilsson might possibly follow her example. She described her as being like Jenny in firmness and high principle, and said that the Parisians thought her "trop sage et sérieuse," and that she better suited the English idiosyncrasy. Later in the evening I was playing in the nice little salon de conversation, when my countess came in and recognized the "Song without Words," and asked me for more. So I sang "Comfort ye." "That is fine music," she said; "whose is it?" I answered and explained. "Really! so that is from the 'Messiah'! I never heard it. The English are *passionés* for Handel's music, are they not?" So then I played the overture to "Samson," and sang "Let the bright Seraphim." She admired both extremely; it was totally new to her; she had never heard Handel before, and thought he wrote chiefly church music! Yet she was thoroughly "up" in Mendelssohn and Mozart, and knew all the operas that ever were written apparently. And never heard Handel!!

July 6. VEVEY TO ST. GINGOLPH AND VILLENEUVE.

A spree! H. C. could not realize the fact that the opposite shore was seven miles off, and its mountains eight thousand feet high, and thought it would assist his realization to row across. But M. and M. L. don't like boats, so they decided to rest for the day, while I had no objection to anything, and volunteered to go anywhere. Our little boat sported an American flag, and a pretty striped awning, which we were glad of as the sun was hot.

The mountains grew and grew, and seemed to get larger, much faster than they got nearer ; so we began to take in the idea of the seven miles and the eight thousand feet. St. Gingolph is made no fuss about in the guidebooks, and consequently is not prepared for tourists as yet ; but we have not seen many things more beautiful than the Gorge de la Morge at the entrance of which it lies. Our inquiry for saddle horses, or mules, or donkeys, rather astonished the natives at the inn ; but they were polite, as all the Swiss are, and sent post haste to a butcher who owned one donkey, and to somebody else who was supposed to have a horse. The messengers returned in a depressed state of mind ; the horse could not be found at all, and the donkey was gone to the mountains. So we were obliged to walk, and set off up the gorge to a certain village *somewhere,* named Novelles, which we should reach if we had patience and perseverance.

The said virtues were exercised for about two hours and a half, and then were rewarded by a village and a most welcome auberge. At least that was the ultimate reward, but there were plenty of proximate ones. The valley winds up between mountains, wooded below, and grand precipitous rocks above, snow-wreathed and ice-creviced. The Morge, a wild, leaping, racing torrent, rushes down to the lake, forming the boundary between Savoy and the canton de Vaud. The path was steep but very lovely; visions of the lake at every turn to the left, and visions of the mighty rocks above at every turn to the right, both seen in a framing of luxuriant foliage. But it was dreadfully hot, and no vestige of human life appeared turn after turn.

At last the coming event cast its shadow before in the shape of a chalet, and some haymakers whom we hailed. In their musical-toned civility they told us the auberge was only ten minutes farther; and a good-humoured Savoyard ran up and told us he was the "maitre de l'auberge," and encouraged us along, chatting most cheerily. He introduced us to his domains in great glee through a rugged yard, and up what looked as if it led to a henroost, saying "Entrez, mademoiselle!" to a little dark kitchen with a pot hanging over a gipsy-like fire of sticks on a great hearthstone; then another and quite triumphant "Entrez!" to a "salon" beyond, with three little tables and six little benches. He scampered about, getting necessaries together, with the aid of his equally good-tempered but quieter helpmeet. First he produced a bottle of Swiss wine, then a loaf of capital black bread, and a plate with three funny little cheeses and one knife. On second thoughts he ran away and returned with a sharp-pointed pocket-knife, which he deposited most engagingly before me. "Pour vous, mademoiselle; un *joli* petit couteau!" He offered an egg; and while it was boiling sent round the village for butter, *hoping* he could get some, but the butter was made half an hour higher up the mountain. H. C. seemed satisfied now that the eight thousand feet were no myth, for he "should have thought that walking three hours straight up hill we should have got to where they make the butter!" Presently my egg appeared in a little brandy glass, but a spoon had not occurred to him, and a cupboard had to be rummaged to find one. In course of time the butter arrived, quite superlative and only just churned, so we were in clover.

I catechized him next as to whether there was any mode of descent other than our tired feet. On this subject he was sanguine but mysterious. Mademoiselle might trust him, he would arrange, "tout irait bien," only a little time was necessary, his horse was gone to pasture. We were not particular, I told him, a hay cart would do. He danced in and out to keep us quiet; it would soon be ready, mademoiselle would be charmed, she would laugh at his beautiful new carriage, she would remember it, etc. After one of these intervals he appeared in a clean white shirt, and told us in immense glee that the *horse* was nearly ready except a little glass of wine! He rushed into a dark lumber room and drew a glass from a little cask, then danced into the salon and filled his mouth with the remains of our bread and cheese, while his wife sewed a button on his wristband.

Outside the door stood, or rather lay, our conveyance. Its foundation was a hay sledge, two little wheels behind with two thick runners, joined by rough crossbars. On this our host had tied with ropes an old wine chest; across it was a plank, with a manifest bolster on it as a cushion. Two long crooked sticks were tied to the runners for shafts. "Montez, monsieur, we will go like the' chemin de fer, vous verrez!" So in we got; the plank

5

and bolster being wider than the box, there was room
enough to sit, while our feet converged to a focus of
about twenty inches in the narrow bottom. He waved
his cap to his wife, with whom he was evidently on the
best of terms, and set off full tear, down hill. It was no
use shouting "Doucement!" he only looked round
and laughed, and tugged away at the shafts, over
boulders and holes, and swinging round corners on the
very edge of the deep gully, till really if we had not
been incapacitated by laughing from either thinking or
doing anything else, we should have been seriously
frightened.

On retrospect, I can't think how we escaped with
whole bones. I never felt anything like the jolting;
our cheeks shook like jelly. H. C. said it was complete
electrification. Our "horse" only stopped when quite
out of breath and steaming with perspiration, eager to
know how many minutes he had been, and pluming
himself on his speed, and still more on his invention.
He would have it patented, and send it to the next *Exposition* and make his fortune, and so forth, joking away
his breath so that his next start was a trifle more moderate. As for admiring the valley, which *he* found time
to do, waving one hand and giving an extra tug with the
other, "Ah que c'est un beau pays, mais que c'est mag-
nifique!") it was out of the question, all we could do
was to laugh and hold on, and try to balance the machine.

About a quarter of a mile from the bottom, just as we
were getting used to the said balancing, and our steed
perhaps getting more careless, we were swung round a
corner and over some unexpectedly large stones, when.

suddenly we felt a most queer giving-way, earthquaky sensation, and roared for a halt simultaneously. Just as the man contrived to stop, the whole concern came bodily to grief, *all to pieces at once* in a most suprising style, cords yielded, shafts broke, nails came out, and boards subsided into one shapeless heap, from which we extricated ourselves with nothing more than a bruise or two, laughing more than ever, for it made the thing so very complete to have such a proper and thorough break-down, it was the only finishing touch it wanted. It was no use reconstructing the machine, so H. C. paid the man and wanted to dismiss him; he knew well enough the five francs for which we agreed before we saw the concern was more than the job was worth, so he proposed to go down to St. Gingolph to have a bottle of wine with us at his own expense, as a wind up of accounts! He seemed rather hurt at his kind invitation being declined, but soon got over it, and made his adieux, begging us to make his compliments to all at Vevey, and inform them what a first-rate carriage would be at their disposal if they would make an excursion to Novelles.

We got to Vevey just in time to cram our things together and set off by the evening steamer to Hotel Byron, another of these Swiss palaces between Villeneuve and Chillon.

July 7. HOTEL BYRON TO CHILLON AND BOUVERET.

Very hot and very hazy. Walk to Chillon, dungeons, oubliettes, hall of justice, and everything *à la carte ;* every one knows it all. But no one told me one little thing, a surprise of colour. In the dungeons, at first seemingly quite dark, one's eye soon accustomed itself to the faint light through the tiny slits in the enormous walls, and then one perceived a most singular reflection from the blue lake on the grey vaulting, tremulous and delicate and curiously metallic, an effect impossible to convey in words.

After a broiling walk to the landing place near Montreux, we boated across to Bouveret on the other side of the lake, crossing the mouth of the Rhone. Leman lies in azure peace, utterly tranquil and innocent; all at once you are in the midst of a mighty wild brown roaring current. The boatmen say, "Don't be afraid, only sit still," and they pull with all their might. In a minute or two you shoot into uncontaminated, still, blue water again. The current is so impetuous, it flows thus unmingled for a mile and a half. It suggested plenty of analogies, but I have no time for them here. We landed and took a stroll at Bouveret, returning by boat to Hotel Byron, landing on our way upon the Ile de la Paix, the "little isle" in "The Prisoner of Chillon." Three poplars grow on it; I send you a specimen spray.

July 8.   HOTEL BYRON TO MARTIGNY.

We went by rail thirteen miles up the Rhone valley to Bex, and I rather wished George Stephenson had never been born as we whisked through the grand scenery; however, it was a very hazy day, and perhaps but for railroads I should never have come to Switzerland at all! At Bex we took an open carriage, past St. Maurice and the Gorge du Trient, nine miles. The view up the valley must be magnificent, but the heat haze almost hid it; the side views were superb, of the

Dent du Midi, 10,000 feet high, and of the Dent de Morcle, 9,000. This Rhone valley, at least up to St. Maurice, is the grandest thing we have seen, next to my glorious Jungfrau.

In the afternoon we went up the Gorge du Trient, at each turn different and wonderful. The sun never penetrates some parts, and only touches any for about an hour. We came, said the guide, " juste au bon moment," sunshine bringing out the strange curves and angles in strong relief, and contrasting the exquisitely brilliant green of the ferns and bushes wherever they *could* cling, with the depth of shade of the caving rock, and the cold grey rushing torrent of the Trient. This gorge is nine miles long, but only passable by gallery for half a mile. After a scramble on the rocks outside, and a rest in cooler air above, we drove to Martingy.

July 9. MARTINGY TO HALF WAY THROUGH TÊTE NOIRE.

Hot and hazy again ; but we discovered that the haze belonged to the valleys, and the higher we rose the clearer it became. We took mules, and had a three hours' ascent to Col de Trient ; then one hour's descent to Tête Noire, where we dined ; then another hour's descent to the Hotel des Cascades, a little white inn facing a waterfall down a wild rocky gorge, close to the junction of two wild streams. This glacier water is a peculiar colour, which no word describes so well as Job vi. 15, 16 : " The stream of brooks which are *blackish* by reason of the ice, and wherein the snow is hid." You never see the same " blackish " look in any other water but these glacier streams ; and " by reason of the ice wherein the snow is hid" is a wonderful touch of true and poetical description.

M. and I both heard the curious *latent music* of the water when our ear was pressed on the pillow, "just like a piano," she said, and truly! It really was like a distant piano playing a monotonous yet sweet melody, always nearly but never quite the same key of G, and harmony merely tonic and dominant in turn, a move of the head occasionally producing the subdominant!

July 10. TÊTE NOIRE, COL DE BALM, CHAMOUNI.

A day after my own heart! Breakfast at six, and start on foot at half-past. A lovely fresh morning, making the rather sombre valley bright and beautiful. After twenty minutes' walk the road took a slight turn.

"There is Mont Blanc!" shouted M. L., pointing to a little shoulder of white peering between the near hills and the Aiguilles Rouges, which closed the view ahead.

"Nonsense!" we exclaimed, but we hoped we were wrong.

"It is," she persisted; "clouds can't deceive *me ; that's* Mont Blanc. I know it!"

A few yards farther settled the question ; in the opening shone the monarch himself, up to his very crown, distant but majestic, clear and dazzling. And I knew that my allegiance must be transferred from the Jungfrau, that henceforth she was only second. Every half mile gave us more of the snow glories for which I have been absolutely hungering, more aiguilles, more shining whiteness. Mountains, real ones, are more to me than any other created thing; the gentle loveliness of lake scenery or forest, or pastoral picturesqueness, is delightful ; but nothing sends the thrill all through one's very soul that these mountains do. It is just the difference between the Harmonious Blacksmith on a piano, and the Hallelujah Chorus from a grand orchestra. One day among the mountains is worth many of other beautiful scenery ; I say *among* advisedly, for a far-off view is not the same thing ; it is the difference between *anticipation* and *possession*, future and present. However beautiful a distant view may be, one wants to be nearer, to be *there*. It would be well if all instinct of anticipation were as true and as truly to be satisfied as this!

A rapid descent fronting the glacier of Argentière brought us to the village of St. Pierre at 9.30, after a walk of seven miles and a half with occasional rests.

After a decidedly severe déjeuner we set off on mules to the Col de Balm, which is just seven thousand feet high. Though clouds were thick on the mountains, and a haze filled the valley, the view toward Chamouni was magnificent. I might as well have sat backwards at once, for my head felt nearly wrenched off with turning it behind. About half way up we had perhaps the grandest idea of Mont Blanc, towering with an inconceivably majestic sweep of outline above everything else.

From the top of the Col de Balm, which is a *pass* over the lowest dip of the great mountain wall, we ought to have seen the Rhone valley and away to the Great St. Bernard ; but on that side we only looked down and away into mist. After refreshing ourselves at the chalet, we wandered to some great snow patches just for the pleasure of walking into it on the 10th of July. M. said she should "eat some snow and then go to sleep on the gentianellas," which I literally did. The sun was blazingly hot, though the air was cool, and our cloaks were only needed for pillows.

After our rest H. C., M. L., and I went up a summit above the Col de Balm, which commands one of the most sublime and perfect panoramas in the world I should think. Here the grandest mountains in Europe are pressing close around you, a perfect abyss into the Tête Noire on one side, the perfectly graceful sweep of the valley of Chamouni on the other, aiguilles that defy the Alpine Club, glaciers between and below them, linking the winter above with the summer below, all one ever dreamt of Alpine splendours crowded into one scene and oneself in the very centre of it, far above the waterfalls and the noisy torrents, far away from the chatter and clatter of tourists ; what if one did see it at some disadvantage as to the list of peaks which ought to be visible ? even with the cloud veil on her forehead, it was the most glorious revelation of Nature I have ever seen. And what was our *seat* here, up above more snow than we saw all last winter ? A regular carpet of flowers, chiefly forget-me-nots, gentianellas, brilliant potentillas, violets, pansies, and daisies, and many lovely flowers I did not know. The grasses too were various and pretty. What an addition to the enjoyment of the *great* the *small* can be ! And there I wrote these lines:

SUNSHINE and silence on the Col de Balm !
  I stood above the mists, above the rush
  Of all the torrents, when one marvellous hush
Filled God's great mountain temple, vast and calm,
With hallelujah light, a seen but silent psalm.

Crossed with one discord, only one. For love
  Cried out and would be heard : " If ye were here,
  O friends, so far away and yet so near,

Then were the anthem perfect." And the cry
Threaded the concords of that Alpine harmony.

Not vain the same fond cry, if first I stand
  Upon the mountain of our God, and long
  Even in the glory, and with His new song
Upon my lips, that you should come and share
The bliss of heaven, imperfect still till all are there.

Dear ones ! shall it be mine to watch you come
  Up from the shadow, and the valley mist,
  To tread the jacinth and amethyst,
To rest and sing upon the stormless height,
In the deep calm of love and everlasting light ?

It seemed a pity to lose the chance of a sunset behind, but it would not do to be benighted there and on Saturday evening too, so we rode quickly down * and took a carriage at Argentière for Chamouni, which we reached when the twilight was deepening into dark. From our window in the Hotel de Londres we looked out and saw

---

* As we came down the Col de Balm we heard a chorus of cow bells rising from the valley. Our guide said there were two hundred cows in the invisible herd, all wearing bells. The confused, pleasant, *quick* sound was very novel ; and though the bells are various in pitch, all melted into one general musical effect, without any clashing of tones, just as the song of many birds does :

    " The tintinnabulation that so musically swells
    From the bells, bells, bells, bells !"
                  —*Edgar Allan Poe.*

A little farther on we neared a tiny hamlet, and up above us came a wonderful tinkle, tinkle, tinkle. Presently a goat peered over the edge of a ridge and ran down followed by one hundred and twelve companions ; they were not the least timid, and passed close to us, each one looking curiously at us, as if aware we were not " *du pays.*" They were going home, and knew the way quite well.

the mountains marvellously beautiful with just the same sort of pale solemn light we saw on the Jungfrau at night. It was quite dark below except for the lights in the village; but up above against the dark sky, Mont Blanc, the Dome du Gouté and the Aiguille du Midi seemed robed in that singular holiness of light, utterly calm and pure, entirely celestial, which to both of us is more than rose tints and gold; there is nothing like it except the smile of holy peace on the face of one asleep in Jesus. Presently we saw a little twinkling on the edge of the glacier, and wondered what it was. On Monday we knew more about it. While we watched it, another little light, but purer and clearer, rose into the intense depth of blue between the Aiguille du Midi and the Rochers Rouges. You will know how a star can rise when you have seen it on a clear night, when a snow mountain seems its stepping stone to its place in the sky.

July 11. SUNDAY AT CHAMOUNI.

M. L.'s birthday, which she began by seeing Mont Blanc crested with sunlight before five o'clock in the morning. The services in the little English church were most refreshing. The clergyman, Mr. Cripps, of Nottingham, led the chanting and hymns without accompaniment, and every one seemed to join heartily, with an unusual proportion of men's voices. Both tunes and chants were judicious, such as all must know and all could sing. The morning sermon was on Isaiah xxxiii. 17: "Thine eyes shall see the King in His beauty, they shall behold the land that is very far off." The evening from Revelation iii. 20: "Behold, I stand," etc. Both were extremely interesting and useful, with loving encouragement and earnest warning, such as one does not hear from every pulpit. The evening was radiant in rose tints, and when they had faded away we came in from the balcony and sang hymns with the clergyman and others.

July 12. PIERRE POINTUE AND PIERRE À L'ECHELLE.

A real fine clear day at last! We inquired about the twinkle on the mountain, and found it was the lamp at the little auberge at Pierre Pointue, the first stage up Mont Blanc; this was attractive, so we went. A remarkably steep ride through the forest, and then far up above it, brought us to Pierre Pointue in three hours. H. C.'s mules always *go*, though he does not appear to use any extra means, so he was there long before. M. L. and I have taken pains to acquire the mule language and its correct intonation; but all our Hu! Allez! Hupp! Carabi! Hui, hui! Allons! *Arrrdi!* is lost on them, and they pursue the even tenour of their way. Pierre Pointue commands a fine view of the Glacier des Bossons (a very fine one) and the snowy shoulder of Mont Blanc. We dismounted, and I had a real *bona fide* scramble an hour and a half higher up with H. C. and M. L. across the ends of snowdrifts, and right through torrents, and up rocks and places you would not think feasible anywhere but in Switzerland. We rested and lunched with immense satisfaction on the rock called Pierre à l'Echelle because the ladders for the ascent of Mont Blanc used to be kept there before the Grands Mulets were set up with a hut. We were now about eight thousand six hundred feet high, and I at least was proportionately happy. It was marvellous how far up the lovely rhododendrons grow, but the forget-me-nots were almost as daring, and the Alpine ranunculus grew higher still, the special glacier flower, said Joseph Dévouassoud. It was a wild scene, the grim Rochers Rouges and Aiguille du Midi just above, the whole Dome du Gouté shining close beyond the great glacier, an awful slope of snow and stones below us, and ever so deep down the Chamouni valley, which we must have seen as the birds see it.* On our way down our youngest guide, Aristide Couttet, proved himself a true boy in spite of his learned name, shortening his route by sliding down all the snow slopes anywhere near the line of march; it looked such fun I envied him; but though I "take kindly" to mountaineering, I am not advanced enough for snow slopes. We walked nearly all the way down from Pierre Pointue, as it was so steep for riding, visiting the Cascade du Dard on the way. So we really have been more than half way (in height) up Mont Blanc, and would have gone to the Grands Mulets had we been prepared for it.

---

* If there were any birds to see it! But there is a curious paucity of them in Switzerland. We hardly ever saw or heard a bird of any kind. If we did, it was quite a thing to be remarked upon to each other. H. C. was always on the look-out, he seemed to miss the birds and living creatures generally. Nature has devoted herself to the inanimate instead of to the animate; one never sees a wild living thing except insects, which quite make up as regards numbers and beauty; no game, no rabbits, nothing!

July 13. LA FLÉGÈRE.

It was intensely hot, so we had a quiet morning for
writing and resting. La Flégère was selected for a nice
little afternoon excursion, only five and a half hours,
starting at 3.30. See how we have improved!
This is an hour more than our first mountain ride to
Mürren, and that we thought a very trying day's work.
The ascent is on the opposite side to Mont Blanc, and
the whole chain should be visible, but unfortunately it
clouded over long before we reached La Flégère, and
we could only imagine how grand the scene would have
been with the evening light full upon it. Still it was
worth going, and we gained a better idea of the real
height as we rose ; it is impossible to realize the height
of mountains from below, the higher we are the grander
they look. Is it not so in other things? A certain pro-
portionate elevation is essential to appreciation. We
climbed above La Flégère, eagerly watching for the
expected break in the clouds above the monarch, which
did not come. Suddenly we heard a low roar ending in
a grand crescendo, with a character of its own quite
distinct from thunder, echoing along the whole chain,
so that we did not know where to look for our long
hoped-for avalanche! M. L.'s eye caught it just in
time, rushing from the cloud upon the Aiguille Verte ;
we only saw a rising of white snow-spray where it
rested. Twice more we heard the same curiously
impressive sound, but not so loud or near. Barring the
avalanche we reckoned this our least interesting mountain excursion.

July 14. MONTANVERT AND MER DE GLACE.

Our last *Alpine* day ! Always excepting Mürren, the five days from Martigny to the end of Chamouni were the very essence of our whole tour ; getting up to Pierre à l'Echelle was the centre and culmination, but Montanvert was a capital wind-up.

We started at 6.20, breakfasted at the auberge more than six thousand feet high, and then with H. C. and M. L. I went across the Mer de Glace. We did not slip once, though we had the gratification of seeing two gentlemen tumble down. It feels queer for the first few minutes, but one soon gets one's balance and one's glacier feet. Only near the farther shore there are some decidedly interesting bits, where one has to walk along a ridge just wide enough to tread, with beautiful blue crevasses yawning on each side ; if you slipped, on the right you would go down a house-roof slope of ice first, and then into the crevasse, and on the left you would go straight down at once perpendicularly. Where the ice is blue at all, it is wonderfully blue, shading into an intensity and depth of colour no painting could exaggerate. But on the whole the *dirt* is annoying, and I cannot entirely respect the glaciers in consequence. The correct thing is to send the mules round to Chapeau on the farther side, but this seemed rather extensive, and involved the Mauvais Pas, so M. and the mules waited our return at Montanvert. But, once across, it stood to reason I wanted to go on, and bit by bit we approached the Mauvais Pas to my intense delight. It is a way, half staircase and half shelf, about a foot wide, round the face of a perpendicular rock overlooking the glacier, and at some height before reaching Chapeau, and looks most charmingly awful. It is not really dangerous, unless one is disposed to be giddy, for there is an iron rope fastened to the rock all the way within reach of one hand, and with a stick in the other you cannot well come to grief if you step cautiously.

Of course this was quite irresistible, so down I went and back again, leaving Dévouassoud with M. L. ; he had long ago given up looking after me, but presently a gentleman came up and wanted the guide to go with him, which he did by H. C.'s permission. We were rather amused at this. It was a pull to get back again to the crossing point, but it was worth coming, for we saw the pinnacles and pyramids of ice at the lower end of the glacier, and heard the constant fall of blocks and stones. "Always movement here," said the guide.

In re-crossing we diverged to see a bottomless-looking hole in the ice, from which rose a tremendous roar from the hidden river three hundred feet below, raving like an imprisoned giant. We had a shower during our walk, but this was all right, for we got some "effects"; it was specially fine when a few minutes' sunshine lit up the whitest part of the glacier near the ice needles, and a heavy cloud threw the opposite side of the valley seen just over the ice into the deepest violet shade. Just as we got back to the auberge it began to rain, and we waited two hours till it cleared.

On our way to Chamouni, I got Aristide Couttet to tell me the rules and arrangements about guides, which is all code and tariff here, and he explained clearly and intelligently. But do not visitors sometimes go to the mountains without a guide? He answered just what I wanted him to say. "Oh yes, madame, but it is very foolish ; they only lose their way, and it is very danger-ous ; accidents happen when they *will* go without one, but if one has a guide all goes well" (*tout va bien*). "We have a Guide, Aristide ; do you know who I mean ? " "Oh yes, madame ; you mean Jesus Christ, He is the best Guide." He seemed quite delighted to go on with the subject, which we did for some time. "One does not fear death if one has that Guide," he said ; "He gives us salvation" (*Il nous donne le salut*). I gave him some little Scripture papers ; he glanced over them, and putting his finger on some verses about the Saviour (John iii. 16 was one), he said, "*C'est bien joli, cela !* "

The storms must be awful here in winter ; we passed hundreds of great pines broken short off at the roots, or torn right up. Dévouassoud said it is most dangerous to pass the forests when they are laden with snow, if a storm rises. The evening was cloudy but pleasant, and we spent it on the flat parapeted roof. I gathered sev-eral flowers on the Mauvais Pas, and the guide gathered a plant he had never found before, but it had once been shown him by another guide. It is a little green thing, and as M. does not know it, it must be rare.

Jos. Dévouassoud has been four days' excursions with us, and he asked us to write him a testimonial in his book, so I wrote :

> CAREFUL and gentle, respectful and steady,
> Always obliging and watchful and ready ;
> Pleasantly telling, as children say,
> All about everything on the way ;
> Good for the glaciers, strong for the steeps ;
> Mighty for mountains, and lithesome for leaps ;

> Guide of experience, trusty and true,
> None can be better than Dévouassoud !

I gave him a free translation which pleased him amazingly.

July 15. CHAMOUNI TO ST. GERVAIS (15 miles).

A brilliant morning after the showers, and Mont Blanc far too dazzling to look at steadily. We thought we had left it all behind, and so were astonished and delighted, when about half way, to find perhaps the most perfect single view we have had at all, even allowing for an exceptionally clear atmosphere. The whole drive to St. Gervais is a succession of beauty, both near and distant, and I was really sorry that, for the first time, we had a dashing driver. H. C. was exactly suited but wanted to know how often he had to get absolution for breaking Protestant necks ! St. Gervais aux Bains is an enormous mineral water establishment, partly hotel, partly medical pension. It is built in a narrow wooded gorge, and has a fine waterfall just beyond it. The visitors' rooms occupy two long wings with open galleries running along the front of each story ; it is like streets of bedrooms, and the view of the same as you pass to your own is comical. It was not full, but there were two hundred and twenty visitors. In the afternoon we went to the village of St. Gervais, a stiff walk up zigzags out of the gorge ; the view at the top was indeed a lovely upland dip below Mont Joli (8,000 feet) with a glimpse of the Mont Blanc chain at one end, and the fine valley of Salenches, bounded by jagged purple hills against the evening sky, on the other. We went to

6

see Cheminées des Fées, most curious pillars of gravel, with roofs of the same, standing straight up, separate from the side of the rock against which they are seen.

Our Alpine work is really over, and I had a token thereof. I had made quite a small idol of my alpenstock, with its long spiral of names beginning with Lauterbrunnen and ending with the Mauvais Pas; it was so handy and helpful; but having served me up to the last day, it closed its account by falling out of the carriage and getting smashed. I have enjoyed the Alps exceedingly, not less than I expected, and yet it has been in rather a different way. When one hears very perfect music, pleasure overshoots itself into pain, the exquisite thrill is just too much, one longs to dare to let it all out in tears, the cup of enjoyment overflows as the hand trembles with delight, and the nectar is lost through its very abundance. But if one has a share in the performance of the very same, the enjoyment is *more* complete because less intense and concentrated; the physical action of hand or voice is the safety valve, and just takes off the too keen edge, just keeps the thrill of pleasure from rising, yes *rising*, into pain. It is exactly thus with these mountains. The strange, unique, solemn beauty would be too oppressive, the sense of it would weigh one's soul down into awe, would be like a mighty hand upon one's breast, stopping the very breath of one's soul. But the physical exertion is just the needed balance; one is in motion, there is effort, there is even the sense of inhaling a different and most exhilarating air; one is thus kept within the region of real enjoyment; one has not time for the snow silence to fall on one's heart. The pleasure is more perfect for one's whole being, just because it is more imperfect for the higher part of that being. If one were borne on an angel's wings up to Pierre Pointue, one would hardly dare speak in the sudden presence of the snow glory ; but as one comes up on a mule and grasps an alpenstock, one is more inclined to shout and laugh with delight, and hasten to scramble higher.

July 16. St. Gervais to Geneva.

A splendid morning, but oh such a hot drive ; none the cooler for leaving the snow mountains farther behind. But they are beautiful to the last, even at Geneva where they edge the horizon like bright clouds, rather golden than white. On this hot day even the enormous Hotel de la Métropole was a most welcome refuge from the heat, welcome actually to *me !*

July 17. Geneva.

A morning's shopping and strolling. In the evening a drive to the cemetery at Petit Sacconnex, where, after some search, we found the tomb of (Mrs.) Maria Vernon Graham, with the text 1 Thess. iv. 17 ; also Dr. Barry's tomb. We called on Mrs. Pennefather (S. A. de Montmorency). Major Pennefather said it had been a most exceptional summer, and that, till the last few days, Mont Blanc had not been visible for six weeks !

We went to an open air concert on Rousseau's Island at 8 P.M. It was very un-English, but very pretty. The little island lies just in the point where the Rhone rushes out of the lake, and is connected with the city by a bridge. On it is a wooden café and several trees. A little semicircular orchestra, roofed, but open in front and brilliantly lighted, was faced by about four hundred chairs placed under the trees. The lake and river, dark or glittering, reflected the bright rows of light from quays and bridges and hotels ; and the moon, after two months' absence, shone through the branches and lit up a reach of the Rhone.

The music was rubbish, mostly from French operas, but very prettily played. One piece, a string sextet, was of higher order and a real treat. The conductor stood facing the audience instead of the orchestra, though he occasionally turned to the instruments which led off any special point. It was not the least like English conducting ; the time seemed less marked than the expression ; a soft passage was given with the slightest little movements of the hand, down, down, down, no right, left, etc., at all ; then you saw the crescendo coming, by the stronger motion.

Between the parts we did "as they do at Rome," or Geneva, and had coffee and ices at one of the little round tables in the moonlight.

July 18. SUNDAY AT GENEVA.

We were told we should hear a very superior preacher at the Temple de St. Gervais, so M. and I went at 10 A.M. We were early, but the large church was already crowded ; it is one of the oldest in Geneva, and it was pleasant to think that many of our Reformers had worshipped in it. All the windows were darkened with red curtains to keep out the glare of heat. M. Tournier gave out Romans iii. 22, 23, but as usual it was "an oration and not an exposition." He opened by saying,

"What is Christianity? What is the church?" A pause. "This is the great question on which men's minds are divided." The first part of the sermon, an answer to the first question, was singularly eloquent and forcible, the answer being that it is the religion of Jesus Christ, and *that* is "the religion of redemption." He alluded to the rationalistic controversies of Geneva, and implied that there is much present agitation on the subject.

After service we had passed a little figure in the crowd; I turned back, it was Andrienne Vignier. She is staying two miles off, but had walked through the heat to hear M. Tournier. She only came from Naples a few days ago, and her accounts of it were sadly amusing. We remarked on Switzerland being so noisy. "Noisy! go to Italy, *alors!* There it is all noise. Music? *Mais oui!* the people all sing. To be sure, ha, ha! Imagine the roaring of wild beasts let loose, and you have it. They have three notes in their voices, and those three come through their nose. The donkeys are far better; they bray in a long melancholy note, quite sentimental, as if they mourned the wrongs of the country. But when the people fight it is more lively; they always fight when they have nothing else to do. They throw things at each other, generally their wooden shoes; and they take such good aim, *olà!* they never miss." Then she described the family to which she has devoted herself, body and soul and purse, for three years, all for love of the mother, her old schoolfellow, for a nominal salary. "There are ten of them, and they all have *dispositions volcaniques.* You hear such a noise" (here she makes sundry illustrative and most unearthly sounds), "it is an eruption, each is a little Vésuve in herself, and when it is over in one quarter it begins again in another."

"Talking of Vesuvius, did you see much of it?"

"We saw the whole proceedings of the mountain day and night, without putting on our shoes."

"And what impression did it give you? what was it like?"

"Hell! just hell, *précisément!* But the whole country is its portal; one must not think of being happy there, it is all misery and wretchedness. These three years have been just agony, and I am completely imbécilified!"

She came with us to the hotel, just her old self, as rapid and as funny as ever, only spicing her accounts with more French words and idioms. In the evening we went to English service, but it was almost too hot to listen.

July 19.   GENEVA TO NEUCHATEL.

Andrienne came early and took us to the Musée Rath, a public collection of statues, pictures, etc. A poor Swiss woman found her way in, and was like a child among the pictures, full of interest and delight. I told her about some of them, and she followed me all the time for the chance of more information. I stood some time before a beautiful copy from Carlo Dolce, "Christ with the crown of thorns," and she liked to hear about the "old, old story."

In the heat of the morning I went to the Rhone swimming bath, which was delicious. At one end the river comes in in a regular waterfall three feet high, through which you can see the light, blue and shining; fancy sitting under this azured crystal. It was such fun to swim down the long bath, it was one's beau ideal of bathing, and the cool, transparent, exquisite blue is so much nicer than salt grey waves.

We left Geneva by two P.M. steamer for Morges, and, though hazy, the view was very beautiful, especially with the assistance of M. L.'s ex cathedra announcements as to *which* were mountains and *which* clouds, among the dim golden-white horizon fringings to the south! We reached Neuchatel about ten, after more than an hour on the very edge of the lake by moonlight, a very pretty line of rail.

July 20. NEUCHATEL.

Simply broiling! The rest shopped all the morning, gifts for home, etc. ; I stayed in the comparatively cool and very pleasant Hotel Bellevue saloon, close to the lake and public gardens. Mr. and Mrs. Maynard are here, which is a great treat ; his chaplaincy is now over, so we were only just in time to meet them. We wished to go to Chaumont in the afternoon, but all the carriages were engaged, so we had a row on the lake instead. We tried to make out Mont Blanc and the Jungfrau, but it is tantalizing to try to identify those majestic presences among far, faint, shadowy cloud outlines, after one has stood face to face with them ; it was looking at the wrong side of the tapestry. The moonlight was perfect ; what would we not have given for an hour of it at Thun, or Lucerne, or Chamouni, or Vevey?

July 21. NEUCHATEL TO DIJON.

What would Frank have said? I was coward enough to decline going with the others to the cathedral on account of the heat, and had a luxurious morning of writing and chatting with Mr. M. The heat was intense. Mr. M. said he "wished last Sunday that he could have preached *in* the lake!" Fancy preacher and congregation up to their necks! it would have been emphatically "a refreshing service."

Our afternoon train saved us much heat, for after sunset it was cool and pleasant, and we did not get to Dijon till nearly eleven P.M. The first hour and a half from Neuchatel till near Pontarlier is right across the Jura chain, not grand, but extremely beautiful, especially at first, when the line rises steeply along the side of a splendid gorge, wooded, except where the limestone rocks are too precipitous to give any hold for firs. And it is wonderful how little hold seems necessary for tree roots in Switzerland ; they cling to rocks where one would have thought not a bush or even a plant could find footing, and shoot up straight and stately, vegetable aiguilles.

As we left Neuchatel we looked out for the possibility of a definite farewell to the Alps. What a strange, sad fascination there is about a *last* glimpse! Above the hazy horizon-were some little, pale whitenesses; was it to these that our good-bye must be said? So we called in our mountain oracle, M. L., who answered authoritatively "that they *were* Alps certainly, Mont Blanc *probably*." So we watched on till they were lost : all silent. But is it not then that thoughts talk loudest ?

Shall we ever see them again?

" *The works of the Lord are great, sought out of all them that have pleasure therein.*"

II.

THE MOUNTAIN MAIDENS.*

(ZELLA, DORA, LISETTA).

A CANTATA.

PART I. SUNRISE.

(1). DAWN CHORUS.

THE stars die out, and the moon grows dim,
  Slowly, softly, the dark is paleing !
Comes o'er the eastern horizon-rim,
  Slowly, softly, a bright unveiling.

The white mist floats in the vale at rest,
  Ghostly, dimly, a silver shiver ;
The golden east and the purple west
  Flushing deep with a crimson quiver.

The mountains gleam with expectant light,
  Near and grandly, or far and faintly,
In festal robing of solemn white,
  Waiting, waiting, serene and saintly.

---

* The music to this cantata, for treble voices, by Frank
Romer, is published by Hutchings and Romer, 9 Conduit Street,
Regent Street.

Lo ! on the mountain-crest, sudden and fair,
Bright herald of morning, the rose-tint is there ;
Peak after peak lighteth up with the glow
That crowneth with ruby the Alpine snow.

Summit on summit, and crest beyond crest,
The beacons are spreading away to the west ;
Crimson and fire and amber and rose
Touch with life and with glory the Alpine snows.

(2). CHORALE.

Father, who hast made the mountains,
　Who hast formed each tiny flower,
Who hast filled the crystal fountains,
　Who hast sent us sun and shower :
Hear Thy children's morning prayer,
Asking for Thy guardian care ;
Keep and guide us all the day,
Lead us safely all the way.

Let Thy glorious creation
　Be the whisper of Thy power ;
New and wondrous revelation
　Still unfolding every hour.
Let the blessing of Thy love
Rest upon us from above ;
And may evening gladness be
Full of thanks and praise to Thee.

(3). RECITATIVE.—*Dora*.

Our pleasant summer work begins.　You go,
O merry Zella, with the obedient herd
To upland pastures, singing all the way ;
And you, Lisetta, to the sterner heights,
Where only foot of Alpine goat may pass,
Or step of mountain maiden.　It is mine

To work at home, preparing smooth white cheese
For winter store and often needed gain ;
And mine the joy of welcoming once more
My loving sisters when the evening falls.

(4). SONG.—*Dora.*

The morning light flingeth
  Its wakening ray,
And as the day bringeth
  The work of the day,
The happy heart singeth,
  Awake and away !

No life can be dreary
  When work is delight ;
Though evening be weary,
  Rest cometh at night ;
And all will be cheery
  If faithful and right.

When duty is treasure
  And labour a joy,
How sweet is the leisure
  Of ended employ !
Then only can pleasure
  Be free from alloy.

            [Repeat ver. 1].

(5). SONG.—*Zella.*

Away, away ! with the break of day,
  To the sunny upland slope !
Away, away, while the earliest ray
  Tells of radiant joy and hope.

With the gentle herd that know the word
  Of kindness and of care,
While with footsteps free they follow me
  As I lead them anywhere.

Away, away ! with a merry lay,
And the chime of a hundred bells ;
Away, away ! with a carol gay,
And an echo from the fells.

To the pastures high, where the shining sky
Looks down on a wealth of flowers ;
To the sapphire spots, where forget-me-nots
Smile on through the lonely hours.

Away, away ! while the breezes play
In the fragrant summer morn ;
Away, away ! while the rock-walls grey
Resound with the alpenhorn.

To the crags all bright in the golden light
With floral diadems,
As fresh and fair, as " rich and rare,"
As any royal gems.

Away, away ! while the rainbow spray
Wreathes the silver waterfalls ;
Away, away ! Oh, I cannot stay,
When the voice of the morning calls !

(6). RECITATIVE.—*Lisetta.*

Adieu, my Dora ! Zella dear, adieu !
The quick light tinkle of the goat bells now
Reminds me they are waiting for my call,
To follow where small flowers have dared to peep
And laugh, beside the glacier and the snow.
I shall not go alone, your love shall go with me.

(7). DUET.—*Zella and Dora.*

Adieu, adieu till eventide !
The hours will quickly pass,
The shadow of the rocks will glide
Across the sunny grass.

We shall not mourn the lessening light,
For we shall meet at home to-night.

Adieu, adieu till eventide !
   The hour of home and rest,
The hour that finds us side by side,
   The sweetest and the best.
For love is joy, and love is light,
And we shall meet at home to-night !

Adieu, adieu till eventide !
   'Tis but a little while !
We would not stay the morning's pride,
   Or noontide's dazzling smile ;
But welcome evening's waning light,
For we shall meet at home to-night !

PART II. NOON.

(8). SONG.—*Lisetta.*

IT is night upon the mountains, and the breeze has died away,
And the rainbow of the morning passes from the torrent spray,
And a calm of golden silence falls upon the glistening snow,
While the shadows of the noon clouds rest upon the glen below.

It is noon upon the mountains, noon upon the giant rocks ;
Hushed the tinkle of the goat bells, and the bleating of the
    flocks ;
They are sleeping on the gentians, and upon the craggy height,
In the glow of Alpine noontide, in the glory of the light.

It is noon upon the mountains. I will rest beside the snow,
Glittering summits far above me, blue-veined glaciers far below ;
I will rest upon the gentians, till the quiet shadows creep
Cool and soft, along the mountains, waking me from pleasant
    sleep.

(9). NOON CHORUS.

Rest ! while the noon is high ;
   Rest while the glow
Falls from the summer sky
   Over the snow.

Rest ! where the alpenrose
   Crimsons the height,
Piercing the mountain snows,
   Purpling the light.
Rest ! while the waterfalls,
   Murmuring deep
Far away lullabies,
   Hush thee to sleep.
         Rest ! while the noon, etc.

Rest ! where the mountains rise,
   Shining and white,
Piercing the deep blue skies,
   Solemn and bright.
Sleep while the silence falls
   Soothing to rest,
Sweetest of lullabies,
   Calming and blest.
         Rest ! while the noon, etc.

(10). RECITATIVE.—*Lisetta.*

Where am I ? I was sleeping by the snow
Upon the alpenroses in the noon.
But am I dreaming now ? The sun is low,
'Tis twilight in the valley, and I hear
No music of the goat bells. Oh, I fear
It is no dream ; but night is coming soon,
And I am all alone upon the height ;
And there are small faint tracks, too quickly lost,
That need sure foot and eye in fullest light ;
And crags to leap, and torrents to be crossed !
I go ! may Power and Love still guard and guide aright.

(11). Song.—*Lisetta.*

Alone, alone! yet round me stand
  God's mountains, still and grand!
    Still and grand, serene and bright,
    Sentinels clothed in armour white,
    And helmeted with scarlet light.
      His Power is near,
      I need not fear.
Beneath the shadow of His throne,
Alone, alone! yet not alone!

Alone, alone! yet beneath me sleep
  The flowers His hand doth keep;
    Small and fair, by crag or dell,
    Trustfully closing star and bell,
    Eve by eve as twilight fell.
      His Love is near,
      I need not fear.
Beneath the rainbow of His throne,
Alone, alone! yet not alone!

Alone, alone! yet I will not fear,
  For Power and Love are near.
    Step by step, by rock and rill,
    Trustfully onward, onward still,
    I follow home with hope and will;
      So near, so near,
      I do not fear.
Beneath the Presence of His throne
Alone, alone! yet not alone!

PART III. SUNSET.

(12). SUNSET CHORUS.

IT is coming, it is coming !
That marvellous up-summing
Of the loveliest and grandest all in one ;
The great transfiguration,
And the royal coronation,
Of the Monarch of the mountains by the priestly Sun.

Watch breathlessly and hearken,
While the forest throne-steps darken
His investiture in crimson and in fire ;
Not a herald trumpet ringeth,
Not a pæan echo flingeth,
There is music of a silence that is mightier far and higher.

Then in radiant obedience
A flush of bright allegiance
Lights up the vassal summits and the proud peaks all around ;
And a thrill of mystic glory
Quivers on the glaciers hoary,
As the ecstasy is full, and the mighty brow is crowned.

Crowned with ruby of resplendence,
In unspeakable transcendence.
'Neath a canopy of purple and of gold outspread ;
With rock sceptres upward pointing,
While the glorious anointing
Of the consecrating sunlight is poured upon his head.

Then a swift and still transition
Falls upon the gorgeous vision,
And the ruby and the fire pass noiselessly away ;
But the paleing of the splendour
Leaves a rose light, clear and tender,
And lovelier than the loveliest dream that melts before the
      day.

Oh to keep it, oh to hold it,
While the tremulous rays enfold it !
Oh to drink in all the beauty, and never thirst again !
Yet less lovely if less fleeting,
For the mingling and the meeting
Of the wonder and the rapture can but overflow in pain.

It is passing, it is passing !
While the softening glow is glassing
In the crystal of the heavens all the fairest of its rose ;
Ever faintly and more faintly,
Ever saintly and more saintly,
Gleam the snowy heights around us in holiest repose.

O pure and perfect whiteness !
O mystery of brightness,
Upon those still majestic brows shed solemnly abroad !
Like the calm and blessèd sleeping
Of the saints in Christ's own keeping,
When the smile of holy peace is left, last witness for their God !

(13). SONG.—*Dora.*

The tuneful chime of the herd is still,
  For the milking hour is past,
And tinkle, tinkle, along the hill,
  The goat bells come at last.
But sister, sister, where art thou ?
We watch and wait for thy coming now.

The crimson fades from the farthest height,
  And the rose-fire pales away ;
And softly, softly the shroud of night
  Enfolds the dying day.
But sister, sister, where art thou ?
We watch and wait for thy coming now.

7

The cold wind swells from the icy steep,
   And the pine trees quake and moan ;
And darkly, darkly the grey clouds creep ;
   And thou art all alone.
O sister, sister, where art thou?
We watch and wait for thy coming now.

(14). DUET.—*Zella and Dora.*

. We will seek thee, we will find thee,
   Though the night winds howl and sweep ;
We will follow through the torrent,
   We will follow up the steep,
Follow where the alpenroses
   Make the mountain all aglow,
Follow, follow through the forest,
   Follow, follow to the snow !
And our Alpine call shall echo
   From the rock and from the height,
Till a gladder tone rebounding,
Thine own merry voice resounding,
   Fill us with a great delight.
        Lisetta ! Lisetta !
Hush and hearken. Call again !
        Lisetta ! Lisetta !
Hearken, hearken. All in vain !

We will seek thee, we will find thee,
   In the wary chamois' haunt ;
Toil and terror, doubt and danger,
   Loving hearts shall never daunt !
We will follow in the darkness,
   We will follow in the light ;
Follow, follow till we find thee,
   Through the noon or through the night.
We will seek thee, we will find thee,

Never weary till we hear,
Over all the torrents rushing,
Joyous answer clearly gushing,
　Thine own Alpine echo dear !
　　Lisetta !　Lisetta !
Hush and hearken.　All in vain !
　　Lisetta !　Lisetta !
Hearken, hearken.　Call again !

(15). TRIO.—*Zella, Dora, and Lisetta.*

LISETTA (*pp*).　I am coming !
ZELLA and DORA (*f*).　She is coming !
LISETTA (*p*).　I am coming !　Wait for me !
ZELLA and DORA (*p*).　She is coming !
LISETTA (*mf*)　I am coming !
ZELLA and DORA (*f*).　Come, oh come, we wait for thee !
　　Nearer, nearer comes the echo ;
　　　Nearer, nearer comes the voice ;
　　Nearer, nearer fall the footsteps,
　　　Making us indeed rejoice.
LISETTA.　I am coming, wait for me !
ZELLA and DORA.　Come, oh come, we wait for thee !

ZELLA, DORA and LISETTA.

We ⎰   her, ⎱ we ⎰   her, ⎱
  ⎱ have sought   ⎰   ⎱ have found   ⎰
They ⎱   me, ⎰ they ⎱   me, ⎰
　　Fear and danger all are past,
Now with joyful song ⎰ we lead her ⎱
　　　　　　　　　　 ⎱ they lead me ⎰
　　Safely, safely home at last !

(16). CHORUS.—*Finale.*

　Safe home, safe home !
Fear and danger all are past,
We are safely home at last !

Oh, the lovelight shed around,
In a rich and radiant flow,
When the loved and lost are found,
Is the sweetest heart can know.
Fairer than the dawn-light tender,
Fuller than the noontide glow,
Brighter than the sunset splendour,
Purer than the moonlit snow.

Now let the wild cloud sweep,
Let the wild rain pour !
Now let the avalanche leap
With its long, grand roar !
Now let the black night fall
On the mountain crest !
Safe are our dear ones all
In our mountain nest.

Safe home, safe home !
Fear and danger all are past,
We are safely home at last !

III.

EXTRACTS FROM LETTERS WRITTEN TO J. M. C. IN 1871.

***

LETTER I.

June 29, 1871. Sitting in an arbour outside the station at Belfort, the only strong place left to the French in this region.

DEAR MIRIAM:

We have had a most interesting journey, and I feel quite historical. We crossed from Newhaven with a crowd of returning French, and reached Dieppe about 9.30 A.M., had coffee, and went on *vid* Rouen to Paris. H. C. would be charmed with Rouen, and I bracket it with Edinburgh and Berne as the three most pictur-esque towns I know. We had just time to go, *vid* rue Jeanne d'Arc, to St. Ouen, which is a crystallization of all one's floating visions of lovely architecture. E. Clay had laid in a splendid stock of little French books and tracts, which we were to divide between us; and as we thought Rouen was not a usual place for tract distribu-tion, we gave away many, and you cannot think how delighted people seemed. One tall grave man, of su-perior rank, watched us, and came up to E. asking if she had many. We were afraid he meant to interfere, as he looked very official ; however, he only wanted to ask "if we would kindly give him one for himself, two if we could." He took them, and thanked us as if we had given him some great thing.

We left Rouen at 2 P.M., and made friends with two very taking French girls returning to Paris after the war ; one of them had immense lovely eyes. They told us all sorts of war experiences. One had an uncle in La Roquette, who escaped by bribing the guard the night before he was to be shot ; her own house left standing and untouched, but houses on each side burnt to a shell. The other had a brother who had three horses killed under him, but escaped unwounded ; a cousin was killed in the first battle, an uncle escaped from his chateau two minutes before the "Communistes" entered and killed three men instead of him ; this girl said her family had lost nearly all their property, the other had fared better. They both reviled the Emperor, and said it was all his fault ; that he was resolved on war in order to preserve his dynasty ; but they would not own that the Communists were French altogether, "it was the bad of all countries who constituted the *Communistes* and they disowned them as *compatriotes*." As we neared Paris they pointed out where the line had been broken up, and soon after we crossed the Seine by two bridges (an island being in the middle) of the most fragile and temporary-looking appearance, at about two miles an hour, with awful squealings of the engine all the time. The ruins of the broken bridge were about fifty yards higher. Then we saw war effects visible and terrible ; for some miles all through those bright-looking suburbs it was one succession of desolations, great ragged holes in the roofs and walls of some houses, and others mere shells, gutted entirely, and others laid open like the front of a baby house, a whole wall having fallen, and showing the skeleton of the stories.

It was far worse than I expected to see, and the two poor girls were sadly distressed and flushed, and their pretty eyes full of tears. ﹅ We were so sorry for them.

At Paris, 4.20, we could not get a cab, and walked with a porter about a mile and a half to the station for Basle (*viâ* Troyes). Most of the way was just Paris of old, gay and clean and lively, but here and there houses were pitted with bullet marks, and over nearly all the churches we saw the mark of the Communists in large-lettered " *Liberté, Egalite, Fraternité.*"

At the rue Strasbourg station we decided to go by the night train, and meantime set off to see the more special ruins. We walked nearly two miles before we could find a vehicle, and then drove to the Tuileries ; the principal walls are standing, but through the burnt-out windows I noticed especially the superb rooms I went through with you, not a floor or a cross wall was left. Then the gardens looked so knocked about, and soldiers' tents looked queer and ominous. The Palais Royal seemed much the same, and the stumpy pedestal of the Colonne Vendôme looked most melancholy.

Our driver was a Communist, I fancy, and a lively one. We bemoaned the Tuileries.

"Ah !" said he, laughing, " it's all right, that makes work for the labourers."

He showed us the Colonne Vendôme that *was*, with absolute glee, saying, " We have taken it down that another may be put up ! "

"Where is the money to come from?" I asked.

"Oh, there is always money enough forthcoming when we want it!"

"Were you in Paris during the siege?"

"Surely! it is my country, my Paris."

The unsubdued care-for-nought look of the man gave me a notion of French levity. He showed us the rue de la Paix, where the awful massacre began, and the bullet marks on the houses. In contrast to all this the boulevards looked just as gay as in 1869, crowded and bright; no end of people drinking coffee and wine at the little tables under the trees, theatre placards in all directions, and all just as usual; *only* it was less *coloured*, for we took special notice that at least seven out of eight women were in mourning; no crape, perhaps they can't afford it, but plain black; this was most striking, and a great contrast to the colours of 1869. We saw a good many dirty and dismal looking soldiers, and were told that these were returned French prisoners coming in by every train.

We left Paris by eight P.M. train and arrived at Belfort at nine A.M., nearly an hour late. All beyond this (Belfort) is in Prussian hands, so the French officials don't or won't know anything about it, and show no timetables, and give no answer but shrugs to any question, or they refer one to "those Germans" at the other end of the station. It is quite sadly comical.

We both vote a night journey a great success; after 9.30 we had the carriage to ourselves, and were quite luxuriously comfortable. Mrs. Snepp gave me a hood which was a great comfort, and E. admires it extremely.

The guard was most polite, and, though he did not

resort to the simple expedient of locking us up, he took trouble in warning people off as if they were *canaille* compared with English ladies, there being no other specimens of the article on this route. One unadvised individual opened our door, and the guard rushed at him with "*March-t-en! il y a deux mesdames banquées; march-t-en! hui?*" Is not *banquées* a good word? We don't know whether we slept much, because we seemed to be aware of the stations, at most of which there was tremendous hullabalooing, occasioned by soldiers returning from Prussia. We quite roused up at 3.30, and fell upon gingerbread and biscuits, and then subsided till after six, when we got up for good, and found ourselves nearing and then crossing the lovely Vosges mountains.

I forgot to say that between twilight and moonlight, about nine P.M., we passed a most desolate and scathed region, and were told it was the battlefield of Champigny. Anything grimmer and gloomier you could not imagine; ground broken and scarred, nothing but weeds growing, a few deserted cottages with great gaps in roofs and ball marks with great cracks radiating from them in the walls, and many, terribly many, irregular-shaped mounds at irregular distances, where heaps of dead were buried just where they fell. It was so ghastly, and made war seem so real.

After we had breakfasted here, we sauntered towards the fortifications, and distributed little books as we went along, and never had such a time of it! The people were so eager after them, we only wished we had hundreds more; several superior people came and asked for them, though we only offered them to the poor. Some asked for "another to give to a friend"; one workman at the fort seemed delighted, and begged us to give him some for his fellow workmen; there were a great many at work above, he said, and they would be so glad of them. We went into a place where some wounded soldiers and some women at work were sitting; they spoke most gratefully, and rose, and bowed. "Merci infiniment, infiniment!" said one man. We exhausted our stock, and after having pottered about the fortifications we parted, as E. wished to go farther, and I came back to write. As I passed through the town I found lots of people on the look-out for me, to ask for more little books; at one point at least thirty people clustered round me, begging for more. I had only three French hymns left, and they were so disappointed that, after talking a little to them, I told them they might come to the station for some. We took the opportunity; for plenty of people give tracts on the Swiss routes, but here they are evidently a novelty.

Belfort is terribly battered about; the large church is just a ruin, not a square yard of roof whole; the houses nearest the fort are simply heaps of ruins. The weather is just warm enough to be pleasant for sitting out of doors without wrap. E. and I are mutually satisfied with our equipments, which are nearly alike; and having nothing but what we can carry ourselves on emergency is most delightful, and we have been "first come first served" several times already. The "unprotected female" line answers first-rate; every one is civil and attends to us. I hope somebody will write to us at Zermatt; I ought to get some encouragement to write my circulars. Love all round in general.

Your loving sister,   F

P.S.—Mrs. S.'s maid supposed, of course, we should have a courier ; did you ever ! I think E. and I could train a courier if wished ; but the idea of *our* being taken in tow by one !

LETTER II.

Beyond ERSHFELD. *June* 30.

E. and I were in such a state of felicity that it went beyond talking, and we walked in a silence of delight. We are (for siesta) encamped under two trees and a huge boulder, a little more than half way from Altdorf to Amsteg (nine miles), at a most lovely bend of this valley which the "Practical Swiss Guide" well describes as "solemnly beautiful," the Bristenstock towering close in front of us, a cone of snow. Can't you imagine me perfectly suited ! But I will go back to where I left off. When E. came back to me at Belfort, she said she was convinced no one but an "unprotected female" would have been allowed to go where she did, up among the fortifications and on the top of the walls ! The sentinels merely looked at her, but no one spoke to her. She had found a whole street in entire ruins.

We left the Belfort station at two, and arrived at Basle at five. I must own to having been a little nervous at crossing the broken and only partially repaired bridges and viaducts ; we crossed one great breach at an immense height, on what seemed merely temporary beams, so that we looked out of the window into the valley below, without any apparent thing under the

carriage! At one station we passed an ambulance train
very slowly, so that we could see well into each
" doktor's wagen," full of all sorts of surgical-looking
things, and a " kitchen carriage," full of stoves and pots
and pans, and others evidently for the wounded with
beds in them.

Had we ordered special trains, we could not hitherto
have done better; and at Basle, where we thought of
sleeping, we had just time for a comfortable meal at the
station, and then a train was going direct to Lucerne;
this was irresistible, and we did not feel tired, so on we
went. It was a most exquisite evening, brilliantly clear,
and the rail from Basle to Olten one series of changing
lovely views. Just before Olten we had a sudden revelation of Alps; for about five minutes a distant range
of snow mountains shone out with sunset full upon
th~m, perfectly golden. It would have suited John
Bunyan; you know what those visions suggest, as
nothing else on earth ever did or does to me. Except
the lake of Sempach, which we skirted, there was
nothing else special till about 9.30, when E. announced
Pilatus! which was just ahead, delicately outlined in the
moonlight, and looking very spiritual and holy! We
went to the Cygne at Lucerne; I was in bed at eleven,
and slept like a dormouse for eight hours. It was
delicious! Fancy our not having been undressed since
Monday night! When I awoke I looked out on the
most glorious morning view of the lake and mountains.
Last week there was rain and snow here; now all is in
perfection, very clear, the green vivid and fresh, waterfalls full, and all the near mountains with extra snow,
Pilatus all capped and streaked, and looking finer than

ever in consequence. Again boat departure was just right, 9.30, giving us time to get money changed, etc. Our sail down the lake was simply perfection, and we saw the Bernese Alps, Jungfrau, and all as distinctly as possible ; you remember we never saw them at all in 1869. To add to it, a school came on board, going to Fluellen for a treat, and struck up some uncommonly pretty Swiss national songs in three parts ; and seeing our interest, the children lent us their books to follow the words, which were also very pretty. The effect of one in particular was quite upsetting, it was so sweet and charming.

You remember H. C. suggesting a "lift" on the steep side of the Rigi. Well, they have outdone him, for they have actually got a railway to the very top! on the Mont Cenis principle of a toothed line in the centre, and a wheel to catch, which continually locks itself, so that the carriages cannot run back, but regularly climb up ; they told me that at one part, which, we could see, the incline is actually one in four !

We omnibused from Fluellen to Altdorf, being a hot flat two miles, and then sent on our bags by diligence, and walked up the valley.

N.B.—I am writing now at Amsteg, 7.30 P.M. It is grander at every turn all the nine miles, and we are so glad we walked it ; don't fancy we overdid it, for we took six hours, resting two hours half way, besides shorter rests ; and this Swiss air is atmospheric salvolatile. We dined half way at a tiny village quite unknown to guidebooks, and the affair was charming. A nice gril of twenty waited on us, but thought it part of her duty to entertain us, and came and sat down all the time, making herself most agreeable. "Yes, plenty of English passed by, but none ever stayed there." She was greatly entertained with *us* evidently, and watched everything like a child. She and a younger sister had never seen india-rubber bands, and were quite delighted when I gave them a few. E. gave them some Gospels, and they promised to read them.

July 1. We were in bed at nine last night and up at five this morning, and off a little before seven. Morning superb, and the pass just magnificent ; we took it easy and did not get over the seven miles to Wasen till nearly noon. But then how could we hurry? There were gorges to look up, and high bridges to look down, and snow summits through every opening, and light and shadows playing over all. Not having cut out too much work for to-day we had time to take any number of mental photographs. At Wasen we went to the inn, a real Swiss one, and dined at 11.45 on cold kid and ham and Italian wine, and were charged tenpence each. (I will always quote English money). Though Belfort is obviously the most direct route to Switzerland, it must be rarely used by English, for at the station we had coffee, eggs, *and* ablutions, for tenpence each, and a dinner of cold beef for elevenpence each. Our whole expenses from London to Wasen have not been £5 apiece, and here we are in the very heart of Switzerland. Yet we have had everything we wanted, and the only difference is that we are waited on by the most obliging Swiss girls at these small inns, instead of by napkined waiters at the great noisy grand hotels.

Amsteg, where we slept, is most picturesque, at the

junction of the Maderanen Thal with this grand pass, but we did not get a good night owing to the roar of the Reuss, which equals that dreadful Arve at Chamouni for noise, and I dislike this as much as I did in 1869, and am longing to get up above it. We are now camped out. It is very hot, and E. is gone a little way from me, I think sketching. E. is an unexceptionable companion for me, and we agree precisely in all our ways and fancies in this expedition. Tell H. C. the hay is being cut, and it is the fashion here to set it up in most queer cocks about six feet high and two broad ; they are put on stakes with four cross-bars, rather crooked and not at any particular angle to each other, so it seems to *stick* and let the wind blow through it most "convanient."

7.45 P.M. Geschenen. Here we are in immense clover! Soon after we moved on from our camp, a storm came grandly down the valley ; we took refuge in the outside gallery of a chalet, and watched it in comfort. It was so fine to see it rush past and leave us in the sunshine, while it swept like great dusky wings down the pass. We soon got on to this place, which is *ideal*, of a different kind to the exquisite loveliness of the lower part of the pass. It is a wee village, shut in by the wildest, most savage-looking heights, mostly topped with snow, awful rocks and a great avalanche gorge on one side, a wild valley narrow and solemn on the other, shut in at the end by what looks like a very large glacier, which they say no one has ever yet crossed. We are close to a bridge over a very deep and narrow gorge, and about a hundred yards off can get back into the great St. Gothard pass, which is very

grand both up and down. And here we are going to
spend Sunday! Don't think us heathens, but we could
not possibly get to an English service to-morrow, and I
really think it will be as good as going to church just
for once! Our inn is very simple, but spotless; the
host is very young and very eager to oblige; and the
hostess must have taste, to judge by the way she has set
off the deal furniture with pretty white netting and
crochet. We are the only visitors in the place, and consequently receive the utmost attention.

We are three thousand five hundred feet high here,
having risen nearly two thousand feet in our nine miles'
walk yesterday, but we are not at all tired, and having
Sunday to rest we are planning greater things for next
week. We are quite early enough; the diligence only
ran to-day for the first time over the Furca pass, there
was so much snow; and now it is so warm I am thankful for cool attire.

Monday, 11.45 A.M. Hurrah! Seven thousand
eight hundred feet high, and going to stay all the
afternoon and night here! E. and I are quite shocked
at our giddy and exhilarated state of mind. We feel
just like children, and except a little undercurrent of
general thanksgiving, we don't feel solemn at all, and
have been in the wildest spirits, especially since we got
over seven thousand feet level. But I go back to
yesterday; it was the very perfection of a day, clear
sunshine with enough cloud floating about to give most
satisfactory effects, the temperature delicious. E. and I
strolled up a valley finished up with a weird-looking,
half-veiled, and very precipitous glacier, made ourselves

cosy nests among boulders and moss, and had a small service on our own account, after which we separated for the rest of the morning, coming back to dinner at three.

Geschenen is the most picturesque place I ever *stayed* at, four gorges opening from it, and most emphatically *gorgeous* as to scenery. Our hosts are so devoted to us that we might be personal friends paying a visit! Our bill from Saturday afternoon to Monday morning, beginning with a meat supper and including quite a good Sunday dinner of trout and beef, was altogether 14s. 4d. for both of us. We generally only have one course, which saves time as well as money.

LETTER III.

FURCA PASS (7,800 feet). *Monday,*
July 3d, 1871. 6 P.M.

We have had a real proper day, and finished up by having to get into bed (while sundry garments are dried), where I am now writing! After yesterday's rest we started this morning at 5.30, having sent on our bags to Viesch, carrying our few necessaries. We walked the five miles and a half by 7.30. The pass from Geschenen to Andermatt is savage and grand beyond description ; the Reuss is a succession of cataracts, so that any fifty yards of it would make the fortune of any English place. The Devil's Bridge is simply awful, rocks tremendous and overhanging, the depths below grim and terrible, and the river coming down in furious leaps.

8

The road is marvellous engineering; in one place it is strongly roofed over to protect it from avalanches. The weather was quite suitable, stormy and gusty, with sudden and fitful gleams of light breaking through wild grey clouds. We had a foretaste of climbing, for we made various interesting short cuts, and were just in time at Andermatt (4,500 feet) to catch the diligence for the Furca.

This road was only opened last summer, and most of the way lay along the edge of precipices; and the latter part had been injured by avalanches, and was cleared out between walls of snow. You can hardly imagine the wildness of the place, utter desolation of snow and rocks all round, and grey depths to peer down into; the Rhone valley in front and the wild pass behind, the most utter contrast to the *rich* magnificence of our walk from Amsteg.

The inn here was very small, but is being enlarged. We have a very comfortable little room with a table and sofa, and are royally lodged, for here the Queen slept when she was in Switzerland, in this very room!

Hitherto, being the only English, we have been taken into the best rooms at once. After a good feed at 11.45 we both went sound asleep, and awoke up quite fresh at two. It looked tolerably fine, so we took a guide (which is absolutely necessary) up the Furca-horn, a peak just above. It was the best climb I ever had, beat our Pierre à l'Echelle experience. There is no vestige of a track, and most queer places and snow slopes to cross; the latter were most entertaining. The guide went first, feeling every step lest he should get a plunge; we following exactly in each step, occasionally up to our knees.

I enjoyed the scramble exceedingly, and got on capitally. The view was sublime, nearly a panorama of the very wildest Alpine scenery, and the Galenstock, a lovely shaped peak of 11,000 feet just above us, the Rhone glacier deep below, and on the other side the Maienwand, an awful precipice, at the top of which, in a dip, is the Todten See (lake of the dead); the Grimsel, and Zitterhorn, and Finsteraarhorn beyond. But we only stayed a few minutes, for most awful-looking clouds were gathering and we heard distant thunder. It soon began to sleet violently, and our guide took us down a longer way, but safer for descent, in a cloud which rushed up and enwrapped us. I was not sorry when we got down safe and sound. We enjoyed some coffee, and I am now writing most luxuriously in bed. It is snowing and raining alternately most furiously, but this is a pleasing variety in our experience! They are closing the outside shutters of three of our windows, as it will probably be a rough night; the other window is sheltered and can be left for light. Have we not speedily got into the real thing?

The Alpine flowers have had the boldness to come out actually right among the snow; wherever a patch is thawed there they are, forget-me-nots and gentians, and most lovely lilac and yellow anemones, both all fringed and furred with curious soft hair; also some tiny bells of delicate mauve, the prettiest little things imaginable. These and the anemones are true ice flowers, the guide said, growing where not a blade of grass has started yet.

I have been reading this over to E., and she is afraid I shall have frightened you by my account of to-day, and that you "will be sending some one to look after

us!" This would be an undesirable arrangement, a
we don't wish to have any one *to look after!* Seriously, however, I do not consider we have done anything
dangerous, and I mean to keep the promise I made to
that effect.

At the Æggischhorn Hotel, 7,372 feet high.
Wednesday, July 5.   3 P.M.

Yesterday morning the storm was past, but the Furca
was all in a cloud, so though we were up at 5.30 we
did not start down till 8.30, when it cleared rapidly and
the rest of the day was bright.   The first six miles took
us close by the side and to the foot of the Rhone
glacier, which is an enormous *precipice of icebergs,*
with a comparatively flat foot beneath.   We had
what the aborigines call dinner at 11.30, then we strolled
on about another six miles down the Rhone valley.   As
we got down to about 4,400 feet the hay region begins.
It looked beautiful, but will not be ready to cut for a
fortnight.   It seems more than half flowers,.but they say
that is good for the cattle.   In the afternoon we got
some goat's milk, which is horrid stuff, but very refreshing.

We arranged to reach Obergesteln about three, for
the diligence to Viesch (twelve miles), but a 'cute Swiss
waylaid us, and proposed taking us in a little carriage,
which would be much pleasanter.   I had some misgiv-
ings as to whether it might be anything in the same
style as our spree at Novelles, (tell H. C.,) inasmuch as
the man candidly owned it would take him an hour to
catch his horse, which was "somewhere" on the other
side of the valley "at play."   We were in no hurry, and

the view was pretty, so we waited for him and trusted! It turned out to be quite a nice little carriage, with a most lively horse, and H. C. would have appreciated the driving, which was like the spin we had down from Chamouni to St. Gervais. The drive was delicious, and the evening lovely. Viesch lies in a charming hollow, just below the Viescher glacier and the Viescherhörner, which are over 12,000 feet. Its own level is 2,800, so we had descended 5,000 feet in the day. Our bags were waiting for us as usual ; sending them on by "post" is most convenient, and saves all trouble and porterage ; the average expense is about tenpence a day.

The Viesch hotel is primitive, and the maid scampered out to fill our ewers and water bottles at a general village spring and large trough formed of half a hollow tree. The morning was lovely, and we were up before four, and off at 5.15 for the Æggischhorn, and by 5.30 the sun was over the shoulder of the opposite mountain, and struck us with such power we were glad to get into the pine woods and be sheltered. This was the hardest walk we ever had in our lives, the steepest possible track nearly the whole way, rising straight up to 7,372 feet. It took us exactly four hours, including one-half hour's rest and several odd minutes' halt. We had some refreshment, and then lay down and went fast asleep for two hours and a half, waking up quite jolly, and as if we had had another night, just as we did at the Furca, but are just in the same fix as there! It clouded over when half way up, and since we got in has been raining heavily, just clearing suddenly once, giving us a grand view of the óther side of the valley entirely filled up with rolling grey clouds far below us. So we have no alternative but to take a day's rest, a day in the ordinary sense, as we had got here at 9.15, but we had done enough for one day before that, for though not seven miles of actual distance, it is more real work than over twelve down hill yesterday. We shall not get our letters till Tuesday, and shall have been a fortnight entirely cut off from communication; but we find it so much best to plan only a day in advance; the local information we get as to what is before us is much better than guidebooks, and we can also do more or less as we feel inclined.

We have not come in contact with a single English tourist, nor heard a word of English yet. The winter on the Furca would be too lonely even for us; they say two men and a big dog stay up there all the seven months' winter, and only come down once or twice, so that they are often three months without seeing any living thing, except hares, which sometimes stray over. On the St. Gothard pass, which is not nearly so high, there is regular sledge traffic all the winter, and men constantly employed to keep a track open.

In coming down from the Furca we passed in many places between great walls of snow through which the road had been cut; in one place the wall was at least fifteen feet deep.

I find letters are going to be sent at 5.30, but I pity the bearer, for we are in a dense fog, and we see no sign of clearing for to-night.

LETTER IV.

July 7, 4.30 P.M. Sitting on the
rocks above the Bel Alp Hotel,
about 7,500 feet high.

Hitherto we have gone on in a grand crescendo, and have not finished it yet. Yesterday, Thursday, we jumped up at four A.M. for the sunrise, but seeing nothing but fog retired again. From six to ten it was great excitement to watch the cloud possibilities. They seemed to be going head over heels just below us, whirling and drifting and breaking and closing in the most chaotic way, in every shade of grey from nearly black to dazzling white. Just before ten they rolled off altogether, and as we were quite ready for this we set off for the Æggischhorn. There is a guide here, Fischer, who is famous, and the best in the district ; but he was pre-engaged ; however, we got Alexander Binner, a very fatherly and watchful specimen, quite a ladies' guide. He insisted on our starting slowly, and consulted and patronised us in general. We have to learn by experience ; we thought we were excellently got up for the work by wearing waterproof dresses with a flannel jacket underneath, but we soon found it necessary to *peel*, and actually went up in our petticoats ! You can't think how hot one gets in climbing, even among the snow. A little way up we heard a great yell (guides here make a point of yelling if they spy one a mile or more away), and presently we met a young Alpine Clubbist, whom E. found she knew by name as a distant connection of hers ! The guides rushed at each other most affectionately, and to my delight I found they were the celebrated Ulrich and Christian Lauener, whom I have often seen mentioned in books. The young fellow had been sleeping with them in the cave of the Faulberg, in order to go up the Jungfrau at two A.M., but the fog prevented.

I cannot in conscience say I kept my promise that day, because in one sense there was "danger," for had we slipped in some places it would have been no trifle ; but I never felt giddy, and I have a sure foot I am certain, and never feel the least nervous. Alexander told us *after*, that when he heard we were new to real mountain work he made up his mind we could not reach the top, but after he had seen us get over the first snow and rocks he was quite satisfied ! Fischer told Alexander I "went like a chamois," and that he was astonished how quickly and easily I got up a very difficult climb where he watched me from above. I tell you this because I always had an instinct that I should find myself a rather extra good climber if I ever had the chance of really proving it. The "P. S. G." calls it "a severe climb " in any case, and the snow makes it now far more difficult and interesting. We crossed and ascended some great snow slopes like those awful-looking things one sees in Swiss photos ; one crossing was quite a third of a mile along the middle of a slope of steep unbroken snow, about six hundred feet high. The guide goes first, treading down the snow over soft places, and we follow *exactly* in his track ; but each step is a separate business, you stand firm and take time to plant each foot, not the least like walking, and as long as one does this there can be no danger, for if there are hidden holes the guide of course tumbles in first, and we stand still while he gets out and tries for a better footing. E. got one plunge into soft snow up to her waist, but that sort of thing does not hurt, and getting wet is no consideration at all ! Near the top it is very precipitous, and we climb with hands quite as much as feet.

The top itself is 9,649 feet high, and commands one of the very finest views in Switzerland. You look sheer down on the Aletsch, the largest Swiss glacier, fifteen or twenty miles long, with great ice tributaries. Above it, close beyond, N. and N.W., the grandest heights of the Oberland, Aletschhorn, Finsteraarhorn, Jungfrau, Mönch, Eiger, etc. South-west rise the Weisshorn and the Mischabel, a many-peaked giant and the highest Swiss mountain, and between them, quite lonely and most grim-looking, the Matterhorn. South-east lies the whole Rhone valley, bounded by Monte Leone, a superb snow ridge, and other half Italian mountains. The St. Gothard range follow, and the Viescherhörner quite near, and be-tween 12,000 and 13,000 feet high, fill up the circle. Just imagine ! Col de Balm is nowhere compared to this ! We stayed an hour on the top in brilliant sun-shine, seeing the view as favourably as possible short of a sunrise, and devoured hard-boiled eggs, red wine, and bread enough to last one a week at home. Of course we were in an awful pickle when we got down, about 3.30, and went to bed and to sleep while our clothes dried ! For the first time we went to table de-hôte, and were lucky, for there were only two besides ourselves, and they Alpine Club men, and it was as good as a book to hear them. E.'s friend had such an escape two days before, that even Lauener turned white ; the largest avalanche the guides ever saw, four hundred feet wide, came upon them "like a flash"; they saw it, and were just in time to clear it; in three seconds it was at rest, 1,500 feet below. He said "one half minute later on the path, and they must have been all killed."

In the evening we strolled out and saw an exquisite sunset; Weisshorn and Mischabel especially splendid in golden rose light, not the least speck of cloud, and the sky all flushed with wonderful tints like an aurora. You can't see these things unless you sleep up high; the finest valley sunset is quite a different article.

July 8.—Yesterday we were greatly disgusted at over-sleeping ourselves, so that we started at six instead of four A.M. We got Fischer for this walk, one of the noted guides; such a nice fellow, has been up the Jungfrau seventeen times, five times in one summer. Though it was a good five hours' walk to Bel Alp, not counting any stoppages, we were not at all tired, it was so delightful. The first two hours lay through the high summer pastures, and we passed some fine herds of lovely cows, so much prettier I think than ours, especially those which look like soft fawn-coloured satin; all had bells of course. We stopped at a chalet on the Riederalp, and had milk, rich and sweet, and Alpine strawberries. Then we crossed the ridge between the Rhone valley and the Aletsch, and had a long descent to the glacier through pine woods with little glades and vistas, and no end of flowers and *perfect* peeps of the snow mountains. It was too good to hurry through, so we sat down, and Fischer sang us a Swiss song with jödeln *ad lib.* I got him to dictate me the words, and

then I learnt the tune ; the " jödeln " is harder than
Handel, and most awkward to get into. The glacier
was absurdly easy to cross, being rough and dirty, and
we did not even go near any big crevasses. The last
hour was more fatiguing than all the rest together, as it
was fearfully hot, and a very steep shadeless path up the
sunny side of the glacier bank ; so we rested repeatedly,
but got to Bel Alp at noon.

To give you an idea of the sun's power among the
snow : I went up the Æggischhorn without gloves, this
gives a firmer grasp of the alpenstock ; but it resulted
in my right hand being so burnt that I have worn a wet
handkerchief on it for two days ; it is just as if it were
badly scalded. What niggers we shall be in complexion
when we come home !

Bel Alp is after the fashion of the Rigi, only more
than two thousand feet higher, and snow peaks are much
nearer, indeed close. People *pension* here a good deal.
Summer chalets are dotted about all round ; there are
plenty of cows, and to my great entertainment goats,
who climb most charmingly among the rocky bits behind the hotel. Again we had a lovely sunset, and the
whole day not one speck of cloud ; it is very hot by
day, but gets deliciously cool and refreshing at night.

To-day, July 8, has been the best of all ! We had
secured Anton Walden, the best guide here, for the
Sparrenhorn, which is nearly ten thousand feet high,
right above the hotel. Another lady, a Miss Anstey,
wished to join us ; her mother, an energetic elderly
lady, up to a good deal, but not to *this*, making a great
favour of it, as she was so very glad for her daughter to
have the opportunity. So we chummed, and made all

arrangements overnight, ordering coffee at 3.30 A.M. We made our actual start at 3.54. Now I have seen it at last, a *real* Alpine dawn and sunrise to perfection ! When we came out we saw the "daffodil sky" which Tyndall describes, in the east, a calm glory of expectant light, as if something positively celestial must come next, instead of merely the usual sun. In the south-west, the grandest mountains stood white and perfectly clear, as if they might be waiting for the resurrection, with the moon shining pale and yet radiant over them, the deep Rhone valley dark and gravelike in contrast below. As we got higher the first roseflush struck the Mischabel, and then Weisshorn and Monte Leone came to life too ; real rose, with something you had to persuade yourself was rose colour, only it was rose-*fire*, delicate yet intense. The Weisshorn was in its full glory, looking more perfectly lovely than any earthly thing I ever yet saw, when the tip of the Matterhorn caught the red light on its evil-looking rock peak. It was just like a volcano, and looked rather awful than lovely, and gave me the impression of an evil angel impotently wrathful, shrinking away from the serene glory and utter purity of a holy angel which that Weisshorn at dawn might represent if anything earthly could.

The eastern ridges were almost jet, in front of the great golden glow into which the "daffodil sky" heightened. By 4.30 it was all over, for as soon as the sun was up the colouring all changed to ordinary daylight hues, and thenceforth we devoted ourselves to getting up the Sparrenhorn and that alone ! I think one cannot take in overmuch beauty at once ; I hardly looked at anything for a long time after this great dawn splendour was over.

Now we found the practical advantage of starting
early. The Sparrenhorn is a little farther, a little higher,
and a little more difficult than the Æggischhorn, and yet
we did it in about the same time, with much less fatigue,
and without getting into any pickle as to raiment. For
the snow was quite hard frozen, and, being very uneven,
was quite easy walking, except when very steep, and
then Walden picked out little steps with his ice-axe
almost as fast as we cared to mount them. Coming
down I had the felicity of two real good glissades, which
were immense fun, besides some sliding. One glissade
I did quite alone ; the other was a capital long one with
Walden's hand, and it was such fun, *he* caught his foot
and was all but down, and I held *him* up ; he laughed
no end at this, and gave me full credit for it. The view
from the top was much the same style as from the
Æggischhorn, not so panoramic, but *very* fine. There
was plenty of rock climbing, quite to my mind. Miss
Anstey is sister of an Alpine Clubbist, and seems very
strong and up to mountaineering ; but E. and I agree
that we have no personal acquaintance, at least in the
lady line, who would do to make a third with us, all
things considered ! However, no one can judge of what
they can do here by what they can do in England, as
to strength. We got to the top at 6.30, and were down
again by 8.45, just as most of the folks here were breakfasting.

I fully meant to go to sleep all the morning, but did
not feel the least tired or sleepy, only a little stiff ; so I
have had a general lazy day out of doors by myself, getting flowers, reading and writing, and have postponed
my lying down till after dinner.

I had some little talks with Anton Walden, who is superior and intelligent. In response to some remark, he quoted a verse from Hebrews to my surprise. He explained this by telling me that an English lady visitor here had sent him a beautiful New Testament; "it is forbidden to read it, but I read it nevertheless." I told him I did not know it was forbidden in Switzerland. "Oh, yes!" he said, "it is entirely forbidden. The one end and aim of the priests here is to keep the people in stupidity and ignorance, so that they may do what they like with them. They cannot bear that any one should read the New Testament for themselves, they know that would not do; but there are a few *free spirits* among us who read notwithstanding." I spoke to him about asking for the Holy Spirit to teach one whenever one read the Testament (which is all he has), and he said : "Yes! that was just what he thought too; he had found that out of his book, and had prayed for the Holy Spirit." Was it not nice?

This hotel is the best placed I ever saw, it is cornerwise somehow, so that every window commands a fair view of something fine; we have a corner room with windows looking two ways, both beautiful. It will be a delightful place for Sunday. There is a chaplain, Rev. Mr. Phillips and Mrs. P.; but I am disappointed to find that he is not C. C. C. S. There are about fifteen people in the house, not more, it is such a late season.

LETTER V.

Rain always comes conveniently for us! So now having got here all right without a drop this morning, and being comfortably housed entirely to our mind, it is raining furiously, and the edges of the clouds are, I think, literally not more than twenty yards off, up the mountain side. You wished that "the Angel might go before us," and certainly the prayer seems to have been answered, for anything more entirely *hitch-less* than our whole progress has been could not possibly be ; even the little bad weather we have had always comes when it is rather agreeable than otherwise, and it is quite extraordinary how every little decision as to where or how or when to go, or do anything, invariably turns out to to be apparently the best and pleasantest we could have done : really far too uniformly so for us to attribute it to anything but the "good hand of our God upon us." The Furca-horn adventure was the only seeming exception, and that was rather fun after all.

Sunday at Bel Alp was splendid : quite different mountain effects, grand but distant tempest clouds massed in great castles and towers and peaks over and among the mountains, always giving more grandeur and beauty than they ever hid, while all continued serene and sunny at Bel Alp till quite late evening, and deliciously warm without being oppressive. About nine P.M. a thunderstorm came over, which laid the dust and cooled the air for Monday's hot transit over the Rhone valley, and ensured a brilliant morning.

The services were the most rapid I ever was at, just one hour and twenty-five minutes in the morning, including sermon and Communion, and forty minutes in the evening, including sermon. Rev. J. E. P., of W., gave us about ten minutes of commonplace and stiff sermons. Mrs. P. chose hymns, very nice ones, out of S. P. C. K. : " How sweet the name," and such like ; went the round of the few ladies in the hotel to get some one to start the singing; no one would, and she came to E. last of all, who of course referred her to me.

Monday, the 10th, we ordered coffee at five, but did not get off till nearly six, which we now consider a sadly late start ! H. C. ought to come to Switzerland again on purpose for Bel Alp, it combines so many things. Beside the superb views and excursions, one gets such a charming bit of Swiss pastoral life. The hotel stands alone, with grass and heather and flowers all round ; and dotted all about beyond are numbers of the summer chalets, with no end of funny little children. In the middle of the day we see only a few odd cows and goats, but in the evening the creatures come pouring in from the bits of high pasture in all directions. They all come of themselves, are never fetched, and never miss or come late. In the evenings we could hardly pay attention to anything but the goats ; they came trooping down the rocks, generally gambolling, and most amusing in their ways. They are most inquisitive and very tame, always came up to look at us in a most comical way, and often let us pat and play with them. There were numbers of pretty little kids and calves too ; all this was so new and amusing.

Bel Alp is the best place I have yet seen for com-

bining real mountain life with most comfortable accommodation and very moderate charges. It only cost us
exactly £1 each for three whole days, including wine
and everything ; we were quite sorry to leave.

We walked or scrambled all the way down to Brieg,
nearly five thousand feet lower ; and did not halt,
unless for a minute to look at a view, for three hours
and twenty-five minutes, and were not a bit tired !.
Then we indulged in diligence six miles to Visp, an
odious place in spite of the mountains around, all marsh,
and flies, and heat, and malaria. We had dinner and a
short rest, and then walked up the first stage of the
Zermatt valley to Stalden, about five miles and a half, a
lovely spot at the junction of the Zermatt and Saas
valleys. Here we had coffee and rest again, and I got a
native shoemaker to arm my boots with immense rough
square Swiss nails, which do not slip either on ice or
steep grass slopes.

We intended staying the night, but felt so very lively
that we actually set off again by six P.M., and walked to
St. Nicholas, another six miles and a half. Altogether
we must have done over twenty miles' walking in the
day. Of course we went to bed when we got in at 8.15,
but I did not feel at all used up, and we walked a good
seven miles this morning just as if we had done nothing.
We could not possibly have done it but for the very oppor-
tune weather, for a most handy thunderstorm came on
while we dined at Visp, which cooled the air ; I can do
nothing in heat, but almost any amount if cool. Our
long early walks are what enable us to get over the
ground so well. We are both disappointed with
Zermatt at first sight, but then the Matterhorn and

9

Monte Rosa have not been visible yet. We took a carriage from Ronda after our early walk, so as to get in here fresh, and speer about for quarters to suit our views, which we soon found. " Hotel des Alpes " is unpretending, but very clean ; we have a little room each, close together, deal furniture, but all new and sufficient ; we have two windows each, commanding three different looks-out, and are higher up than any other hotel here, and have the most charming Swiss waitress. We are to have everything, for excursions or not, for four shillings a day each, and we thought this was to be the dearest place of all ! We drank some milk, and told them to give us anything they liked for dinner at one. Whereupon we had five courses all to ourselves ; we told them three would do in future. (Oh if you could but see the rain !) We have no defi-nite plans, as we cannot cross the St. Théodule except in settled weather, nor do the Allée Blanche, but we shall call for letters at Aosta not later than the 21st. E.'s uncle and cousin are at a large hotel here ; they have come nearly the same way as we have, but their journey has been a succession of mishaps and the most complete contrast to ours, yet *they* are travelling *en grand seigneur.* Their story made us realize how much we have to be thankful for.

LETTER VI.

July 13, 10 A.M. Sitting above the
Riffel Hotel (8,000 feet).

I am intensely hoping Miss Anstey may be here to-day (which is not unlikely), as, if so, I go at once to the very top of all my Alpine ambition. She and I are wild to go up the Cima di Jazi, 13,000 feet! and yet the safest in all Switzerland for anything that height. We should sleep at a chalet two hours and a half up, for the ascent to take only four or five hours in the morning. E. will not attempt it, as long ascents try her breath, and I am not so demented as to go without a lady companion, so if Miss A. does not turn up I shall resign the idea. Wednesday was too doubtful a morning for any serious excursion, so we went for a walk, and E. turned off to call on her uncle, and I found an old woman knitting and tending goats in a lovely dingle, so I sat down by her and read out of the German Testament, apparently to her intense delight, and had a most interesting talk with her. After that I had nothing particular to do ; the Görner glacier was looking most bewitching, hardly three miles off, so what could I do but walk towards it and to it ? I did not meet a living soul, and enjoyed immensely being so utterly alone in a most wild and beautiful spot, where a seemingly full-grown river rushes mightily out of a great dark-blue ice cave, with great ice pinnacles up above, and the full catalogue of Alpine beauty all around.

I am so desperately cautious, that being alone I did not attempt to go upon the glacier itself, although one part looked perfectly safe and easy, but only scrambled a little about the terminal moraine. I gathered a white lily, only one, most lovely and lonely, like our yellow garden lilies. Zermatt is in a different zone of flowers ; yellow globe flowers, large campanulas, two very bright rock pinks, and some intense crimson rock flowers preponderate. On my way back some little white clouds, which looked far too innocent to be hiding anything, suddenly broke off, and there was the Matterhorn right above; the weirdest, most unreal-looking spectre of a mountain you can imagine. It is unquestionably the most striking single object I ever saw or expected to see. How it ever entered any mortal brain to think of scaling it I cannot understand. It stands quite alone, no connection with any other mountain or range, and seems not simply peaked and perpendicular, but actually to hook over. Why it does not tumble over bodily seems a mystery.

In the afternoon we took a horse between us to the Z'mutt glacier, the path thither being the object rather than the glacier, which, though curious, is very ugly, covered with reddish stones. It took us about four hours and a half, but we did not get the full benefit of our nag, as the path was so atrocious that the guide actually did not let us ride more than twenty minutes of the way back. Part of it was so narrow that two people could not possibly walk abreast, with a precipice at least a thousand feet straight down from the edge. But it was a most paying excursion as to beauty, and totally changed our ideas of Zermatt; it is considered only a second rate excursion by many, and yet it is one of the very finest things either of us have seen. We went close under one side of the Matterhorn, which looks unique from anywhere; its base there consists of extraordinary square-cut snow terraces, one above another, perfectly perpendicular. We waited for a cow to be milked for our benefit at a pitch dark chalet, where the poor people live without either window or chimney.

This morning we walked up here, handing our waterproofs and knapsacks half way to a luckily met baggage mule. Every ounce seems to make a difference to my walking powers up hill; I have even cut up my "Practical Guide," and carry three leaves at a time to save weight. Sometimes we catch a small boy and charter him to carry these wretched waterproofs, which are never anything between an unmitigated nuisance and an absolute necessity. We are camped out now for the rest of the morning; there are patches of snow round us, but the sun is hot and the air fresh and delicious.

Friday, July 14, 8.30 A.M.—10,200 feet high at this moment! on the Görner Grat, said to be simply "the finest mountain panorama in Europe!" Not many letters are dated from here, I fancy, for it strikes me we are doing a rather original thing in spending a morning and writing up here.

To go back; yesterday afternoon we merely took a general scramble to see what we could, and had no end of fun in jumping little snow torrents, and contriving how to get across melting snow and round snow beds. You can't think what a *boy* I feel; it does so entirely occupy my mind where to set the next step or take the next jump; no need to tell me not to think or talk; why, we should sprain our ankles if we gave our minds for two minutes to anything. Mr. Snepp wanted me to write hymns, but, dear me, he has not been in Switzerland! My only chance for that would be if we got entirely shut up in the clouds for two or three days.

We made all arrangements overnight; our guide was to call us (it seems to be the guide's duty, not at all the chambermaid's!) if it was fine, not otherwise. We ordered coffee soon after 2.30 A.M. They were not punctual, and we had the aggravation of waiting till 3.5 before we could get fairly off. However, we had the consolation of breakfasting with a party of gentlemen starting for Cima di Jazi, and a gentleman who, with two guides, was off for Monte Rosa. There was a faint clear light in the east, and the snow mountains glimmered like ghosts; but otherwise it was quite dark, though it rapidly brightened. We made a great effort to go fast, and succeeded in gaining the first Görner Grat just before the very first touch of rose came. It is really exciting and wonderful and thrilling, beyond almost anything, to see that *first* marvellous rosefire suddenly light up peak after peak. I think it beats the Hallelujah Chorus! We waited half an hour till the sun was fairly up, as we should have lost by going on. Everything was frozen, and a great deal of hard snow to cross, so odd on the 14th of July!

About five o'clock we got up here; it is an exceptionally glorious morning; at first a few tiny clouds floating about and waving like streamers from the highest peaks; now it is absolutely cloudless, unbroken deep blue above, and a perfect circle of the highest mountains in Europe enclosing enormous glaciers around us. Monte Rosa, the nearest of all, looks a stone's throw across a glacier valley. Till just now, when some tourists came up, we have not heard a sound except a very distant waterfall several thousand feet below, and one adventurous little bird that must have lost its way. We sent our guide off, so as to stay *ad lib.* There is a little space at the top here, partly rock and partly stony, where we walked like hyenas backwards and forwards (about three yards) to keep up circulation till the sun got power, which it did soon after six. Then we read a little, and then I went to sleep for three-quarters of an hour, then another hyena promenade, then breakfast on hard eggs and bread and red wine. Then some German tourists came up as hungry as wolves, and were quite thankful for a bit of bread we could spare. It is quite hot now, and not a breath of wind; had there been we could not have stayed so long; the clearness is extraordinary, so different from yesterday, when the peaks kept up a sort of sublime bo-peep among the clouds. An avalanche somewhere towards the Matterhorn has just fallen with a long deep solemn roar; no one saw it, only heard it. There is snow all around us, *i.e.* on three sides; on the fourth there is none, because it is a precipice.

Monday, 11 A.M.—Up atop of the Hörnlein, a sort of impudent sucker sprouting from the root of the Matterhorn. I could not finish half I had to say on the Görner Grat, as some Americans came up and made an awful clatter and quite broke the spell of the place. We consequently started down soon after ten, and entirely lost our way, got into a sort of labyrinth of snowdrifts and rocks; you see this unprecedentedly late snow makes everything unusually difficult. We got into no *danger,* only a little extra delay and fatigue.

In the afternoon we came leisurely down from the Riffel to our pet hotel at Zermatt, where we had an amusingly gushing welcome, as we are in great favour, especially with two particularly nice Swiss waitresses, who simply worship us. It is quite odd the fancy they have taken to us ; they watch for our return from every walk, and run to meet us and carry up our things.

Saturday we really kept our resolution to be quiet, and only camped out all the morning a mile off in a pine wood, and had an ordinary walk in the evening. Sunday was just brilliant all day ; a nice little church, Chamouni style, but very few there. Chaplain Mr. A., a young curate ; sermon no harm, but very young and mild. Service otherwise very nice ; good reader. E.'s uncle and cousin staying over Sunday ; the latter a warm-hearted little thing and a recent Young Women's Christian Association member.

This morning, Monday, brilliant again. When I came down to breakfast, about 4.40 A.M., the Matterhorn looked like an obelisk of solid gold, a most peculiar effect, for on that side we see no other snow peak, and all below it was still in shadow, deep green and brown, and nothing between this and the one immense golden rock.

We have come in for a piece of peculiar good fortune. We had no intention of doing anything grand to-day, but took food and went without a guide to the Schwarzee, a lovely little lake, perhaps seven thousand feet high, reflecting the snow summit exquisitely. By our host's directions we found the way easily, and got there at 8.30, having started at five. On the way we fell in with cows and goats and a boy, so we made him milk a goat for us into E.'s tin cup, while we held its horns !

We only got one little cupful apiece, and wanted the child to catch and milk another. He declined entirely, saying the others were not his own, and therefore he could not : only that one belonged to him. Was not

this wonderfully honest? Of course we took care he
did not lose by it. We camped at the Schwarzee, but
very soon saw Mr. Whitewell (E.'s connection) coming
near with two guides and a porter, on his way for five
hours up the Matterhorn, intending to do the worst part
early to-morrow. He had never been up this Hörnlein,
which is not much out of the Matterhorn route, so we
had the advantage of following him and his guides all up
here to my great delight.

We are in such good training that we did it easily
enough, especially as there was very little snow to cross ;
but I don't think you have the least notion of the sort of
places we get up now. Tell H. C. we should not now
count Pierre à l'Echelle at all among our proper good
climbs! Anything under nine thousand feet does not
count at all! Mr. W. and his party are gone, and we
have been some time quite alone ; and there will be no
more tourists, as it is too late for early birds; and it is far
too much for an afternoon excursion. The view is nearly
as fine as from the Görner Grat, but not so panoramic,
because we are close under the Matterhorn.

Tuesday, July 18.—We stayed a good while on the
Hörnlein, and when we did come down we found we had
the hardest work we have yet done ; we clambered up
so delightedly that we never took in what a complete
precipice it was, and infinitely harder to come down than
going up could be. However, we got down without the
least slip or nervousness. It is simply a question of
making each foot sure before you remove the other or
replant your alpenstock. We find the Hörnlein is about
the height of the Görner Grat, and anywhere else it

would be a very grand rocky peak; but as it juts out in front of the Matterhorn, it seems part of it, and does not interfere with the unity of the enormous single peak.

We were out from five A.M. to 6.30 P.M., pretty well of oxygen for one day, and we did not feel over-tired.

To-day we are really taking it quietly, as we must be off at two A.M. to-morrow for the Col de St. Théodule, the highest of all the passes, 11,000 feet. All the telescopes in Zermatt are at work upon the Matterhorn. This morning Mr. W. was visible not very far from the top, *i. e.*, three movable black dots supposed to be himself and the guides. We have done all the excursions here except Cima di Jazi, as Miss Anstey has not turned up. Zermatt itself is not equal to Chamouni on the whole, but some of the views when one gets to them (the mule paths and others are the worst I ever saw) are as grand, and much wilder and more astonishing. The contrasts are very great, some of the loveliest, quietest little dingles imaginable. You might be in England or Wales, all green and ferny and shady, little tumbling brooks and stepping stones; and then you look up and see something fifteen thousand feet high through the branches!

LETTER VII.

July 20. *Noon.*
CHATILLON, *in the Val d'Aosta.*

We are safely and pleasantly over our grand affair and one great extravagance, the Pass of St. Théodule, and after floundering in snow yesterday morning have been eating ripe figs, apricots, and pears *this* morning.

We ordered coffee at 1.30 A.M., and got fairly off by two,
with a most gushing farewell, the host insisting on pre-
senting us with a bottle of some special red wine for
our journey as a token of regard! We had quite a
cavalcade, a guide *en chef*, Schaller, and another engaged as porter, but who did not think fit to carry my
carpet bag, and transferred it to a sub. Also a man
with E.'s horse, and another with my mule. It was clear
cloudless starlight, and therefore not dark, when we got
away from the lights of the hotel. It was very curious,
this silent march under the stars, and quite novel, along
a roaring glimmering white river and over a little foot
bridge, and then up into the blackness of the pines, and
at last out above them just as a little quiver of paleness
began to show where the dawn was to be looked for.
We saw some shooting stars, and then E. saw a meteor,
and towards three A.M. I saw a splendid meteor in
the north-west, as large and bright as a crescent moon,
but lasting only two or three seconds. The progress of
dawn was most interesting, so gradual and lovely ; but
the sunrise itself was not so fine as some we have seen ;
being golden only and not rosy. But we had to perfection that pale, clear, saintly, expectant light on the great
white mountains, which I think so peculiarly beautiful,
before any colour comes upon the world, and some
singular reflections of gold clouds upon snow slopes,
themselves in shadow.

We did not ride all the way to the foot of the Théodule glacier as a few do, for Schaller said it was really
dangerous, and very little saving of fatigue, being sheer
scrambling over rocks ; so, though the creatures had
shown themselves astonishingly knowing in picking a

way over most dreadful places already, we dismounted and dismissed them. Most of the path had been just a track creeping along and up the side of tremendously steep slopes, with the great Görner glacier down so many hundred feet below. Even I submitted to have my animal led by a little chain, a thing I never gave in to before. How horrified you would have been at my attire! for on alighting we took off every possible thing, even the skirts of our dresses, and I proceeded with simply my grey linen unlined body on, and not even a necktie, between four and five A.M., and over ice and snow. It is experience that it is the best plan, one walks lighter, and the exertion keeps one warm enough, while if one wears jackets, etc., one only gets hot, and then runs the risk of getting a chill. I believe girls catch more colds than boys, because they have so much extra on to go out in, and consequently get warm and thereupon get chilled. I remember my own agonies at being "wrapped up" when I was a little girl, though I was not extra coddled in that way.

The almost unprecedented snow here greatly diminished instead of increasing our difficulties, for the upper glaciers are firmly snowed over, crevasses and all, so that our grand affair turned out less difficult than some smaller-sounding things we have done. Schaller was very wroth on reaching the glacier to find that the rope had been forgotten by Biner, but the snow was in such good condition that it proved to be not at all necessary, though usually an essential for this pass. It was a long pull of nearly three hours up the snow, never steep enough to need steps cutting with ice-axes, as on the Sparrenhorn, and not in any way exciting, except for the wonderfully wild snowy scene all round, right up among the enormous heights of Monte Rosa, Matterhorn, etc. We were surprised how little fatigued we were, but this was probably owing to Schaller's determined management of us; he would not let us go beyond a very quiet pace, said we should get palpitation at that height if we did, and insisted on our eating a little and drinking red wine. He says it is a great mistake in mountaineering to go on *till* you get a little exhausted.

On the top of the col we halted (and then was the time to put a shawl on!): such a strange wild scene, a vista into a great misty depth, was Italy; but otherwise it was all grand and solemn and pure, snow summits far too high for either dirt or noise. There is a hut on the top, the walls of which were built by De Saussure nearly a hundred years ago for his scientific experiments, *now* the guides went and smoked in it! It is the highest dwelling (so called) in Europe. In ordinary seasons a man would be found here, and wine, but no one has come yet this year, and the floor was ice, with the old straw for beds frozen into it. I picked up a feather very near the hut, which I send as a relic to Johnnie; can he tell what bird it belongs to? I don't think many of his relations will send him feathers from eleven thousand feet high. We only stayed about twenty minutes, for the snow softens every minute, and in the afternoon might be even dangerous. It was about eight when we started down on the Italian side, and we were soon plunging and floundering in soft snow. I found I had a great advantage in being so much lighter than the others, though I got let in sometimes.

About eleven we got to Brend, a nice little inn below the snow and above the first chalets. Here we went to sleep, guides and all; and to my extreme astonishment, when we fairly roused up and felt like *morning*, it was nearly three P.M. So we had made up for our short night, and felt quite fresh, and as if another day had begun. After dinner we had a lovely evening walk down through magnificent gorges to Val Tournanche, only five or six miles more; and we were perfectly ready to start again at 5.30 this morning, and walked more than thirteen miles down to Chatillon, dined there at eleven, and have had an hour's siesta after it.

It was "like a book," only a great deal better, to watch the gradual development of vegetation during our uninterrupted descent of ten thousand feet. On the col not even a lichen, then down through Alpine lichens and mosses to gentians and glacier anemones, every mile bringing us into a different zone of flowers; then pines, then birch and hayfields, then ash and standing corn, then walnuts and chestnuts and reaped corn, and now vines and every kind of Italian greenery and fruit. It was more than passing in a day from January to July, for the extremes are greater than English winter and summer; perhaps from Spitzbergen to Italy represents it better, without seven-league boots. It was well that it was quite cloudy part of our way, or we should have found the snow more trying than we did, even with veils and dark spectacles; we had a few showers, but nothing to hurt or hinder. Down here they have had none, and it is as hot and dusty as can be, with flies equal to Visp or Egypt. It is a very picturesque place, rather like Freiburg, only Italian in character; a beautiful bridge of one high arch spanning a tremendous gorge close to the hotel, and peeps of snow mountains over an almost tropical valley.

> *July* 22, 7.30 A.M.   Perched on rocks just above Courmayeur ; Mont Blanc, aiguilles, and all, glorious before us !

I hated Chatillon, could not settle ; hotel dusty and awfully hot, just what 1 dislike ; so we left at 4.30 by diligence, and reached Aosta at 7.30. We were obliged to go inside ; however, I was consoled by getting an opportunity of airing my Italian with some Turin people ; I got on better than I expected, and think I should soon get pretty fluent. I am disappointed to find that in this Val d'Aosta they speak almost entirely French ; and if not this, Piedmontese, which is a hideous patois, as ugly as Welsh, and not at all like Italian. Next morning we did Aosta pretty thoroughly before 9.30 A.M. First we had a superb walk up to a church, St: Marguerite, which commands a magnificent view of the whole valley (weather magnificent too ; always is when we want it !) It is very beautiful indeed, wide and grand, with two rivers winding below three separate sets of grand snow mountains in the openings of the lower ranges, town itself a picture, with towers and bridge, and plenty of walnut and chestnut trees and vineyards, to fill up.

We were in ecstasies with a little village perched on a green shelf of the mountain, every separate house a picture with galleries and gables, and the spaces between one mass of arcading of vines trained on stone pillars and wooden trellises above, surpassing the prettiest Italian pictures you ever saw. It is literally "sitting under his vine"; and the natives did look so cool and pic-turesque in the shade, quite enviable. This expedition took us about two hours, and then I actually went all about the town. This is the first time we have slept in one since Lucerne, and the first time we have slept below three thousand feet ; but then Aosta is really uncommon, not merely Italian, but full of such fine Roman remains as I did not know could be seen out of Rome, massive arches and towers in wonderful preservation and most interesting. We gave an old woman twopence and my bag to put what she liked in. I thought she would never stop, and on counting for curiosity, there were thirteen plums, fourteen apricots, and five large pears! Walking along this valley does not do after seven A.M., so we went by diligence at 10.30 seventeen miles to Morgex by about three o'clock ; some folks could have "walked backwards" quite as fast. We heard a great deal of talk about the king, who is now "in the mountains" hunting a beast of the chamois kind, but peculiar to one mountain district south of Aosta. He seems immensely popular here ; they told us with great satisfaction that he always speaks Piedmontese "*en famille* and to *us*, though he can speak all the other languages," and that he is "*un vrai montagnard*," and enjoys above all things getting away to the mountains, and that he camps out quite near the snow for three days at a time, and is "a wonderful shot and never misses," and various other items of praise.

Morgex was very lovely, but horribly hot, and I have had quite enough of Italian valleys and am delighted to be nearer the snow again at Courmayeur, which was about seven miles farther. I must have been either a ptarmigan or a chamois, if I transmigrated, before turning up as F. R. H. ; mountains do suit me, and no mistake. At Morgex I tumbled about on a mattress all the afternoon ; it was too hot to sleep, and too hot to go out, and even too hot to have the windows open. However, the enormous shadow of Mont Blanc brings early evening, and soon after six the whole valley was in shadow and we had a nice walk.

Owing to a fortunate mistake, we have had the most exquisite sunrise of all. We ordered coffee at 3.30, and to be called at three, thinking, as these Italians are un-punctual, we might get off at four. They did call us, and we thought it a very dark morning ; and when I had finished dressing, I looked at my watch, and it was just 2.20. We were not sorry, for a Mr. Wade we met at Aosta (brother of the ambassador at Pekin) warned us that it would be an awfully hot walk if once the sun got over the shoulder of the mountain. So we set off at three under the stars again, with a delicious breeze com-ing straight down from Mont Blanc to meet us. The dawn was perfection and cloudless, except some fairy flakes of pink and gold, and one little pale bell of cloud half way up the monarch. *But*, when the rose-fire touched Mont Blanc itself, and spread down to meet the little cloud, the glory of it was entirely indescribable. E. said, " the most heavenly thing upon earth," and there it must rest, for one can't say more. I always thought people coloured these sunrises a little, but that is sim-ply impossible ; even Ruskin will not over-paint them. " Fade into the light of common day " has great signifi-

10

cance ; for though the splendour lasted longer than usual this morning, it is only a matter of fifteen minutes at most ; and if one misses *that,* one may just as well not get up till eight.   Had we started at four, we should have had little if any view of Mont Blanc, owing to the bend of the valley ; as it was, we reached the very finest point of view at the right moment.

Courmayeur is most charming, grand and lovely combined, decidedly beats Zermatt.   Fortunately Mr. Wade recommended us to Hotel Mont Blanc, which we never should have found for ourselves ; a quiet hotel-pension half a mile away from Courmayeur, and on the grandest site, quite to our liking ; we are pensioned at about 5*s.* 3*d.* a day.   We are camped out for the morning ; there are no goats to play with, but pretty little green and brown lizards scampering about the rocks, which do as well, and make a change !

A wrinkle for Maria, which seriously I should think worth introducing for poor people at Wyre Hill !   At our pet hotel at Zermatt we had *hay* duvets ! of course too hot for July, but must be most comfortable in winter, and quite as much warmth as a good blanket.   Just a large doubled square of coloured print, neat and clean, lightly filled with loose hay !   What a boon they would be in hard winters, and they could be made of any old stuff for almost nothing.   I shall try it myself for very poor people, if it comes a hard winter.

The bread on this side the Alps is most queer ; the waiter brings a small clothes-basket full of bread, and puts a handful like a little sheaf by each party on the table.   It is in strips about two feet long, size of my little finger, very crisp and nice.   They give other bread or roll, but these sticks are evidently the leading idea.

The hours here are most original. We are supposed to have coffee early, when we like ; then at 10 A.M. a déjeuner table d'hôte ; this was, first a white grainy compound with grated cheese supposed to be soup, then sliced German sausage and bread and butter, then very good cutlets and fried potatoes, then stewed pears, then cheese, then apricots, etc. The second table d'hôte is at five. There are about thirty-two Italians and Piedmontese in the house, no English ; they are rather noisy, but very amusing to watch. After breakfast we strayed into the salon de lecture, and found a tolerable piano, the first we have had ; so naturally I sat down, there being only two ladies in the room, played a bit, and finally sang. I was rather startled after the latter performance to hear a vehement round of clapping. I had no idea of it, but the room had filled quietly ; I had my back to them, and found I had a room full of Italians as audience, quite a new thing for me! and they seemed amazingly pleased. Actually the waiters brought more chairs in, seeing the concourse, to my great amusement ; so what could I do but yield to the requests, and sing two more songs! We are not the least tired as yet, but mean to have three hours' siesta ; we always make up our short nights.

LETTER VIII.

CouRMAYEUR, *Wednesday, July* 26.

We could not have beds in our pension, and the hotels were full, so we slept in a pigsty of a cottage where nothing was clean except the beds. It was too late to make a fuss, but we made up our minds to live out all day and decamp on Monday morning.

Sunday was tolerably pleasant. Services quite delightful, though there were only seven English and a few foreign *spectators.* Chaplain Mr. Phinn, from Dorsetshire; two lovely little sermons, all one could wish, and not stiff and unappropriate like some others we have had. The hymns went so capitally in the morning that Mr. P. put on four hymns in afternoon service; he is almost a match for Mr. Snepp at it! And really we seven English, and Mr. P. included, made the little Vaudois chapel ring again, and did a good deal better than many a congregation of ten times as many. Mr. P. knows many of dear papa's own tunes well, and his especial favourite is Zoheleth, which he says every one is struck with who hears it, as far as his experience goes.

We were to have gone early on Monday to Mont de Saxe, but a really tremendous thunderstorm came on with torrents of rain, so we got up late, and did not finish breakfast till nearly seven. It was fair then, but too late for Mont de Saxe, which is a special sunrise affair, so we walked off to the Pavillon de Mont Blanc, which is exactly parallel to Pierre Pointue on the opposite side, and about the same height. Not having slept properly for three nights, we found it rather a pull, and clouds came down on the aiguilles, and Mont Blanc might have been in England for all we saw of him, and an old Swiss farmer told us there would be *"le vent et la grêle et la pluie* and all that was bad." So we raced down again and got to the hotel before two. Thereupon it cleared up and was a lovely afternoon, and we wished we had stayed. Next morning we started with a mule and guide for Mont de Saxe ; it was fair enough till we were near the top, and then it began to snow, and snowed all the time till we got down to rain level, and then it rained all the day in such a style that you would not think it could go on like that for ten minutes longer. We gained our hotel by eleven.

My proofs had come late the evening before, so I sat down to make the best of it in the salon de lecture (as we had no room), but did not get on at all well, as the Italians fidgeted in and out and played cards and piano. We had decided we could not go on this way any more, so poor E. went off to Courmayeur in the rain, and after going everywhere, finding all full, to her great delight got a comfortable and fairly quiet room, only very dark and no look-out, at the Hotel Royale. Still we hailed this and departed as to a sort of refuge, and had a very good night.

The Italians made a great fuss at our departure, and want me to come back and sing again. Each time 1· touched the piano the whole company flocked in from all sides, it was most amusing ! All are staying *en pension*, which is why we could have no room. At table d'hôte at Hotel Royale Mr. and Mrs. Phinn's places were next ours, and Mr. P. talked most interestingly ; such a nice man. They had called on us at Hotel Mont Blanc, which is what a chaplain ought to do, I think, so I was gratified.

This morning proved perfectly magnificent, which was tantalizing, but I determined to buckle to and had a good steady five hours' work on my proofs in an open air gallery without any distracting view except a brilliant sky.

Friday, July 28.—Still at Courmayeur! So far I had written in a delicious den, a discovery of E.'s, a shallow cave under a rock a little way up Mont de Saxe, cool and shady, and commanding a grand front view of Mont Blanc, with a little white pillar of cloud on the very top.

Yesterday I had a very satisfactory proof morning. In the afternoon we had a stiff climb up the shoulder of Mont Chétif, whose Courmayeur face is a striking precipice, and whose top is a curious cone of rock ; there is a tolerable path up a gorge which leads to a ridge below the cone : from this you get an astonishing face to face view of the most precipitous side of Mont Blanc (too steep for any snow to stick), and the immense ice-fall of the great Glacier du Brenva. The summit of Mont Blanc was almost entirely veiled, but that seemed almost to enhance the weird sublimity of the view.

Mr. and Mrs. Phinn asked us to come to tea to meet Costabel, the Vaudois missionary pastor, stationed at Courmayeur. This was very interesting. He is a simple, good man, very cordial and communicative, and he told us a good deal about Vaudois work, etc. ; the talk was all in French. Costabel is very isolated here, and has only a few poor Christian friends, and never any superior society unless English find him out. Mr. P. has thoroughly taken him up, and they go long walks together. He told us the fear of death among the people here is awful, that he is frequently present at the most painful death scenes. During life and health they leave everything to the priest, and believe that he will make it all right for them, and except complying with certain forms do not think or trouble themselves about religion at all. Then when they are dying they get alarmed, and see that this natural shifting of their religion upon the priest will not do, they lose confidence in him, and have no other; they want peace and have none; they would like to feel assured, but they have no assurance, and die in the agonies of terror. It was terrible to hear Costabel's description of what he says is the rule as to death-beds. "Unto the poor the Gospel is preached," and he says it is so here, that only the poor will listen to him and those in the outlying villages where no priest resides.

We find the people here quite different from the Swiss, and not so ready to accept Gospels, etc. It is the first place where on offering one we have been asked "if it was a Protestant book." However, they always end by taking them.

We did so hope to have got away this morning, and now I fear we cannot get to Chamouni at all. The Allée Blanche is a route which is worse than lost by going in bad weather, and Courmayeur is in such a hole that you cannot get out of it without going over some great pass, unless you do two days' diligence to Torca and round by Turin, or go back to Aosta and over the Great St. Bernard to Martigny. Although Courmayeur has been the scene of our only mistakes and misfortunes, I more than ever think that either for strong or weak folk it is the very best place I know of for making a long stay; the walks and excursions are inexhaustible, grand ones for mountaineers and lovely little easy ones for invalids. Valleys and gorges fork in all directions. It is totally different from Chamouni, which is one grand valley, and even better than Zermatt in this respect.

It is on a gentle slope, some height above the noisy foaming Dora, and so has not the perpetual roar which is such a drawback to Swiss enjoyment. If the rivers would but go to sleep at night, what a relief it would be! I shall take your advice about not overdoing one-self the last thing before coming home; I found my broken nights took down my strength to English level, and I was quite fagged in getting up Mont de Saxe, but one good night set me up again. I certainly have not been so well for years, and I am so sunburnt it will take two winters to bleach me.

CHAPIU. *Saturday*, 5.30 P.M.

We have got off at last; the weather was not hope ful, but we ordered a mule and provisions, and set out at five A.M. in the highest spirits, and there was the most transparent dawn-sky imaginable, not a cloud, and a delightful north wind, which is an infallible sign of first-rate weather.

As we passed our old hotel (Mont Blanc) we found a caravan of about eighteen mules and nearly as many guides, and all the Italian gentlemen pensioning there (no ladies) were going to the Col de la Seigne for the day. ·

I wish H. C. could have seen the shiftless southerners attempting to mount; four of them had actually got on a low wall to mount from while the guides were trying to poke the animals close enough for them. We hastened on, not wishing to get mixed up, and kept ahead the whole way, five hours, though we were alternately on foot, and got to the top just before them. We chose our spot to lunch, and they camped at a little distance, with many bows and "Bon appetit!" and other small foreign civilities as they passed us.

When we had finished and were moving off they shouted to us to stay, and all rose and came to us, offering wine and fruit, and saying they wished to propose a toast and drink with us before we left. It was far too gracefully done to refuse; so red wine was poured, and all raised a most cordial "Vive l'Angleterre!" with great enthusiasm and clinking of glasses, to which we responded with "Viva l'Italia!" which seemed to please them. Then an old priest said, "Mesdemoiselles, êtes-vous catholiques? Viva Roma," to which I replied in Italian, "We can at least say, *Viva Roma capitale d'Italia!*" which response he quite understood, and said, "Ah well, ah well! viva Christianity!" to which we of course responded *con amore*. Then two or three more, probably freethinkers I am afraid, said "Oui bien, but no more popery," and other similar exclamations, at which we were very much astonished, as at least three priests were in the party. Then we were allowed to depart with no end of hat-wavings and good wishes. It was such a curious little episode, occurring too at such a superb spot, and close to the cross which marks the boundary and bears on one side "France" and on the other "Italia."

We reached Chapiu at two, and we hoped it might be possible to put on steam and get over the Col de Bonhomme this afternoon, but we found it could not be done before dark, so we were obliged to give it up and stay over Sunday at this funny little lonely inn.

It has been a glorious day, almost too clear, as it rather takes from the sublimity, the summits looking so near. We passed the Lac de Combat, an exquisitely soft tinted lake, pearly blue, but less intense than Geneva, reflecting a grand and lovely group of snow summits and ridges, more like a fairy fancy than a reality in its unique loveliness.

That lake was red in Napoleon's days, and a wretched garrison was kept freezing there four whole winters, guarding the pass at the boundary. The ruins of their rough fortifications are reflected in one corner, a melancholy contrast.

The col is 8,450 feet high, but the ascent was unusually gradual, and we were as fresh when we got to the top as when we started. But then we had ignominiously descended to having a mule between us, so it was only two hours and a half walking for each.

LETTER IX.

HOTEL GIBBON, LAUSANNE. *Thursday, Aug. 3.*

I actually have had no one-half hour to begin this conclusion of my reports, for, in spite of all my resolutions, we have had three tremendous days. How was a mortal to resist doing all one could at Chamouni?

Sunday at Chapiu we turned out for a little air the first thing, came back in the rain, and had to stay in the rest of the day. We intended to have spent part of it in Scripture reading among the few scattered chalets within reach, as Costabel told us the inhabitants are mostly mere heathen, and not even looked after by any priest.

Monday dawned sulky, but not bad enough to stay at Chapiu, where the bread was sour and the other viands pale and greasy, and we, having the best room, were accommodated with one deal bench instead of any chairs. So we set off before sunrise, in hope, and after an hour's steep climb met the clouds, which were relieving themselves of sleet. We soon got to the highest chalet and took shelter. Such an interior! Fancy a good-sized barn, one half consisting of a platform three steps high, the other with floor of bare earth. We were civilly invited to ascend the steps and sit on a box, which we thankfully did, for we dared not stir for dirt and fleas. On this platform, which had one window a foot square, were five beds, three of hay on the floor, covered with one filthy sheet and a great brown coverlet ditto, the other two a sort of boxes of hay. Presently the beds were made, and the process was simple, consisting of a shake and poke to the hay, which sent out a cloud of dust. Two children were awoke and dressed; their toilet, performed by the father, occupying about a minute, and chiefly consisting of putting on cap and shoes. We watched the proceedings on the earthen floor half of the house with amusement. The inhabitants all had breakfast in a desultory way, milk and curds and bits of black bread, supped out of great porringers with gigantic spoons. There were five men and a woman, all occupied with the milk and cheese business, and grouping themselves picturesquely in the light from the door, and a wood fire on the ground made near-enough to a hole in the corner of the roof to give the smoke a chance. Over the fire a cauldron, at least four feet in diameter, swung about by a great creaking beam, a most witch-like affair. After nearly two hours the storm moderated, and the guide said we could go on.

When we had done all the worst of the ascent, the rain having happily ceased, I suddenly fell sick. It was a fix, for we were too high either to stop or go back, and I could not stir, but lay down on the wet stones, whereat the guide was frantic. "Madame serait malade, if she did not get up and walk." (They consider themselves as responsible for their travellers). Most opportunely E. descried at some depth below two gentlemen and a mule; by the time they reached us I was rather better, and they were most amiable about lending me their animal, making out that it was only laziness to have had one at all. We continued the ascent; and, to my amazement, getting among the snow again so revived me that when we got as far as the mule could go (in about an hour) I felt all right. The "traversée," as they call it, of the Col de Bonhomme was the wildest of wild scenes, cutting across the west shoulder of the Mont Blanc chain, all rocks and snow, most formless and chaotic, and famous as being about the most difficult to find the way. Our benevolent friends had a Zermatt guide, who was supposed to know it well; but they quite lost the way, and were brought back by much racing and halooing by the Chapiu man who was with me and the mule. A thick white icy fog had come on and made the col very characteristic, but we lost the grand views. We came down into the lovely valley of Contamines and dined at Nant Borrant, and after an hour's sleep we walked two hours more down to Contamines, which we reached about 5.30. Such a lovely place, luxuriant and bright, with snow summits closing the valley, and the rosy smile of a great white peak shining down at sunset through a cloud rift.

Next morning was another of the brilliant days of which we have had so many. It is eighteen miles to Chamouni, so we took a horse between us for the first six or seven miles, leaving less than eleven to walk. The top of the Col de Voza is glorious, it is too close under Mont Blanc to see the real summit, but the massive shining snow of the Dome and Aiguille du Gouté are close above ; all the other aiguilles follow in a grand curve, and the fine sweep of the vale of Chamouni is nowhere seen to such advantage. The colouring was vivid, and the atmosphere keenly clear. We scampered down to Les Ouches, and then finished the walk with four miles and a half of level road to Chamouni, which was quite a rest after the mountain work. Having got our letters and looked about Chamouni, we took mules and started up the Bréven ! Not all the way, as we could not reach the top before dark, but to Plampraz, about two-thirds of the way up, a first-rate place for sunset, rather higher up than La Flégère, and exactly opposite the great Glacier des Bossons and the very heart of Mont Blanc.

How we did triumph over the people whom we met going down to table d'hôte at Chamouni, just as the grand show up there was going to begin ! There had been more than one hundred visitors at Plampraz, but all cleared down before sunset, and we had the little inn and the sunset all to ourselves. It seemed too much to have all alone ; how I did want you and all ! That whole magnificent range close opposite to us turned gold, and then fire colour, and then softened into rose, and then tenderly paled away into that most saintly colourless afterlight, which M. L. will remember we agreed in admiring most of all. The valley was quite dark below, and the black pine forests beneath, and the almost purple sky above, formed a wonderful setting for all that superb colouring.

Next morning, Wednesday, we were up just in time for a lovely clear sunrise; but there is no expanse of colouring in the morning, as the eastern tips are only seen sideways. The rose flush was very delicate and lovely, but all over in ten minutes. Then we had coffee, and soon after five started up the Bréven, which I did not intend to do at all, and meant to let E. go alone; but how could I help it on such a morning! It is much more difficult than I expected, as there are several snow slopes, and one where we should have been glad of an ice axe to cut steps; and near the top the "cheminée" is quite a hands and feet climb up a rock. The view from the very summit is a first-class panorama, and quite a different thing from going only to the little inn, which many do, and call it "going up the Bréven." We stayed an hour to take it in, then came down again to Plampraz and had another breakfast.

The next move was to march to La Flégère, about five or six miles, a more tiresome walk than we expected; as, instead of being nearly level along the slope, it was rather sharp up and down the whole way. It was delightful to see La Fiégère again and compare impressions, as it was my first revisited scene. It was beginning to cloud over, and so looked just the same as when we saw it in 1869. I do not think the Mer de Glace part of the view lost anything by comparison with all we had seen ; but the Mont Blanc part of it is very inferior to the Bréven view. We had only time to rest twenty minutes and drink some milk, and then set out again by a cross cut, which for part of the way was no path at all, down to Argentière. We had no guide, and occasionally made a bad speculation and made angles ; however, we reached the Couronne where we breakfasted in 1869, ravenous !

After dinner we took mules for the Col de Balm at 4.30, rather annoyed at being reduced to this ignominy, but we had wearied ourselves in tracking the way to Argentière, and it was a close, oppressive day. I had before inquired for Joseph Dévouassoud ; he was off duty as guide ; however, he got wind of the inquiry, and a description of the inquirer ; whereby he arrived at the conclusion that it was the writer of the verses in his certificate book, which verses he seems to have considerably traded upon ! So after dinner he came in delighted and gushing, quite amusing, and got leave from the guide chef to exchange his turn, and so came with us up the Col de Balm. It was cloudy and gloomy when we got up at nearly seven o'clock ; we went immediately up the hill on the left, where H. C., M. L., and I went to get the panorama. It was really very grand ; though I would rather have seen it in clear light, the sombre gloom was not a bad effect, especially on the Tête Noire side, where the gulf was almost black and the mountains just awful, with the white Buet like a dim ghost overlooking them. The Mont Blanc range was a chaos of cloud and snow. We saw most where last time we saw least, *i. e.* down Martigny way ; the Rhone valley mountains being clearer, and some vestiges of sunset light on them. No one else except a very fatigued German slept there; he had walked from Chamouni *viâ* Montanvert, and had quite exhausted himself; "it was far too much to attempt," he said. We were entertained, for we had done considerably more in the day, and were quite lively after it all.

It poured all night, but left off after seven A.M., so we prepared to start; our bill was simply scandalous. We decided to give up the Eau Noire gorge route, and go direct to Martigny. The P. S. G. calls it five hours and a half, but we scampered, wishing to catch the 12.30 train, and we actually did it in four hours, including five minutes' stoppage on the Col de Trient for a glass of wine and water.

Although it poured furiously part of the way, I never was more glad that we had no waterproofs; we could not have done it if we had, and if I come pedestrianising again I shall take none. Getting wet is nothing in Switzerland, one gets dry again directly. It seemed quite too luxurious to get into such good paths again as the Col de Balm; Zermatt, etc., are half a century behind Chamouni in this respect.

It would have been tatalizing to go by rail down the Rhone valley if it had been fine; but it was all colourless and cloudy and rainy, so I was grateful to George Stephenson. The lake of Geneva can't help looking blue in any weather, but it was rough enough to make us glad we had not gone by steamer. Montreux, etc., looked astonishingly tame after the great scenes we have been in. We came on here (Lausanne), as our bags were to be at Poste Restante, otherwise it would have been nicer to go on to Neuchatel. Even the smallest modicum of baggage is sure to be a nuisance first or last. Only fancy us at Hotel Gibbon! the first time we have been in one of these Swiss palaces in this tour, and we feel so out of place! The first thing I did on getting into this grand hotel was to tumble down full length on the polished gallery floor, owing to the nails in my boots. I never had a single fall on ice, snow, or rock! so it was rather odd.

Our evening coffee here under splendid chandeliers and mirrors and carving and gilding was a considerable contrast to the previous night. At Plampraz, which was lowest in the scale, we had no chair or table in our bedrooms, and the limited washing apparatus was on a very small shelf by the bed, which was a sort of wooden crib.

On the whole I set Courmayeur as A 1 of all, and I think Zermatt second, and Chamouni third. But there is no single scene more unique and characteristic than the Mer de Glace at Chamouni, and no panorama to compare with the Görner Grat. Courmayeur has far the most variety, whether for excursions or for strolls, and is quite the place for the longest stay. But Chamouni is the place to begin with, to get into training; Courmayeur to improve upon it; and Zermatt to use and tax all your Alpine powers. You can't think what easy walks all the Chamouni excursions seem to us now! N.B.—I read my letters over to E., so there is a guarantee against exaggeration.

Connie was the only person who addressed rightly to Chamouni; every one else put Switzerland, so causing delay and extra payment, as it is *France*. No one ever will believe that Chamouni is not Switzerland and never was, but Savoy, and now France.

Monday, 7.30 A.M.—Clapham Park. Just as uncomfortable a journey home as possible, a small counterbalance to our previous prosperity. I can't stay for details, but will write when I get to Perry Barr. Horrible crossing. Delightful Sunday here, splendid! most striking sermons, Rev. Aubrey Price; leave here 8.45. Could not possibly post on Saturday.

MY ALPINE STAFF.

My Alpine staff recalls each shining height,
  Each pass of grandeur with rejoicing gained,
  Carved with a lengthening record self-explained,
Of mountain memories sublime and bright.

No valley life but hath some mountain days,
  Bright summits in the retrospective view,
  And toil-won passes to glad prospects new,
Fair sunlit memories of joy and praise.

Grave on thy heart each past "red-letter day"!
Forget not all the sunshine of the way
By which the Lord hath led thee : answered prayers
And joys unasked, strange blessings, lifted cares,
Grand promise-echoes ! Thus thy life shall be
One record of His love and faithfulness to thee.

(163)

HOLIDAY WORK.

I ONLY wish that all the tired workers at home would renew their strength and spirits by such holiday work abroad as lies within reach of many who fancy it far out of their reach. I did not know till the summer before last what a combination of keen enjoyment and benefit to health, with opportunities of usefulness and open doors innumerable, was to be found in a *pedestrian tour by unprotected females!* This, too, without difficulties or discomforts worth calling such, and at a *very* much smaller outlay than is supposed possible by those who travel in the usual expensive way, and think that going to Switzerland for six or eight weeks means spending £50 at the least. Much less than half that sum will suffice for such a tour as ours. And lest it should be thought that exceptional strength is necessary, I may premise that both my friend and myself had been thoroughly overworked, and were obliged to seek rest; that neither of us is very strong, and that a walk of a mile or two is the extent of our English powers.

Of course we chose the inexpensive route, *viâ* Newhaven and Dieppe to Paris, and thence by night train to Belfort, on the frontier, where we arrived at nine A.M., June 29th, 1871. As we had slept pretty fairly, having

(164)

had a carriage to ourselves by reason of the guard's natural sympathy for unprotected females, and having been able to lie down full length by reason of going second class instead of first, we were not tired, and intended to proceed. But the train to Basle and Lucerne had just left. " *C'est une désorganisation complète !* " said a fatigued Frenchman, and rightly. No information whatever was to be had, either at Paris or at Belfort itself, as to trains beyond, unless you got hold of a German official. Moreover, every German train was arranged to depart just before the corresponding French one got in, and *vice versa*, apparently for the purpose of spite. And so it came to pass, as a result of the war, that we had nearly six hours to wait.

When there is no one to wait and be anxious for you, and no one to arrange for but your two selves, and no fixed plan beyond to-day, and that day and all its hours committed to a Father's guidance, disappointment becomes almost impossible, and the crossing of one's intentions constantly results in most evident guiding to something better. So it was with our detention at Belfort, which was no part of our own programme.

We set off through the town to the fortifications. "Why should we not begin at once?" said my friend, E. Clay. So, setting the example, she began offering French tracts and "portions" to almost every one we met. And a wonderful two or three hours we had! Such eagerness for the little books, such gratitude, such attentive listening as we tried to speak of Jesus, such tears as we touched the chord of suffering, still vibrating among these poor people, to whom war had been an awful reality! Surely God sent us! Not one to whom we spoke but told us of husbands, sons, or brothers fallen in the siege or elsewhere ; or else of terrible losses and poverty. Some to whom we gave tracts went away reading, and soon came back begging for another, " pour ma mère," " pour un ami." We went into a large room, where several wounded soldiers lay, while women sat at work ; here again all was earnest attention and gratitude. "*Merci infiniment, infiniment!*" said one poor fellow.

At last we made our way up to the fortifications, where probably none but "unprotected females" would have been allowed! Our *petits livres* secured us the respect of the few soldiers and many workmen. We realized a little of what war means, as we wandered about the half-ruined stronghold, and looked down upon a church with scarcely a square yard of roof intact, and houses in every stage of shatter and desolation, or, at best, poorly patched up for bare shelter.

Before we left, a deputation came to us from a party of workmen who had been reading our tracts during their dinner, to ask for a few more, that they might take them to some *camarades*, who were employed in another part of the town, and who "would be too happy to possess them."

As we returned through the town we found many waylaying us. At one point which they knew we must pass, at least thirty persons were waiting, and pressed round us, begging for more tracts. We had only a few leaflets left, with " Rock of Ages " in French and German, and these they accepted eagerly. I have since regretted that it did not occur to me at the moment to *sing* it.

We reached Lucerne that night, and next morning

steamed down the lake. It would have been contrary
to our travelling principles to pay first-class fare for the
privilege of sitting among the unsociable English, aft,
with funnels and paddle-boxes right between us and the
magnificent scenery opening out before us; so we took
second-class tickets, thereby securing for half-price a
clear front view, with nothing but transparent air between us and the increasing loveliness ahead, and also
the advantage of being among the natives, who were all
politeness to the English ladies. We thus had also the
benefit of some charming Swiss songs, sung by a girls'
school out for a holiday ; they lent us their little song-
book to follow the music, and were delighted at receiving little books in return, which might, by His blessing,
put a *new* song in their mouths.

From Altdorf, at the other end of the lake, our long-
anticipated *real* pedestrian tour began. Our plan was
as follows. Our luggage consisted of a *small* carpet-bag
apiece, every inch and ounce having been considered
and economised, though even these were discovered on
further experience to contain superfluities ! These bags
we sent on each morning by post or diligence if on *grandes
routes ;* by baggage mule, country cart, or small boy, if
off the track : to whatever place we thought we could
reach in the day without undue fatigue ; and here we
always found them all right ; average expense, a few
pence.

We started at four or five A.M., walking on till we felt
inclined to stop and rest : our first halt being given to
leisurely reading and prayer in some grand and lonely
mountain oratory ; a plan which we found more pleasant
and profitable than devoting the whole time to it indoors

before starting. Then we strolled on again, halting or
taking refreshment, just as and when we felt inclined ;
resting for several hours in the heat of the day, and
making another stage or two in the afternoon. We carried tiny knapsacks (bags are a great mistake, being
more fatiguing to carry) ; these held tracts and " portions," a biscuit and a hard egg, and the barest necessaries in case of missing our carpet-bags, or altering our
plan for the night. As Switzerland is the land of hotels
and travellers, such a tour as ours is easier than it would
be elsewhere ; unless you are in *very* out-of-the-way
places, you seldom go three miles without some opportunity of getting a meal, nor six without a fair chance
of beds.

We began very gradually ; our first walk was only two
miles, but in a fortnight we found ourselves doing from
fourteen to twenty miles in the day without getting
tired ! Our early hours were part of the secret ; one
can do double the distance before seven A.M. that one
can after ; the invigorating effect of the crisp, fresh
mountain air from four to seven A.M. is indescribable.
Those who think eight A.M. a pretty fair start never
know what this atmospheric salvolatile is. But you cannot burn your candle at both ends, and must go to bed
accordingly. If you resolutely and *regularly* retire at
eight P.M., and make no scruple about taking a good
siesta in the heat of the day (and you may lie down on
the grass with impunity in *such* open air), it will come
quite natural to get up about 3.30 or 4 A.M. We felt sen-
sitive about Dr. Watts and " wasting our hours in bed,"
if we were not out of it before 5.30 on Sunday mornings.

Oh, the delicious freedom and sense of leisure of those days! And the veritable "renewing of youth," in all senses that it brought! How we spied grand points of view from rocks above, and (having no one to consult, or to keep waiting, or to fidget ahout us) stormed them with our alpenstocks, and scrambled and leaped, and laughed and raced, as if we were, not girls again, but downright *boys!* How we lay down on moss and exquisite ferns, and feasted our eyes on dazzling snow summits through dark, graceful pines, with intense blue sky above, and the quiet music of little torrents coming up from the dell below, and with the "visible music" all round us, in every possible colour-key, of those marvellously lovely Alpine flowers, which people never see who go "in the season," a month or two later. How entirely we were rid of that imp, Hurry, who wears out our lives in England! "No hurry!" It took us a long while to realize that delightful fact. And how we wished that a wish could have transported the whole Association of Female Workers and Young Women's Christian Association, whom we left in London, bodily to the spot, to share the wonderful rest and enjoyment which our Father was giving us! A "*holiday*" most certainly; but how about "*work*"? So much of that, that we never wanted more opportunities, but only more earnestness and faithfulness, and courage and love, to use them. If space allowed, one would like to give each day in order and detail, with its pleasant providences and openings. But we can only indicate briefly some of the different kinds of "opportunity" so thickly strewn in our path.

Our tour was entirely through Roman Catholic cantons; its roughly sketched outline being this: from Altdorf, over the Furca, down the Rhone valley to Viesch; a detour to Æggischhorn and Bel Alp; then to Zermatt; over the pass of St. Théodule into the Val d'Aosta; Courmayeur; over the Col de Bonhomme to Chamouni; thence to Martigny, where we took rail direct home, *viâ* Neuchatel. And all the way, no Bible, no gospel, but souls walking in darkness all around! Will not some of our workers try to go, and tell them of the True Light?

At the little inns where we slept, we nearly always found young waitresses. A few kind words and smiles secured their absolute devotion to us, and we were waited on like duchesses. (N. B.—How much nicer than going to big hotels, with waiters flying about, to whom you are merely No. 79 or No. 43!) They have "no time for religion in the summer," but attend extra masses in winter to atone for it. But they find time to listen with surprise as you speak to them of salvation. They are afraid to die; "*Ah, la mort, c'est terrible!*" And it is at least something new to hear of a "sure and certain hope." We speak to them again in the morning before we go, and sometimes find that they have been lying awake thinking of what had been said. We give them a Gospel of St. John, and our own reading has not been less profitable because it has not been in our own Bibles, but in this "portion" for poor Thérèse, marking as we read such bright star-texts as may catch her eye, and guide her to Jesus.

Here I may say that during our long mid-day rests we made it our special occupation to mark the most striking passages and texts in the "portions" we were going to give away. These were *chiefly* St. Luke and St. John, while to persons of superior intelligence and education we often gave Romans, but *always marked.* Even curiosity will induce people to look attentively at marked passages.

At Zermatt, where we stayed five days in the clean, cheap, and unpretending Hotel des Alpes (which we strongly recommend), there were two maidens, and we agreed each to make special effort with one. Alexandrine had evidently never thought about religion ; but Marie, a singularly gentle and lovable girl, seemed an instance of " soil prepared." She had thought much of death, and with terror ; she had tried to be worthy of heaven, and had failed, and wondered why she felt so bad when she really wished to be good. She said she knew that Jesus died for sinners, but had no idea what good that was to do for her, as of course she must gain her own salvation, and *then* He might save her. She had never seen a Testament, and no one of the many English ladies whom she had served had ever spoken to her about these things.

Every evening she contrived to come to my room, and we read the German Testament and prayed to gether. She listened eagerly, and as if it were indeed a matter of life and death. I cannot say that when we left she was able to *rejoice* in Christ, but I think that she had, though tremblingly, touched the hem of His garment ; she was trusting to none other, and saw that it must be " Jesus only," and the whole desire of her heart seemed to be toward Him.

We often turned out of the path to go to parties of haymakers. They invariably received our books with pleasure, and their acknowledgments were most courteous. If we stayed to read a few verses, they never seemed to feel it an interruption. We gave them the book out of which we read, with a leaf turned down, that they might look again at the passage. One morning I sat down by an old woman, who was knitting, and watching goats. She was an "old maid," very poor, and full of troubles. She often thought of heaven, she said, and how different it would be there, and she prayed that God would show her how to get there. She was sure she should be happy if she was where the good Lord Jesus was. It seemed to me that the poor old creature had some real love for Him, and was perhaps a·true child of God, though with little light; so, acting on impulse, yet with misgiving as to its being the right choice, I read to her very slowly most of the 8th of Romans, pointing with my finger to every line as she looked over me, dwelling on and repeating the most comforting words. I was little prepared for the effect of the thought, so entirely new to her, "*no separation.*" She took hold of it with unquestioning faith and with wonderful joy. "Has He said that, that I shall never be separated from Him? Ah, how beautiful; ah, how good! I can suffer now, I can die now!" And the poor wrinkled old face was positively radiant. Her tears of gratitude, when, after a long talk, I said she might keep the little book which contained such precious words, were touching indeed. At my last glimpse of her she was poring over her Romans, heeding neither her goats nor her knitting.

Children were generally proud to be taken notice of by the "*Engländerinnen,*" and so were the parents, if, on making friends with a family group, we asked the little ones to show us how nicely they could read. As they mostly read clearly and well, this seemed to answer better than our own reading, for it gave additional motives for attention, and easy opportunities for questions and simple comments.

It is a good plan to learn by heart some of the leading gospel texts ; even a very few so learnt, prove valuable weapons, and without this one feels comparatively swordless, as one cannot give a rough and ready translation with the same confidence as the exact words of the French or German version. Sometimes we quoted such a text where we could have but a minute's conversation, and if our friends seemed at all struck with it, we gave them the portion containing it, telling them that if they would look carefully they would find those words in the little book. We sometimes, on looking back, saw them sitting down at once to search for it. "*My word shall not return unto Me void*" is a grand promise ; and in the faith of that it was a comfort to quote and reiterate short and easily remembered texts, when our supply of "portions" ran short.

All very well ; but what are those to do who speak little or no French and German ? "Where there's a will there's a way," and plenty of ways too. You can mark the "portions" ; you can offer them ; you can point out passages, and get the person to *read it to you ;* or you can set the children to read for you ; and while that promise standeth sure, who shall say that such work shall be in vain ? What does it matter about *our* words, if we can, even silently, give *His* words?

We never came upon ground trodden by any other

sower, except among the guides, and we did find a few of them who had at least "heard of these things." They are intelligent and superior men, and seemed more often ready and disposed to converse *seriously* and *freely* on important subjects than any class of men there or elsewhere.

At Bel Alp, a mountain pension about seven thousand feet high, one of the loveliest spots in the darkest canton, we engaged a guide for the ascent of the Sparrenhorn, which is nearly ten thousand feet high. (Unless going above snow level, or crossing a glacier, we never required Swiss guides. A tolerable map and the "Practical Swiss Guide" were enough for all other routes).

We started at 3.45 A.M., and from the stillness of the hill-side overlooking the great Aletsch glacier watched an Alpine dawn. In the east was a calm glory of expectant light, as if something altogether celestial must come next, instead of a common sunrise. In the south and west, "clear as crystal," stood the grandest mountains, white and saintly, as if they might be waiting for the resurrection, with the moon shining in paleing radiance over them, and the deep Rhone valley, dark and gravelike, below. Suddenly the first roseflush touched the Mischabel, then Monte Leone was transfigured by that wonderful *rose-fire*, delicate yet intense. When the Weisshorn came to life (most beautiful of all, more *perfectly* lovely than any earthly thing I ever yet saw) the Matterhorn caught the same resurrection light on its dark and evil-looking rock peak. It was like a volcano, lurid and awful, and gave the impression of a fallen angel, impotently wrathful, shrinking away from the serene glory of a holy angel, which that of the Weisshorn at dawn might represent, if any material thing could. The eastern ridges were almost jet, with just a tinge of purple, in front of the great golden glow into which the "daffodil sky" rapidly heightened, till the sun rose, and the great dawn splendour was over. Would you not like to go and see such a sight?

During this excursion I had several little talks with our guide, Anton. In response to a remark, he quoted a verse from Hebrews to my surprise. He explained this by telling us that four years ago an English lady had spoken to him about his soul, and on her return to England had sent him a New Testament. This he had read daily. He had *no other help*, but found in it that he might pray for the teaching of the Holy Spirit, and from that time had constantly done so. He had learnt from it the need of a mediator, and that there is but *one* Mediator, and now prayed no longer to the Virgin or the saints, but only to and through the Saviour. He had no doubt but it was God's own word, because he felt its power and preciousness. "Life was a different thing to him now," he said, and it was evidently a life of faith on the Son of God. Possibly this may meet the eye of the faithful sower who dropped the incorruptible seed which has borne such "fruit unto life eternal."

What if but one of the words spoken or books given during a whole tour should be thus blessed! Would it not be worth all the effort, and the screwing up of courage, and the battles with shyness and nervousness and reluctance which have to be fought again and again?

Ye who hear the blessèd call
  Of the Spirit and the Bride ;
Hear the Master's word to all,
  Your commission and your guide :
" And let him that heareth say,
Come," to all yet far away.

　　.　　　.　　　.　　　.　　　.

Brothers, sisters, do not wait,
  Speak for Him who speaks to you !
Wherefore should you hesitate ?
  This is no great thing to do.
Jesus only bids you say,
" Come ! " and will you not obey ?

VI

AN ALPINE CLIMBER.

Ho ! for the Alps ! The weary plains of France,
   And the night-shadows leaving far behind,
   For pearl horizons with pure summits lined,
On through the Jura-gorge in swift advance
Speeds Arthur, with keen hope and buoyant glee,
On to the mountain land, home of the strong and free

On ! to the morning flush of gold and rose ;
   On ! to the torrent and the hoary pine ;
   On ! to the stillness of life's utmost line ;
On ! to the crimson fire of sunset snows.
Short star-lit rest, then with the dawn's first streak,
On ! to the silent crown of some lone icy peak !

'Twas no nerve-straining effort then, for him
   To emulate the chamois-hunter's leap
   Across the wide rock-chasm, or the deep
And darkly blue crevasse with treacherous rim,
Or climb the sharp arête, or slope of snow,
With Titan towers above and cloud-filled gulfs below.

It was no weariness or toil to count
   Hour after hour in that weird white realm,
   With guide of Alp-renown to touch the helm
Of practised instinct ; rocky spires to mount,
Or track the steepest glacier's fissured length
In the abounding joy of his unconquered strength.

12   (177)

But it was gladness none can realize
   Who have not felt the wild Excelsior-thrill,
   The strange exhilarate energies, that fill
The bounding pulses, as the intenser skies
Embrace the infinite whiteness, clear and fair,
Inhaling vigorous life with that quick crystal air.

That Alpine witchery still onward lures
   Upward, still upward, till the fatal list
   Grows longer of the early mourned and missed ;
Leading where surest foot no more ensures
The life that is not ours to throw away
For the exciting joys of one brief summer day.

For there are sudden dangers none foreknow ;
   The scarlet-threaded rope can never mock
   The sound-loosed avalanche, frost-cloven rock,
Or whirling storm of paralyzing snow.
But Arthur's foot was kept ; no deathward slips
Darkened the zenith of his strength with dire eclipse.

So, year by year, as his rich manhood filled,
   He revelled in health-giving mountain feats ;
   Spurning the trodden tracks and curious streets,
As fit for old men, and for boys unskilled
In Alpine arts, not strong nor bold enough
To battle with the blast and scale the granite bluff.

One glowing August sun went forth in might,
   And smote with rosy sword each snowy brow,
   Bright accolade of grandeur ! Now, oh now
Amid that dazzling wealth of purest light,
His long ambition should be crowned at las
And every former goal rejoicingly o'erpast.

For ere the white fields softened in the glow,
   He stood upon a long-wooed virgin-peak,
   One of the few fair prizes left to seek ;

Each rival pinnacle left far below !
He stood in triumph on the conquered height :
And yet a shadow fell upon his first delight.

    For well he knew that he had surely done
      His utmost ; and that never summer day
      Could bring a moment on its radiant way
    Like the first freshness of that conquest, won
Where all had lost before. A sudden tear
Veiled all the glorious view, so grand, so calm, so clear !

VII

LETTERS TO MRS. HAVERGAL,

OF PYRMONT VILLA, LEAMINGTON,

IN 1873.

No. I.

GRAND HOTEL, Paris, Room No. 446.
May 30, 1873. 7 A.M.

THUS far all safe and well; but I must begin at the beginning, for the sake of M. and E., who will like details. We started May 28, in the morning, went to the Lord Warden at Dover, and crossed to Calais by the 9.35 boat. *Un beau ciel* enough, brilliant sun; but, alas! no enjoyment of it, as we were all ill.

The gangway on to the steamer happened to be pitched unusually steeply, so that it was quite an interesting speculation to Amy and me, whether Mrs. S. would come down or stay in England! and the steamer was tossing about very horribly; but E. did not hesitate an instant when her papa told her to go down it with his hand. When we got nearly to Calais, and Mrs. S., Ann, and I were not sufficiently recovered to stir, poor E., who looked just like a little white ghost, and could really hardly stand· herself, would insist on trying to get to each of us with eau-de-Cologne; it was so pretty to see her. Ann is very sensible, and takes any little inconvenience more philosophically than I ever expected a maid to do.

I had an interesting talk with a young railway official, who came some distance in our carriage, getting in with cap off and "*Pardon, mesdames!*" (I do so like this foreign politeness). He was in Paris during most of the siege, and was "very hungry," and "souffrait affreuse-ment"; at last, owing to his railway position, he had a sudden chance of getting out, which he only did that his mother and sister might have his share of rations; then, when the armistice came, he got into Paris by the very first train with bread and meat for the "*mère et sœur*," and found them both so famished that they could not eat it! and it was weeks before his mother could digest a bit of meat, merely from the derangement of starvation. He thinks this generation won't want to go to war again! I asked him what he thought of the death of Napoleon. "It was the justice of God," he said. "Do you think the Prince Imperial will ever suc-ceed?" "Not just yet, but events move in a circle, and his turn may come." He was very bitter about the war, saying, "And to think that we are all Christians, the French and the Germans!" This gave opening for a little further talk and a Gospel of St. John. He seemed extremely interested in watching me mark a number of passages before giving it to him.

Ceci met us at Paris; she has found nice accommo-dation for Amy in the house of a French pasteur, who is to give her lessons; it is near the Paumiers. This hotel, the "Grand," is supposed to be the finest in

Europe ; it is quite full, so we had to go "*au quatri-
ème.*" However, we go up and down in a lift, and we
have rooms with balconies, looking down into a fine
boulevard, and so high up that we see over most of the
roofs, and get less noise and dust. The inner court of
the hotel is almost like an immense conservatory, tree
rhododendrons in full flower and other things ; the
saloons are gorgeous, with enormous crystal chandeliers
and mirror panels, so arranged as to make the place
look interminable, quite a fairy-land by gaslight.

HOTEL BELLEVUE, NEUCHATEL. *Saturday Evening.*

We could not start till twelve, and then went a drive
round Paris, which looks its very best in spring foliage
and costumes! We went over Notre Dame with a Na-
poleonist guide, who lost no possible opportunity of in-
stilling Napoleonic ideas. " This is the altar where the
Emperor was crowned, on the same spot the Prince Imperial was baptized, and here also he will probably be
crowned! " We eschewed pictures, etc., because a general idea of Paris was the thing wanted. After dinner
Mr. and Mrs. S. and Amy went another two hours'
drive to the Champs Elysées and the Bois de Boulogne,
while Ceci and I went a walk in the Tuileries gardens.

Then comes an adventure! Express for Neuchatel
left at eight P.M., and as it is a long way to the station
and luggage had to be registered, we ought to leave at
seven, and the omnibus was ordered, but it never came
till half-past seven, and then we had to tear like fire-
engines, and got to the station just as the doors were
closing. Mr. S. undertook the live stock, and I the

baggage. " Too late, too láte ! " raved four or five
porters. However, by dint of most vehement pleading
and a little bribery, I got it taken in and registered,
while as I was obliged to have the tickets to show for
this, Mr. S. had a tremendous row with the platform
officials because he had not the tickets to show. Finally, they wanted to bundle Mrs. S. and E. in, and the
train was actually starting when E. came to the rescue
by setting up such a howl of " I won't get in without
papa ; you sha'n't touch me ! " and such floods of tears,
that she actually moved the stationmaster to compas-
sion, and he signalled the driver to stop a minute.
Meanwhile, Mr. S. by main force held the door of the
platform on one side, while an official struggled to close
it on the other. Happily for me, English muscle beat
the French, and as I ran with my very utmost speed I
got inside, Mr. S. loosed hold, and the door closed with
such a slam behind me ! Then we tumbled over each
other into the carriage, and off for Neuchatel (at least
so I supposed ;. the officials had told us we were all
right without change till 9.40 next morning).

For the first hour a young man sat by me, who turned
out to be " ancienne noblesse," son of a *duc*, a vehement
legitimist, and apparently a leader among thirty thousand young men who " have inscribed themselves " on
that side. He had just been laid up for a month
through being wounded in a duel, a sword wound ; and
told me without the least compunction that his adver-
sary had got the worst of it, and would not be able to
walk for two or three years ! Yet he was " bon Chré-
tien," and always kept Fridays and other fast days ! ! I
felt so sorry for him, for he was a fine, intelligent fellow,

but did not seem to have a glimmering of right and wrong ! He turned out somewhere about Fontainebleau, and then we settled for the night (carriage to ourselves). E. proposed having prayers, so Mr. S. read a psalm and prayed. About 3.45 A.M. I roused up, and thought somehow the country looked wrong (it was quite light), so I sat up in some anxiety for the next station. It came : Chalons-sur-Saone ! on the line to Lyons and Marseilles ! So I called to the stationmaster to know what was to be done ; our party were all asleep, and rather astonished to be summarily bundled out. On went the train, and imagine the Snepps and I standing in a small French station at four o'clock in the morning, some fifty miles out of our route ! Happily it was superb weather.

I soon made out what we could do, and it was a special providence that we roused when we did, for, like old Tiff's harness, it "broke in a 'straw'nary good place dis yer time !" and by omnibusing across the town we just caught a train to Dôle, a small town on the Neuchatel line. Then we proceeded across country for three hours in that serene, leisurely way peculiar to continental trains, which might allow of the guard shaking hands with his friends along the road. As we all went to sleep it did not signify. At 7.30 we turned out at Dôle for ablutions and food.

Now just imagine Mrs. Snepp, etc., washing in large brown crocks, with unbleached towels, in the back room of a small French restaurant, the extempore washing apparatus on one table, and basins of coffee with tablespoons on the other (just like Belfort). However, all was perfectly clean, and everybody was amused and liked the novelty. We had to change again at Pontarlier, and then a glorious two hours through the Jura gorge, which I never appreciated before, because I was going away instead of cóming. Mr. S. is delightful to travel with, he is so enthusiastic about the scenery ; he regularly shouted when we came in sight of the snow mountains !

We got to Neuchatel at three, after eighteen hours' journey. E. is extraordinary ; she has not flagged one bit yet, sleeps like a top, and is in first-rate spirits whenever awake, and not the least trouble, and seems to have left all her timidity behind her in England.

We are at the Hotel Bellevue here, where we were in 1869; one of the very choice Swiss hotels, quiet and elegant, on the edge of the lake. It is splendid weather, and Mont Blanc is perfectly visible, and last night (Sunday) was rosy in the sunset.

There are very few people yet, but Mr. S. finds work enough nevertheless ; he had some most serious conversations yesterday, and seems to have made a wonderful impression on a Welshman, an M. P. and a dissenter. He seems so grateful for Mr. S.'s talk, and is quite staggered in his anti-Bible education views.

They went to English service in the morning, and I went to French service, and dropped in for a confirmation of about ninety girls, all dressed in black with white caps and white folded handkerchiefs over them. Pasteur Nagles preached, and it was quite different to any foreign sermon I ever heard, " Lovest thou Me ? " A most touching, personal, spiritual sermon, not at all the usual oration style, but simple and powerful and full of scriptural thought.

Late in the evening Mrs. S. and I went to try and

find Madame Mercier, the Swiss representative of the Young Women's Christian Association, but she is gone away.

I routed Mr. and Mrs. S. up at four o'clock this morning to look at the dawn on the Alps from their balcony; it was very lovely, but not the "real thing," too distant for the grand effects. However, we contemplated it for nearly half an hour, and then went to roost again.

No. II.

PENSION SCHWEIZERHAUS, LUCERNE. *June* 3.

I left off at Neuchatel, Monday. Well, we had views which I never before believed in, of the distant Alps, all the way by train along the lakes of Neuchatel and Bienne, and down the line to Berne.

We lunched at the Bernerhof, which M. will remember in 1869, and then I unmercifully dragged the whole party up one hundred and twenty-seven steps to the roof. It was so clear that it was difficult to realize the Jungfrau as more than ten or twelve miles off, though it was actually forty-five as the crow flies, and seventy-five by road! I believe Emily would wish to go up Mont Blanc at once if we proposed it. It is most amusing how she enters into the spirit of the whole thing, is quite certain she should be neither tired nor frightened to go anywhere, and is quite grand in her responsibility for a share of the small packages, generally marching in front with me, with as much as she can carry.

To return to Berne, we took a carriage and drove

about. Saw the bears and fed them, all correct ; waited
for the big clock with its performances of cocks and
bears and men with drums to strike the hour ; and went
into the cathedral. E. was very decided in her Protestant preference of it to Notre Dame at Paris, which she
did not appear to feel quite safe in !

After a superb sunset we got to Lucerne at eight. I
had written for rooms to the Schweizerhaus, a pension
strongly recommended in the guidebooks, so the host
was at the station to meet us. I advise any one staying
more than a day at Lucerne to try this instead of the
noisy and dusty town hotels on the quay. Fancy a
house about two hundred feet above the lake (ten minutes' walk from the steamboats), looking down over
everything, with no break to the lovely view of lake and
mountains, Pilatus right, Rigi left, and the snowy Titlis
range in the centre ; the foreground trees, etc., down to
the lake ; a small but pretty garden, a verandah with
flower-stands and a balcony the same width over it,
upon which all our rooms open.

Mrs. S. rather needed a quiet morning, so she very
goodnaturedly wished Mr. S. and me to "improve the
shining hours" in some way. Unfortunately Pilatus is
still snowed up, so we contented ourselves with the
Rigi, and started by the 8 A.M. boat to Vitznau to go up
by rail! The sensation and general effect are most peculiar. The "train" consisted of a single carriage,
holding about fifty, with glass at the two ends, but open
all down the sides where windows should be. Across
this are rows of garden seats, bass instead of solid wood,
all facing backwards, so that you all look downhill as
you are being pushed uphill, and look uphill as you

come downhill. The engine comes out of a den of a shed, and is hooked on behind, pushing, not drawing. Such an imp it looks, the drollest and most knowing thing you ever saw in the shape of machinery, with its little boiler stuck up on end, and slanting forward like the tower of Pisa, bunting and pushing in a most comical way, as if it were bending to the strain, with a determined shoulder to the wheel. Underneath are the massive cogged wheels in the middle, on which the whole affair depends, locking into a great toothed rail between the two ordinary rails. It is impossible to help laughing at the little fellow, as after a very small squeal or two off he goes. But one soon learns to respect him! The first fifty yards are a gentle incline, and then comes the first gradient, which produces what is mildly described as "sensation!" All at once the carriage seems as if it were going to be tilted up on end, and the people see over each other's heads just like an infant school gallery, and as we "back" uphill, those must be stolid indeed who can refrain from some sort of noise in expression of astonishment. I don't think I ever was more surprised. I expected some sort of gradual zigzag, a steep incline of course, but nothing beyond a carriage road; but this thing goes perfectly straight up a hill steeper than any I ever saw a wheeled carriage attempt, even the Lynton coaches. When you come to a station it is quite queer to feel the carriage go level again, with an odd little bump as the cog locks. The views as you rise are glorious. The rail is only open to Staffelhöhe, nearly an hour's walk from the top, and navvies are at work on the rest. I never was more sorry for not having brought more spiritual ammunition, for though I had tracts and "portions" for about forty, it was nothing like enough, and all would have accepted them had I had more.

The upper part of the Rigi was rather snowy, and somehow there is not the same pleasure in getting one's feet wet in commonplace snow that ought to be all gone by this time, as in the real thing above eternal snow level. It was very calm and bright and clear, but I never can see that panoramic views are so really beautiful as many others. Half way up the view is nearly always the best. There is a piano in the inn at the top, so Mr. S. must needs have a hymn from "Songs of Grace and Glory," and a "Havergal Psalmody" tune, on it, at 5,900 hundred feet high.

We only stayed about an hour, and then came down by the Weggis path, which we did in a dense fog in 1869. Near the top the gentians, large and small, were in full beauty, and often on the very edge of snow patches.

The weather has quite suddenly cleared up. It was bitterly cold at Lucerne last week, and it snowed on the Rigi on Saturday, so that on Sunday morning there were three feet of snow! and on Tuesday gentians and positive heat! Just below the top we turned out of the path on to a lovely green plateau where the view is magnificent; and here we knelt on the very gentians, and Mr. S. prayed, or rather adored. It was so nice. It was a pretty fair first walk, being a spin of nine miles down, not reckoning the hour's walk up; but I hardly know anything lovelier in Switzerland, which is saying a good deal.

We went out for a nice drive in the evening with Mrs.

S. and E., and saw the Lion, and drove up to the Pension Wallis, where the Queen stayed some days, a quiet, unpretending house, quite five hundred feet above the lake.

Wednesday.—This morning we all set off by the 8 A.M. boat down the lake. For the benefit of those who have not been, I may elegantly describe the lake as three great sausages, the top sausage having two great arms! You sail out through a charming little strait into sausage No. 2, and seem to be quite in a new lake; and the same, only going sharp at right angles, into No. 3. The morning was beautiful; no wind, and bright sun; water, deep emerald. Just after entering sausage No. 3, Mr. S. called our attention to what looked like a most lovely rippling line of emerald and silver, about half a mile ahead. At the same moment the steamer men rushed on deck and hauled down the awnings, and in about a minute, just like a shot, the famous föhnwind was down upon us. We had just had some tea, and it blew a heavy cup and saucer clear off the table; everything loose went flying; the lake was covered with green and white waves all at once. The men helped the ladies down the stairs off the top-deck, and cleared away every footstool and loose seat, even turning a great strong table on its back with legs up, or that would have been blown over too! It must be awfully dangerous for little sailing boats. I never saw one of these curious lake storms before, and though not in the very least dangerous for a great steamer, yet it was most disagreeable, and on the return journey quite upset me for a little while. I could not have imagined such waves on a lake, and it certainly gave new force to the storm on Galilee. We drove from Fluellen a few miles along the opening of the St. Gothard pass, so well described as "solemnly beautiful"; the enjoyment was a little spoiled by the wind which came tearing down the pass, raising dense clouds of dust. Mr. S., however, was in raptures, to my heart's content.

No. III.

HOTEL JUNGFRAUBLICK, INTERLACHEN. *June* 6.

We left Lucerne yesterday morning 9.40 (Thursday), under very doubtful appearances; Pilatus wrapped up in grey clouds, air damp and warm, and drizzle most of the morning. Still it was a new aspect of the pretty arm of the lake down which we steamed to Alpnacht (11.20).

The whole ride was charming, from 11.30 to 6.0, but the pass of the Brünig is exquisite. You wind up for an hour and a half, mostly through trees now in full beauty, with changing views first of the great valley behind you, then of a glorious opening upon the lake of Brienz deep below, then of smaller mountain valleys, and then of the white Oberland Alps and the grand valley of Meyringen. It had rained for a good while, and we feared it was hopeless for anything but driving up into grey clouds, when just as we began the ascent it left off, and kept fair all the way over the pass. Oddly enough it is the second time I have gone over the Brünig with the hope of staying at the top, which was part of our plan ; it does seem such a pity to halt hardly five minutes, for one of the finest views in Switzerland, and then tear downhill again. If we could have been certain of the weather, I think we should have stayed. We had great fun in hoisting Mrs. S. up to the banquette, for the spin downhill (only an hour) ; it was something quite new to see her perched up in that style. I believe she did it as much to entertain us as anything, which was very amiable of her.

The next possibility was to stay at the Giessbach falls at 6.30, and remain the night to see them illuminated, but unhappily it came on to rain again, so we steamed down the lake of Brienz to Interlachen, which we reached at 7.30. We are at my beautiful hotel; the card gives no idea of the views which are all around, so that there are no back and front rooms, but all have fine views. I have just been a little walk up the Niesen with Mr. S. and E. ; it is a glorious morning after the rain, only the Jungfrau wears her veil of bright cloud, and I have only once caught a glimpse of the shining silver horn. But all the rest is as lovely as can be. It is very warm ; too hot to go far out of the shade. I am writing out of doors on the terrace facing the Scheinige Platte and the lake of Brienz. I am so astonished at Mr. Snepp's French ; he never gave me a notion that he knew a word, and now he comes out with all that is wanted for travelling or hotel talk quite fluently, and with a very good accent. But here French is no use at all ; only German. He has a little pocket aneroid barometer, which shows the height above sea level exactly ; it is so interesting.

June 7. *Saturday.*—Yesterday afternoon Mr. and Mrs. S. and E. went to the Giessbach falls; I stayed quiet, as I have not yet taken a blank day since leaving home, and I wanted to be very fresh for an early mountain start this morning to the Scheinige Platte. We had all arranged overnight, guide and provisions; but it turned out a set-in soaking rain, with not merely the mountains covered with cloud, but the lower hills wreathed about with white veils almost down to the lake level.

HOTEL ROYAL, CHAMOUNI, HAUTE SAVOIE, FRANCE.
June 14. Saturday evening !

Actually not a line written for a whole week; but when I detail proceedings you will not be surprised that I found no time for writing. June the 8th was a queer Sunday, for though the whole place is Protestant, there is not a pretence at Sabbath observance, and the great annual shooting match of the canton Berne, lasting a week, began on Sunday at 6 A.M. by firing twenty-two cannons, one for each canton. The whole place was decorated with any amount of arches and other green erections, with mottoes and devices and flags innumerable, especially all over the hotels, both roofs and windows, while Swiss costumes thronged the streets and roads. As we went to church another cannonade of twenty-two rounds came off close by, so that we had literally to pass the cannons' mouths, and the rifle shooting begins with an occasional cannonade.

Our quiet sweet Communion service was a strange contrast to the scenes and noise outside. The reverberation of the cannon among the mountains was wonderful. I must tell you about little E.'s first missionary work, it was so very nice of her and entirely unprompted. A German lady in the hotel was a Protestant, but her husband a Belgian Romanist; they had one little girl, a most clever child, eight years old, speaking not only French and German, but English too with great fluency. She and E. played together all Saturday; and then, overhearing us talk about this poor little child being brought up a Romanist, which of course the priests had taken care to secure, E. got most interested and anxious. "Won't you give her a little tract?" "Won't you talk to her?" "Won't you tell her not to play with her dolls on Sunday?" So all Sunday E. was in a fever to get hold of her, and succeeded at last in bringing her up to my room with an air of great delight. So the little girls sat on each side of me, and we had quite a nice talk, little Célestine quite pleased and interested, and Emily playing into my hands in a very pretty way and quite helping me. However, as I did not say anything about the dolls, E. did that herself before going to bed, and also gave Célestine a little Gospel of St. John. E. enters most eagerly into distribution, comes to me for Gospels for waiters and chamber-maids, and constantly asks me to give them to drivers or railway guards.

Monday, June 9, dawned promisingly, so we postponed Grindelwald till the afternoon, and Mr. S. and I went up the Scheinige Platte, starting about 6.30; as it is five hours up (six thousand feet), and we were not fully in training, we had a horse, professedly between us, but I had the lion's share. The Platte was quite a surprise to me; it is not an inviting-looking hill, a steep, sharp-edged ridge, overlooking Interlachen, ascended by a path of three hundred zigzags through a steep forest ; then another thousand feet among singular rocks and along the edge of sublime precipices (sheer down three thousand feet) and a cone of grass, flowers, and snow ; and then you see on the north the whole of the lovely lakes of Thun and Brienz ; and south, a superb snow amphitheatre : Wetterhorn, Jungfrau, Eiger, etc., with the two valleys of Grindelwald and Lauterbrunnen forking out in green depth of beauty several thousand feet below you.

It was fine and calm, and the grand snow range had just enough of cloud hanging about it to enhance the brilliance of the snow and the mysterious effect which those untrodden vastnesses always have more or less. We stayed about half an hour on the top to enjoy the view and the cold meat and red wine ! and then scampered down, rather aggrieved to find that the horse and guide were great hindrances to speed. We started as soon as possible for Grindelwald, a grand drive of fifteen miles, in two little carriages.

No. IV.

HOTEL ROYAL, CHAMOUNI.   *June* 16.

I left off No. III. at Grindelwald, Monday, June 9. My second impressions of Grindelwald are far beyond my first. I cannot think how it was that it did not make more impression on me in 1869. I had no idea it was so beautiful: three immense mountains, Wetter-horn, Mettenberg, and Eiger, close to and full before one, with a grand snow view of the Viescherhörner through the glacier opening between them.

Our arrangement usually is that Mr. S. and I go off for an early excursion or walk, then Mrs. S. and Emily get more rest.

So on Tuesday. Mr. S. and I started about six, with the most stupid guide I ever had, for the Eismeer, the Grindelwald Mer de Glace. Of course I got my boots nailed overnight, very knowing-looking pyramid-shaped nails, which stick well into snow or smooth grass, and give a good cling to the foot when the slope is very steep; they are put in about an inch apart. The way was a little footpath under colossal rocks overhanging the edge of the glacier, and rising steeply till it brought us up to a level of 5,500 feet. From this point we looked down on a great basin of dirty ice, all over débris washed down from the heights. The motion of the glaciers is very wonderful; the whole mass moves down bodily, at rates varying on different glaciers from ten or twelve to four hundred feet per annum. The new snow keeps forming it above, and at the valley end it keeps melting and breaking away as it reaches the warmer level. It is a strong illustration of the might of silent influence; only the warm air, invisible and intangible; yet it forms an impassable barrier to these millions of tons of solid ice, which must otherwise pour down into the valleys and destroy all life. But the basin of dirty ice (two or three miles in extent) was not all we came to see. It was bounded by a magnificent and dazzling amphi-theatre of snow, with only a protuberant dark rock here and there to throw up the brilliant whiteness, running up to over eleven thousand feet high ; while the entrance of the gorge down which the glacier pours to the valley below is a great rock portal, of which the right doorpost consists of the celebrated precipice of the Eiger, which goes sheer up (too nearly perpendicular for snow to cover) to more than twelve thousand feet high.

Then we had a very stiff scramble of perhaps three hundred feet down to the glacier itself ; and here, but for God's providence and Mr. S.'s watchfulness, I should have had a serious accident. Part of the descent was by two rough ladders against the face of the rock ; the first was easy, but the second not only long, but very steep indeed. The guide went first, and most culpably never warned me that the handrail of the ladder, consisting of two very long slender pine poles, pierced half way, was broken, so that the end of the upper pole was loose and ended in mid-air. Down I went (backwards), one hand adjusting my dress, and the other holding fast to the rail. As I could not see from above that it was broken, and suspected no danger, I was going comfortably down, face to the rock, and in another minute should have come to the sudden end of the rail to which I was trusting, when nothing but a miracle could have preserved me from a very severe fall of many feet on to the boulders below ; but Mr. S. suddenly saw and shouted to me to stop ; I instantly did so, and looking behind saw the broken rail in time not to trust it further. We went some distance over the glacier, and had the satisfaction of hearing several avalanches, and seeing one rather good one. My notion of an avalanche always used to be a gigantic snowball bounding down, but they are really rather a snow fall, just like a waterfall, only snow This one started high up, and poured over several ledges of rock in succession, till it reached the edge of the glacier, where it formed in three minutes a great mound of snow, I should think thirty or forty feet high ; the roar lasted nearly five minutes. It was rather pretty and elegant than grand, to see it come down. From the glacier we could see the ridge where the Rev. Julius Elliott was killed in 1869, within half an hour of the summit of the Schreckhorn (Horn of Terror).

We got to the hotel again at 11.30, and then went all together to see Mr. E.'s grave.   There is a granite slab over it, and a tablet against the church wall with Heb. xi. 5, "For before his translation," etc., and " To depart and be with Christ, which is far better."   The Grindel- wald people keep it in order themselves, and keep " edelweiss " planted round it, the Alpine flower *par ex- cellence*, which is never found below eight thousand feet.

In the afternoon we drove to Lauterbrunnen ; un- fortunately the Jungfrau was clouded, so we lost the special beauty of the valley. We pottered about up and down the village and to the Staubbach ; and then I put some knowing guides up to beguiling Mrs. S. into just trying a chaise à porteur, which previously she would not hear of, and at last had the satisfaction of seeing her trotted out in one.   This led to arranging for a small expedition next morning, which was to pave the way for something better.

Wednesday, June 11, accordingly we had a walk (about three miles) to the Trümlenbach, along the val-

ley, spending most of the way in arguments and per-
suasions for Mürren, which Mr. S. and I were to have
done alone, but which it would have been a thousand
pities for Mrs. S. to have missed. At last, to my exultation, we won the cause, and Mrs. S. consented to come
up to Mürren for the night, seeing that the porte-chaise
somewhat exceeded her expectations. So we started
directly after lunch and took it easy, and by 6.30 found
ourselves at the pretty new inn, 5,500 feet high.

Though a fine and promising afternoon we got neither
sunset nor sunrise, *i.e.* veiled mountains and no tints at
all. Still, unless absolutely buried in clouds, Mürren
must always be grand, the mountains look more colossal
and majestic than from any other place. It is just the
right height to get the double effect of depth and height,
the valley below so near and deep, and the giants opposite so close and precipitous. I enjoyed getting up
into the colder mountain air ; it is different from valley
cold, and seems to brace and exhilarate without chill-
ing.

Though Mürren was unknown not many years ago,
there is now a good-sized new hotel, with two "dépen-
dances" besides, and an immense new rival is nearly
finished, and there is talk of a railway up like the Rigi !
Dreadful as that sounds, one really can't be selfish
enough to grudge any means of facilitating the ascent,
so that thousands may share the sublime view. Any
one who has not been there will hardly understand the
fact that, with this indescribably splendid mountain
view, one is really distracted from it at almost every step
by the flowers. No description can exaggerate these,
either as to variety, loveliness, brilliance of colour, or

number. The whole place is one mass of flowers, thicker than ever you saw the thickest daisy or buttercup field of monotonous yellow or white. Here and there in patches some special flower predominates, but generally all are mixed up together, perhaps twenty species in a square yard, and most of the colours intensely brilliant. I think we must have gone at the right time exactly, for I do not remember quite such splendour in 1869. Chief of all for attraction are the forget-me-nots, much brighter and larger than the English ones, whole spikes of living turquoise waving by myriads, then gentians and pansies, and large exquisite primrose-coloured anemones, and smaller white ones, and pink primula-like clusters, and purple bells most delicately fringed, and intense blue starflowers with a clear white eye, called "heaven flowers," and dozens of others. I brought in a nosegay which Mr. S. said was fit for a queen, only a queen could not purchase such a one unless she came to Mürren to get it ; for they always fade long before we can get down to the valley again. However, even below there is a wealth of flowers which one never sees in England, only just a little commoner than this lovely aristocracy of flowers up above, so delicate and noble. It is worth any one's while to go early to Switzerland to see them ; no one would believe it who only goes in July and August.

Sleeping at Mürren gave a fine chance for Mr. S. and me to go up the Schilthorn (nearly 10,000 feet), the finest non-dangerous ascent in the Oberland. So we committed ourselves to a good guide, who put us through a catechism as to our capabilities and equipments, insisting on gaiters, veils, and dark spectacles, without either

of which three he refused to take us ! As Mr. S. had
no veil, the guide first suggested that it would answer
equally well to wet the face thoroughly and then blow
flour over it ! Fancy being done up in paste previous
to being baked in the sun ! But he said any *Anglais*
would have his face skinned if he went up the Schilthorn without either veil or flour and water. As Mr. S.
did not see the beauty of the latter plan, he offered to
lend him a veil, and produced one, probably green orig-
inally, but resolved by weather and wear into its con-
stituents of blue and yellow with a little surviving
green. This he fastened on Mr. S.'s white hat in a
style that would astonish Perry Barr. Then he agreed
to call us at two A.M. and departed. So at two A.M. up
we got, and soon after 2.30 had coffee, turning out, to
poor Mrs. S.'s utter horror, a little before three. It
was cloudy and dark, but quite hopeful, and might yet
be magnificent. We toiled up for two hours, vainly
hoping that a tantalizing glimpse or two of a speck of
gleaming snow apparently up in the clouds might ex-
pand into a revelation of the whole range in dawn-
beauty, but soon after we came to the first snow even
that disappeared, and the clouds came down upon us
with a very cool welcome to their domain.

We plunged on over a snow slope or two in pouring
rain, and then the guide faced round, and after an ominous silence declared his mind, viz, that it was a great
mortification and disappointment to him to fail, but he
must tell us candidly that we must give up ; the rain
was hopeless, and had already so softened the snow that
it would be entirely impossible for any mortal to get to
the top, and we might as well turn back at once as

struggle on for five hours more and then be defeated. Decision is always better than uncertainty, so we scampered down again as fast as we could, and went to bed at 6.30, while our clothes were dried. It was a great disappointment to both of us, for the Schilthorn is a first-rate thing to do.

Happily it cleared up splendidly by eight at Mürren, though the Schilthorn remained wrapped in dense rain clouds. So after breakfast we· had a very pleasant, though dirty, trot down again to Lauterbrunnen.

After some hurried soup we drove off to Interlachen, where the chief impediments (rightly so named) had been left, and, after a fatiguing scramble of packing and washerwomen and small bills, got off to the train which now, instead of omnibuses, meets the Thun steamers. It is a delightful little two-mile railway, with covered seats on the top of all the carriages, just from Interlachen to the landing place. We lost the lovely lake of Thun, just as in 1869 ; not a mountain top to be seen, driving rain all the way, and wind and motion enough to make us uncomfortable. We got to Berne (same hotel as in 1860) between seven and eight, a tiring day.

Next day, Friday, rail from Berne to Geneva, rain most of the way, so that we could see little of the views, which ought to be very interesting. Saturday (June 14) was just fair enough to justify starting, and at 7.15 we mounted one of those wonderful " diligences inversables " which are peculiar to this one road. They consist of a gigantic coffin below, which holds any quantity of luggage, and acts as ballast to the whole concern. Then over this are five rows of seats, rising behind each other like a deep gallery, so that twenty people (on emergency twenty-five) can all have a full front view at once. There is a peculiar board just over the horses' tails, on which two or three extra of the aborigines càn sit if needs be, but the passengers' seats are luxurious with red velvet. Over our heads is a sort of canopy stretching across glazed sides ; if neither wet nor sunny this canopy can be rolled back altogether, and as the whole of the glass sides can be let down, it then becomes an entirely open carriage, all except the coupé, which is boxed in at the very back with the worst view and the least air, and for which the wise English pay a good deal extra, in order to keep themselves to themselves and avoid the οἱ πολλοι. We had the whole front row, and I enjoyed it extremely.

But, alas ! the grand views of Mont Blanc all clouded over, and finished up with a wet evening. I was particularly sorry for this, because the drive up to Chamouni is unsurpassable, and I think gives the finest "first impression" of Mont Blanc. The Swiss tell me that the weather for the last year or two has never been settled, and has baffled the calculations of the oldest guides. We had decided on the Hotel Imperial, and went, found the front door open and walked in, but rang bells in vain, and then discovered that it was void, nothing " open " except the entrance ! It was so funny. Two others looked " fermés " also, so we went to the Royal and got a very cheerful set of rooms with good view, having choice of nearly all the rooms in the house, as it is so early yet for Chamouni. We all agree, however, that, though too early for high mountain excursions, it is much better on the whole than later, less heat and dust, cleaned-up rooms everywhere, always a choice of apartments, much better attendance than when all is full, less noise and bustle, no crowded carriages, and the glorious Alpine flowers! It was quite pleasant to settle in here, after sleeping in different hotels for eight consecutive nights, and the last three days were more fatiguing than excursions, being travel, which implies "baggages et billets," and the still greater evils of smaller boxes, baskets, and bags, not to mention shawls, umbrellas, parasols, and alpenstocks.

Nothing like a carpet-bag tour, with no packing and unpacking and registering and looking after and carrying about and counting up to do!

It was nice to find a notice up, that, for those who missed family prayer, the chaplain, Rev. J. F. Bickerdike, would hold it every evening, at 8.30, in the reading room. So of course we went, only "two or three,' but it was very nice. Mr. B. is very earnest and spiritually minded; and Mrs. B. very nice too. She was at Mr. Pennefather's Deaconess Institution for some time, and has told us a good deal about Mildmay. She says that every one appeared to have been impressed with the singular heavenliness of Mr. P. during his last year. For many months before his death his special anxiety and interest had been prayer for real spiritual blessing upon the immense amount of machinery and organization which he had completed; work and workers all marvellously organized, and then his one thought seemed to be seeking for blessing upon it all.

Sunday, June 15, was a brilliant morning; Mont Blanc dazzling, though less grand from Chamouni itself than from any other point of view; one is too close under it to form any idea of its height. The little English

church was bright and cheerful ; every one likes it better than almost any other Sunday halt ; and somehow
they always manage to have excellent chaplains, who do
not chill one by reading commonplace little sermons
which were produced under totally different circumstances. It must be a poverty-stricken heart indeed,
which can't speak out of its abundance in Switzerland.
There is a small harmonium, which I played in the
morning: Tallis, Worcester Chant, and Farrant for
chants ; Nottingham to "This is the day the Lord hath
made"; and Hanover to "O worship the King all
glorious above."

The responding and singing were capital, though the
congregation only about eighty.   There are a few
French Protestant families here, who are visited twice a
year by a distant pasteur ; so Mr. B., who is a thorough
French scholar, kindly visits and gathers them to a little
French service, at 7 P.M. (English P.M. service is at four),
but after this is going to have them at 9 A.M. because
that will suit them better.   There is Holy Communion
every Sunday morning.   There was quite a nice gathering at the 8.30 P.M. "family prayers," and we sang
Hymns 17 and 14 from "Songs of Grace and Glory."

Monday, June 16, we planned a grand expedition, the
"Jardin," a wonderful glacier excursion which has long
been an ambition of mine.   It was fine after a wet evening, so Mr. S. and I started a little before six, and
walked to Montanvert, overlooking the Mer de Glace
(six thousand feet), reaching it soon after eight.   We
asked for a guide at once to take us up to the "Jardin,"
and were told by the innkeeper that we ought to have
started not later than three A.M., and that the snow was

far too soft to do it so late as eight, that nobody has been yet this year, and what with avalanches and slips and vagaries of ice and snow and crevasses and " éboulements," he couldn't say whether any of his garçons could find the way at all, and finally declined to sanction our going. This was sure to be right, because disinterested! for he sacrificed his own profits upon guide, provisions, and wine ; and as a first-rate guide soon after endorsed the decision, we had no choice but to give it up. The chef des guides has since told us that he does not think the " Jardin " should be attempted till at least the end of next week. So we contented ourselves with a climb up the height on the right of Montanvert, and then down and across the Mer de Glace.

We were obliged to have a guide across the ice, and he says that at this time of year the route alters almost every day, crevasses safe to-day may be dangerous to-morrow ; and he is responsible for inspecting the route every morning before any visitors cross, setting up little stone waymarks which the other guides understand.

The big " Moulin," which Mr. C. and M. will remember (a great hole in the glacier, down which you hear a tremendous roar of sub-glacial water hundreds of feet below), is all vanished since 1869. We said good-bye to our guide, and trotted down the Mauvais Pas on the other side, striking off into a little path to get down to the Sources de l'Arveiron, where the river rushes out of the foot of the glacier ; and then down into the road and back to Chamouni by about two o'clock.

Tuesday, June 17, a very doubtful morning, and not clear enough for the Col de Balm ; so we started at six for the Col de Vosa. It was damp and muggy; so, after walking nearly seven miles, I gave in and came straight back, while Mr. S. went on up the col alone. Just after I turned back it began a real mountain pour, so six miles walking in this was a tolerable soak; but nothing to Mr. S.'s state, who persevered through an amusing series of difficulties up to the top, and got back nearly two hours later.

This morning again (Wednesday) it is pouring, and seems likely to keep on at it. We have had more or less rain every day for a week now; no signs of fine weather yet.

I have written to see if Mr. S. can extend his tourist tickets beyond the month; if not, we get back to Birmingham on the evening of June 27, and I go on to Oakhampton next day.

I have not had much conversation with the natives, but have had plenty of opportunity of giving tracts and portions. Our driver to Grindelwald had a St. Luke; next evening he took it out of his breast pocket to show me that he had it, saying it was a treasure and he would never part with it. The evening before he had got it out at supper, and read it to the roomful of guides and drivers. Most of them approved, and two or three wanted to buy it from him, but he said he would not give it up for anything. Then he read some more aloud, whereupon a godless guide began scoffing and blaspheming; not ten minutes after, he cut his hand, or rather wrist, so fearfully that he was quite ill, and the driver said they thought he would be laid up for a fortnight, the loss of blood being so great as to be dangerous; I suppose it was an artery. The others were quite impressed, and said it was a judgment of God upon him. This old driver seemed to have the fear of God, and listened earnestly and responded warmly to all I tried to tell him.

No. V.

HOTEL ROYAL, CHAMOUNI. *June* 19.

We are not well off as to weather; Tuesday and Wednesday entirely lost, a continued pour. We reckoned on a probable fine morning after it, and early it was lovely; but we did not arrange to start till 10.30, and we had a hot and unprofitable tug up to the Montanvert, and a dull, cloudy day, not the top of a single aiguille visible. The only fun was taking E. up; she is the strongest child I ever knew, and enjoys the whole thing deliciously.

At the little inn they brought us first a tureen of bright yellow soup, tasting like bad sour milk and oil, which even I could not touch! They call the compound "egg soup," and professed great astonishment at our not liking it. Then they produced a tureen of dish-water with a mild 'flavouring of broth, in which floated irregular slices and lumps of stale bread, with a few blacks and a good deal of smoke to improve the mess. So for once I really appreciated table d'hôte on our return, which is generally an unmitigated bore. Mr. Bickerdike always says grace from the head of the table, and the little gathering every night for "family prayers" is very nice.

Last evening looked very doubtful and heavily clouded ; had any one guessed it would have turned out a glorious morning, we might have arranged for Col de Balm early, and might have been off at five or so. It is now (10.30) though still fine, quite clouded on the Bréven and Col de Balm ; how curious it is that only the early mornings, from four to nine, are ever really clear (with rare exceptions). This afternoon Mr. S. and I are going to make our last attempt at a good excursion ; and having been disappointed of both the others (Schilthorn and Jardin), I do very much hope weather will keep up for this, the only remaining feather for our caps, Les Grands Mulets.

No. VI.

. Hotel Royal, Chamouni.
Monday, June 23.

Hurrah ! we have done it, and could not possibly have had a more successful or a more amusing excursion, " la première ascension " of the year, and consequently all Chamouni excited about it. We had inquired at the Bureau des Guides, and found that the regulation was two guides and a porter at an exorbitant tariff, being a " course extraordinaire." It did seem waste to spend six or seven pounds on one excursion, so we said it was out of the question. However, two strong young fellows not yet admitted as " guides," but only as " porteurs," who had formed part of Mrs. Snepp's carriers to Montanvert, talked to us about it. They had

14

their testimonial books to show, one had been seventeen times up Mont Blanc, and all seemed satisfactory. They undertook to take us up themselves without any further fuss, and so Mr. S. agreed to entrust them with our bones. Their eagerness and delight were comical; there is a certain éclat about "la première ascension," and they would go on any terms, so that they might have the glory of it, and take the shine out of their superiors, the sworn "guides." We saw that we could not be in better hands, as all their interest lay in making it a first-rate success. Our boots had to be fresh nailed, and a bigger spike put in my stick, and various arrangements made, all which they looked after.

On Friday, at 2.30 P.M., we set off, accompanied for the first stage by Mrs. S. and E. and the Bickerdikes, our fellows strutting in triumph with their great ice-axes, called piolets, and a great coil of rope, and our small effects.

The first part was very hot, but we took it slowly; then came forest and ferns; then the path got worse, with tiny torrents crossing it, till, by 5.30, we reached the first snow patches, alternating with flowers, and about six we reached Pierre Pointue, where we were to sleep. I had a little wooden room, with single boards between my head and the back den where the guides snored. Mr. S. had the salon converted into a tidy bedroom by the importation of trestles and boards as soon as our supper was cleared away. As there was no fire, we went into the little kitchen and warmed our feet in the oven, where also our boots were baked previous to being greased for the ascent.

As soon as our guides had eaten, they dashed off to

collect wood and dried rhododendrons for a bonfire, for of course Chamouni must be apprised of our arrival, and as it got dark the flame blazed up well on a jutting rock in full view of the hotels below. Meanwhile we had a grand sunset, several sunset pictures in one, all thrown up by the dark depth of the valley below. On the right the Aiguille Verte and Aiguille du Dru formed an exquisite calm picture apart, both a delicate rose-colour, partly veiled by floating mist of semi-transparent silver. Opposite, intense purple and very stormy-looking clouds massed densely all along the tops of the Bréven range ; but their other side must have been gorgeous, for a weird light was reflected down from underneath it upon the upper slopes of rock and snow as from a great hidden fire, quite different from the *direct* sunlight. Then over the Pic de Varens were great rifts of gold, *quivering* with intensity and showing distant peaks of softer brilliance, changing every minute, as if series of golden gates were being unrolled, revealing gates of opal and pearl beyond them. Then to the left and behind the Dôme and Aiguille du Gouté, lit up with amber and scarlet, the Mont Maudit shone out as a cloud-tipped expanse of glowing snow ; while the true summit of Mont Blanc just glimpsed through cloud, so rich in rose-fire and so beautiful that it was hardly tantalizing that the moment of full revelation never came, and all died away into white and grey as our bonfire blazed up just below us.

Of course I went to bed at once, and soon to sleep, spite of the snoring through the boards. In the middle of the night I heard a continued scratching, suggestive of rats, only it must be a snow species, as ours would not find the climate agreeable ; after a while I found it proceeded from the salon, where Mr. S. was vainly scraping damp matches on the boards that he might see the time. Presently the host roused up and gave a light ; it was 1.10 A.M., so we had yet fifty minutes to sleep. The men did not seem to mind being routed up, it was part of their business, and they subsided again quite good-temperedly, and in three minutes the snoring recommenced. They made it up by overshooting two o'clock, when they should have called us, so Mr. S. himself gave the réveille at 2.10. I rushed anxiously to my window, and rubbed the frosty pane to look out, for it had been hard to distinguish between wind and torrents ; to my exceeding delight it was the latter only, and the morning was perfect, the stars sparkling like winter, Mont Blanc cloudless, and just gleaming with that strange pale light preceding the dawn.

By a little after three we were off. The Cranes will remember the scramble to Pierre à l'Echelle well, a narrow path skirting a precipice ; it is now all snow, up which we worked step by step, each foot planted with a firm poke to ensure the footing, and also improve the track for after comers. They will recollect the snow slopes down which Aristide Couttet glissaded ; it was up these we climbed. At Pierre à l'Echelle we roped, the guides and Mr. S. having leather belts with a metal ring like harness, too heavy for me ; I was simply noosed round the waist with a firm knot. They insisted on a certain order : Désailloud first, then myself, then Payot, and Mr. S. last, saying this was the safest arrangement. About eight or ten feet of rope are allowed between each person ; they showed us it was a real Alpine Club rope,

known by a red thread in the middle of the three strands,
and gave us distinct instructions what to do in case of
one slipping, or snow giving way, and dangling in a
crevasse. The sun had struck the summits with very
beautiful colouring, something between amber and
crimson ; and Mr. S. called a halt and would have the
Morning Hymn! It was very bad economy of wind, I
sang two verses and then "struck." Sticking half way
up a snow slope, holding on by a projecting crag at four
A.M., is not the most favourable position for hymn-sing-
ing, however inspiring the sunrise may be. We worked
up and across the great Glacier des Bossons, incom-
parably grander than the Mer de Glace ; and if you
want a good idea of it, study any of those snow stereo-
scopes, with people crossing crevasses and threading
among blocks and pinnacles of ice and looking down
into gulfs ; they give an excellent idea of it. I could
have fancied I had got into a stereoscope box in a
dream.

The snow was in excellent condition, *i.e.* we did not
often go in above our knees! and every now and then
only went ankle-deep for a treat, and in a few very
sheltered parts we could trot over the crust without
breaking it.

Every few minutes Désailloud shouted " Attention ! "
" Faites tendre la corde ! " (stretch the rope) and that
signified a crevasse. Then we went very slowly, stretching the rope tight between us (which reduces the shock
if anybody goes in), while Désailloud sounded the snow
step by step, sometimes cutting away an unsafe bit, as
it is safer to step or spring across an open fissure than
a hidden one. There is so much snow now that most

of the crevasses are well snowed over, and we needed
no ladders, which are necessary in August. We had to
pass close under the Aiguille du Midi, where the torn
snow showed we were on the track of avalanches ; and
here Désailloud hurried us on, saying the sooner we got
over that ten minutes the better, as there was no fore-
seeing an avalanche. All this time we had the advantage of being in the shadow of the immense heights,
with sharp, frosty air and crackling snow. About 7.15
we came out upon the steep snow slopes on the other
side of the two glaciers we had crossed, and were not
only in full view of the sun, but of Chamouni. In three
minutes the guides caught the sound of cannon, and
listening we heard two more rounds. " On nous voit ! "
they shouted in a state of ecstasy. " Everybody in
Chamouni can see us with the big telescopes ! " They
were so charmed, and I think we found it rather stimu-
lating also, to know that we were being watched from
below. Désailloud gave himself the trouble of hoisting
a great shawl on his piolet as a flag, and carrying it up
three steep slopes in triumph. And they were *very*
steep, though not at all dangerous, as we got footing
nearly knee-deep for every step.

A little before eight we reached the Grands Mulets,
black desolate peaked rocks in the midst of an ocean of
snow, and our arrival was signalled instantly by four
more cannonades in Chamouni. There is a wooden
cabin perched on a shelf of the rock ; the guides knew
where to find the key, and set out luncheon for us quite
tidily, while we sat cross-legged on the two little beds
to warm our feet. Payot acted lady's maid and took off
my boots and stockings (I could not possibly get them

off myself), and kindly lent me a pair of his own enormous worsted socks, warm and dry, which soon warmed
me up beautifully, and then I sat upon my feet and
handed the socks to Mr. S., who was very cold indeed,
so that I was almost frightened for him till a little food
and cognac warmed him up too. I did not feel the
least tired all the way, and could have gone on much
higher with ease ; but as soon as I had eaten I went fast
asleep for a quarter of an hour, which seemed rather
grievous to do in such a scene, but I could not help it,
and woke up as fresh as possible for the descent. In the
meantime our guides had set off on their own account,
scrambling and tearing about just like boys out of
school, yelling madly, coming down again right over the
roof of the cabin, which was all snow like the rest. The
powerful sun during our halt had so softened the snow
that our descent was a simple series of slides and plunges ;
after a few hundred feet we got quite used to the
motion. Real glissades were not safe to attempt, with
the glacier below. We had some lovely effects, such as
I have never before seen, in passing the colossal ice
blocks on the shady side ; the sun behind them touching the transparent edges with a sort of aureole, and
shining through a glittering drip from the overhanging
ones. We wanted to stop and admire, but the guides
said it was "not good" to stand there ; the giants have
an objectionable trick of tumbling over now and then, and
it is as well to keep out of the way. The snow bridges
required a little more caution than in the morning, but
we passed them all quite safely.

At our first halt on the glacier about five A.M., Mr. S.
dropped his spectacles (fortunately not the dark ones),

and the slope being steep and the snow hard they went glissading down two or three hundred feet till they vanished in a hole, all in a few seconds. We could not have found the place again, but on our return the guides pulled up on the lower edge of a great hole about six feet wide, overhung by snow and rock, and announced that the spectacles were *there*, and they would fetch them up! They had made a different return track on purpose. Mr. S. entreated them to let it alone, but they declared there was no danger, and they would evidently have been desperately disappointed of their fun if he had insisted.

They untied me to give more rope, and then Désailloud lowered himself (Payot, Mr. S., and I holding the rope), and we roaring at him not to go, he only laughing in return out of the depths, and shouting that he could *see* the spectacles and meant to have them! There was luckily just rope enough for him to reach them, and up he came, like a monkey, with the spectacles safe between his teeth, all over snow.

They would not untie us when we got to Pierre à l'Echelle, because the snow slopes are so steep (though no more crevasses), which seemed to me the very reason why we should not pull each other down, as we soon proved, especially as I don't like glissading when roped, and one attempt thereat resulted in our all rolling over each other. Presently I thought we were come to a sufficiently easy part to go carelessly, whereupon I slipped, and Payot, who was next me, totally lost himself too, and we had just started a decidedly too rapid spin down a *very* steep incline, when instantaneously Mr. S. did the only possible thing which could have

stopped all four of us; flung himself right on his back
with his heels in the snow, the orthodox thing to do if
only any one has the presence of mind to do it.   This
checked the impetus, and we quickly recovered our
footing.

After this we were unroped, which I greatly preferred,
as the roping is very hampering to individual action on
the snow slopes, though splendidly safe for the glaciers.
Being free I managed some nice long glissades by myself.   Payot and Mr. S. did a magnificent glissade together, going down like a shot in less than two minutes .
a descent which would have taken perhaps twenty minutes to get down any other way.   I need not say that
after these exploits there was not a dry inch on our
clothes!   I was not at all tired on reaching Pierre
Pointue, so after settling the bill we raced down to Chamouni in considerably less than regulation time, owing
to scampers and short cuts, as we were anxious to give
Mrs. S. a pleasant surprise by being back much sooner
than expected.   It was very bright and hot, and we
could never have done half the walking in the valley
that we did on the mountains.   We found we were not
expected till five or six o'clock, so as we marched in
before three the final salute was not ready, but our
arrival was soon known, and the little cannon were blaz-
ing away again!   About half a mile from Chamouni our
guides passed their home and stopped for a minute;
they might as well have left the heavy rope and ice-axes
as carry them to Chamouni and back again in the heat,
but oh dear no, they could not possibly enter Chamouni
without them, heat and weight being no consideration
compared with getting the outward and visible credit

of "la première ascension de 1873"! So they shoul-
dered it all again, and marched in in style.

Our reception was most amusing; even the waiters,
who are an unusually glum set, were beaming, and Mr. S.
was rushed at by the master of the hotel and the secre-
tary of the *Journal de Genève*, all as frantic as if we had
returned from the moon itself. Refusals availed nought,
and they positively insisted on treating us to champagne,
which was taken with the usual foreign glass-clinking
and ecstatic congratulations. Then came an humble
request, would we write just a little article for the *Journal de Genève*, to appear on Tuesday? it would be such
a favour, such a benefit (*i.e.* to the Hotel Royal), and so
forth; and if we preferred writing in English, monsieur
le secrétaire would speedily put it into French. So
when I let them know I was not new at that trade, and
graciously acceded, they congratulated *themselves* with
fresh enthusiasm! I don't know when I ever laughed
more, the whole concern was so funny and utterly novel.
I had not a notion the ascent to the Grands Mulets was
made such a fuss about, but the éclat was owing to its
being the *first* ascent of the season, which had never
before happened to be done by a lady.

But now for Mrs. S., who decidedly won her spurs
while we won ours. To Mr. S.'s consternation she was
out with E. and A. and the Bickerdikes, and no one
gave the same version of her departure, the received
one being that she had gone on a mule to meet us after
being informed by the telescope that our descent had
commenced. So we sent after her, and at last when we
were becoming really anxious the party drove into Chamouni at 6.30.

She was much disappointed and vexed at not being
in time to receive Mr. S. She thought the expedition
to La Flégère the B.'s asked her to take would only be
for two hours. Up they toiled in the heat, mile after
mile of those horrid zigzags ; then the saddle slipped a
little on one side, and the muleteer gave Mrs. S. such a
counteracting push as nearly sent her over on the other,
whereupon she dismounted and actually climbed all the
rest of the way on foot. Then little E. would not ride,
and they chartered a big boy who carried her two miles
on his back ! At last they reached the top, 6,500 feet !
The report of our " ascension " had reached La Flégère,
and the hostess was ready to embrace Mrs. S. on finding that she was wife of one of the " voyageurs,"-the
whole neighbourhood seems to have been on the look out
in a state of excitement. Presently up dashes E.'s boy :
" Les voyageurs sont arrivés à Chamouni ! " dancing
and capering as if he would like to fly down to meet
" les voyageurs." Pleasing intelligence for poor Mrs. S.
on the top of La Flégère ! So down she started full
speed the four or five miles on foot, as it is so steep for
riding down, and sent the aforesaid boy on to get a carriage to meet them at the bottom. So all ended well,
and we had a *lively* table d'hôte at seven o'clock, as you
may suppose, except that I was cross at having allowed
myself to be beguiled into writing for the Geneva paper
instead of taking a siesta as I intended.

They tell me I am *fully* equal to doing Mont Blanc
easily. But now for a piece of wisdom : I really think
it would not be worth while to do it, considering the
great expense and the danger of being overtaken by bad
weather, however delightful if continuously fine. We

have had all the most interesting sights and doings of the ascent, and the only gain would be the being able to say we had done it.

Though not the faintest quiver of nervousness once crossed me to spoil the enjoyment, yet it certainly does not come within the promise I made in 1871 to attempt "nothing dangerous," for there is a certain amount of danger both from crevasses and avalanches which no surefootedness or precaution could entirely neutralise. Neither Mr. S. nor I thought of danger till we were actually up there, so I went with a clear conscience, which would not be if I were to go a second time, and I could not have the entire absence of fear and absolute trust in God's keeping which I had *this* time. Even as a matter of muscle and agility I would not recommend it to any but gentlemen, and by no means to all of those ; it wants a light, quick walker, good lungs, steady head and sure foot, and *light weight* and step for crossing the crevasses. The two days' splendid weather seemed just on purpose for us ; it has changed again and been stormy all day.

Sunday was very pleasant, the number of English nearly double that of last Sunday. Mr. S. read prayers morning and afternoon. I played both times, and we had nice hymns and chants. At table d'hôte we met a Mr. Burns and his family, who knew dear papa at Dunoon.

Our return is uncertain ; probably we shall stay a Sunday at Boulogne, and perhaps get two or three days' sea bathing as a break in the long journey, and a *let down* out of the mountain air. I cannot give any certain address at all !

No. VII.

CHAMONIX. (How I hate spelling it French
fashion ! I never can reconcile my mind
to considering it France.) *June* 25.

Weather continues to be "variable," so Monday we
could do nothing, violent storms all day ; once we saw
a cloud come down into the valley two or three miles
off, and then literally roll along the very ground as if it
would swallow us up ; and when it did reach the village, the pour beat any mountain storm I ever saw.

Tuesday we speculated would be fine, so Mr. S. and
I started at 4.15 for the Col de Balm. We had a lovely
walk along the valley to Argentière (six miles). We
went on two miles more to La Tour, the highest village
of the valley, nearly five thousand feet above sea
level ; and here I decided to stay, while Mr. S. went on
to the top, four miles farther. As usual the lovely morning failed, and clouds came down ; and poor Mr. S. got
no view at all, and had his tough climb all for nothing,
up a path not yet "arrangé pour la saison," which
means any amount of landslips and mud and snow and
torrents and boulders to be walked over.

We got back to Chamouni at 1.30 ; the excursion is
reckoned as nine hours' walking, five up and four down.
So Mr. S. walked twenty-four miles and I only about
sixteen !

I never saw such an awful place for swindle without
redress ! All the hotels belong to a "Société Anonyme,"
so there is no competition and no *maître d'hotel*, whose
personal interest it is to protect and please his guests. I
have actually made them reduce our bill by nearly eighty

francs; all such clear overcharges that they could not maintain them. One item beat anything I ever heard of, " a pencil, fifty centimes!" (*i.e.* half a franc) which turned out to be that a waiter had lent Mr. S. a pencil for half a minute to write a message with, the pencil not having been even asked for and returned on the spot! The only thing they don't swindle in is the guides and mules, which are all tariff, and though high are not utterly unreasonable, and are always exact.

Ann gives a sad report of the servants' table. I am glad she is a Young Women's Christian Association member, and she seems to have been brave and true to her colours. Of all the valets and ladies' maids she was the only one in Chamouni (for all the hotels dine together at present) who went to church, except one apparently well-disposed man, who sided with her and spoke up for religion.

HOTEL DU PAVILLON. *Saturday Evening.*

I thought I should not have much to tell you, but we have had quite an adventure of a sort new to me! I wrote so far, early A.M. on Wednesday. As we wished to be at Geneva by Thursday evening we ought either to have gone down direct on Thursday morning, or started not later than nine A.M. on Wednesday to go by Tête Noire, which is nine hours. Although a little carriage road is open all the way, the ups and downs, etc., are so great that they allow just the same time as for foot or mule passengers.

We did not start till 12.30, and soon found that most of the way the carriage had to go even slower than we could walk! and we walked a good deal. I am not given to nervousness, but really in several places I was more easy in my mind out of the carriage than in ; it always seems to me the most dangerous mode of progression, where a narrow road has only a slight and occasional fence of two fir poles, and there are torrents and real precipices below, especially in early summer when the edges often give way from the rains. Though not a bright day, it was tolerable till about half-past six in the evening, by which time we ought to have been safely housed at Vernayaz, instead of beginning the ascent of the Forclaz just beyond the Tête Noire hotel, which we did not leave till six.

For information of Maria, etc., I will just explain that the Tête Noire is a magnificent high level valley or gorge, winding for four or five hours at a good height among mountains, as picturesque a combination of heights and depths, rocks, torrents, cascades, pine trees, ferns, flowers, and precipices as exists anywhere. The upper end consists of an hour's stiff pull up to the Col de Forclaz, on gaining which you look down over the other side into the Rhone valley, deep below, reached by a rough zigzaging road of about seven miles down.

So we began the descent just as it was beginning to get dark ! It reminded me of Astathes in that pretty little allegory, " The Spring Morning," who set out late on his journey, and came in for storms and wild beasts, where Agape, the early little traveller, passed safely. After about ten minutes, in coming down a very steep bit, something went bang. The driver got out, pottered in the wet, and then " Faut descendre ! " was his laconic information. So " descendre " we all did, in all the drench, and lo ! the drag had broken, right in two.

So he turned us all out, and we had to trudge seven miles down in the deepening dark!

Happily the rain ceased in a short time, or rather we came down out of the cloud, so it was only a question of tramp. It was pretty well at first, but as it got to nine and ten and eleven o'clock it was no trifle, and a sprained ankle would have been no marvel. We had to pick step after step with the utmost caution, among big stones and sudden dips and occasional streams, when we could trace anything; but when we passed under trees, which are luxuriant for the last mile or two, it was absolutely pitch dark, and we could only guide by each other's voices, or the jingle of the horse bells before us, or the rush of a little watercourse beside us. At last we got to the bottom, and were allowed to get into the carriage. I should say that I picked up two or three glow-worms, which were a material assistance in guiding those who walked behind me! By that time the wind had risen, and resisted all attempts to get a light while the re-harnessing took place. The arrangement is, one strong horse that goes all the way, and a mule that is tied on behind for descents, and brought to the fore for levels and ascents, running by the side of the shafts with two or three ropes and straps, which broke three or four times.

After we had our mule tied on we had to go nearly a mile at slow walking pace, "the police forbid any trotting through Martigny!" through wide roads and dead level. At last we got fairly out on the Vernayaz road, anticipating a good trot, when all at once a perfect hurricane came tearing down the lower Rhone valley to meet us, right in our teeth; it not only blew the

clouds away, but bid fair to blow the stars out, and had
it come broadside I believe it must have blown the vehicle over.   And this lasted till some little time after
midnight, when the great white new hotel of the Gorge
du Trient loomed up ghostly and lightless under the
rocks.

We were glad enough to see it, and soon rang the
natives up, who were singularly amiable considering
their sleepiness, stumbling down in various stages of costume and nightcap.   Mrs. S. was very tired next morning, but no one else was a whit the worse, and Emily
got into Geneva the next night as lively as ever.   In the
morning we went up the Gorge du Trient, a colossal
fissure from six hundred to one thousand feet deep, and
often not six feet across, the only access being by a
wooden gallery a quarter of a mile long, hung on iron
cramps and supports above the roaring torrent, which
fills up the bottom of the cleft, with no shore whatever,
a narrow, deep volume of mighty waters.

At the hotel they had a beautiful young St. Bernard,
with her two splendid little puppies, a fortnight old.
Mr. S. wants a dog badly as house-dog, and Emily
wanted a puppy, and it seemed cruel to take such a little one away from the mother ; so, as the people came
to terms, he bought the whole family!   The mother,
Vinesse, is a beauty, with a grand head and gentle,
wistful expression, a dog that would die for you.   The
little fellows are sleek rotundities with big paws, supposed to be going to be very superb specimens.   I am
delighted with them of course.

[The last letter of this series is missing.]

VIII.

JULY ON THE MOUNTAINS.

THERE is sultry gloom on the mountain brow,
    And a sultry glow beneath;
Oh for a breeze from the western sea,
Soft and reviving, sweet and free,
Over the shadowless hill and lea,
    Over the barren heath!

There are clouds and darkness around God's ways
    And the noon of life grows hot;
And though His faithfulness standeth fast
As the mighty mountains, a shroud is cast
Over its glory, solemn and vast,
    Veiling, but changing it not.

Send a sweet breeze from Thy sea, O Lord,
    From Thy deep, deep sea of love;
Though it lift not the veil from the cloudy height,
Let the brow grow cool and the footsteps light,
As it comes with holy and soothing might,
    Like the wing of a snowy dove.

IX

THREE LETTERS,

(FROM A SERIES OF TWELVE) TO MRS. HAVERGAL IN 1874,
DURING A TOUR CHIEFLY WITH CONSTANCE S. C.

THE INN ON THE FAULHORN.
6th July, 1874.

"Sunset on the Faulhorn!" All day there had been strange rifts in the clouds, and sudden pictures of peaks or of abysses framed in white and grey; but towards seven o'clock the wind rose, and there was a grand outpour of colour upon everything, sky, clouds, and mountains.

Imagine yourself midway between heaven and earth, the sharp point of rock on which we stood hardly seeming more of earth than if we had been in a balloon, the whole space around, above, and below filled with wild, weird, spectral clouds, driving and whirling in incessant change and with tremendous rapidity; horizon *none*, but every part of where horizon should be, crowded with unimaginable shapes of unimagined colours, with rifts of every shade of blue, from indigo to pearl, and burning with every tint of fire, from gold to intensest red; shafts of keen light shot down into abysses of purple thousands of feet below, enormous surging masses of grey hurled up from beneath, and changing in an instant to glorified brightness of fire as they seemed on the point of swallowing up the shining masses above them; then, all in an instant, a wild grey shroud flung over us, as swiftly passing and leaving us in a blaze of sunshine; then a bursting open of the very heavens, and a vision of what might be celestial heights, pure and still and shining, high above it all; then an instantaneous cleft in another wild cloud, and a revelation of a perfect paradise of golden and rosy slopes and summits; then, quick gleams of white peaks through veilings and unveilings of flying semi-transparent clouds; then, as quickly as the eye could follow, a rim of dazzling light running round the edges of a black castle of cloud, and flaming windows suddenly pierced in it; oh, mother dear, I might go on for sheets, for it was never twice the same, nor any single minute the same, in any one direction. At one juncture a cloud stood still, apparently about two hundred yards off, and we each saw our own shadows gigantically reflected on it, surrounded by a complete rainbow arch, but a full circle of bright prismatic colours, a transfiguration of our shadows almost startling, each, moreover, seeing only their own glorification! When the whole pageant, lasting nearly an hour, was past, we sang "Abide with me," and then the dear old joyous "Glory to Thee, my God."

ORMONT DESSUS. *September*

This second month of my Swiss journey is altogether different from the first, for now I am making *writing* the first thing instead of idleness. I am doing it quite in moderation, and taking plenty of fresh air as well ; one can be out half the day and yet get four or five good hours' writing as well, under these circumstances, when there are no other calls whatever upon time or strength ; and this combination of work and leisure is very delightful. Besides, I feel as if I had got quite a fresh start with that month's rest ; it seems as if nature had then walked into my brain and taken possession (turning *me* out meanwhile), and given a kind of spring cleaning! rubbing up the furniture, and fresh papering some of the rooms, and cleaning the windows! That perpetual "moving on," which some so delight in, does not suit me nearly so well as staying in a place and taking it easy. The weather has been so much colder and more variable, since I changed my tactics, that the two things coincided beautifully ; for, except two days, it has been too cold the last fortnight for any sitting out of doors.

I don't know why I always seem to shrink from writing much, or even anything, of the "under the surface" life (which is so much more than the "on the surface" and the mere surroundings), in my circulars. They would be much fuller if I told one tithe of the hourly bits of gentle guidance and clear lovingkindness which make the real enjoyment, or of the perpetual little opportunities of a "word for Jesus" which He seems to give me, and often of real work for Him, which yet seems to come so unsought, so easily and naturally, so altogether without any effort, as to be not felt to be any working at all. Now I will give you an instance of how He took me at my word the other day. It was one of the few warm days, and I established myself with pen

and ink in a shady nook by a little, steep, downhill torrent. I had suddenly got that sort of strong impulse
to write on a certain theme, without which I never do
my best, but with which I always do my best poems.

The theme was a grand one (" The Thoughts of
God"); I had thought of it for months, and never before had this impulse to begin upon it; though, once
begun, I expected it to be one of my best poems. I
spent a little time in prayer first, and then the warning
and the promise in Jeremiah xv. 19 came strongly to my
mind : "if thou take forth the precious from the vile,
thou shalt be as My mouth." I felt that wanted looking
into ; I wanted Him to take forth the precious from the
vile for me, and to reveal and purge away, then and
there, all the self and mingled motive which would
utterly mar the work that I wanted to be for His glory.
After that the question came, was I—had He made me—
just as willing to do any little bit of work for Him,
something for little children or poor people, simple and
unseen, as this other piece of work, which might win
something of man's praise ? Then I was intensely
happy in feeling that I could tell HIM that I had no
choice at all about it ; but would really rather do just
what He chose for me to do, whatever it might be.
However, there seemed nothing else to do, so I began
my poem. I don't think I had written four lines when
a labourer with a scythe came along a tiny path to drink
at the stream a few yards below me. He did not see
me, and started when I hailed him and offered him a little
book. He climbed up to receive it, and then, instead of
departing as I expected, deliberately sat down on a big
stone at my feet, and commenced turning over the

leaves, and evidently laying himself out to be talked to. So here was clearly a little call ; and I talked to him for some time, he being very interested and responsive. Just as he was going to move off, two lads, of about fifteen and eighteen, his sons, came crashing through the bushes ; I don't recollect whether the father beckoned them or not, anyhow up they came, and he quietly sat down again, and they sat down too, and seemed quite as willing to listen to the " old, old story " as he had been, only I could not get so much out of them. At last the whole crew departed, and I was just collecting my thoughts and reviving the aforesaid " impulse," when in about ten minutes the younger lad reappeared, with his sister, a girl of about seventeen. They did not say a word, but scrambled straight up to me, and, seating themselves at my feet, looked up into my face, saying by their look as plain as any words, " Please talk to us ! " What could one do but accede ! and they stayed at least another half hour, so quiet and interested that one could not but hope the seed was falling on " good ground." The girl, Félicie, was more communicative than the lads, very simple, but intelligent. By the time they departed a good part of the morning was gone, and the " impulse " too ! but I enjoyed the morning probably twice as much as if I had done a good piece of my poem ; and it seemed so clear that the Master had taken me at my word, and come and given me this to do for Him among His " little ones," and that He was there hearing and answering and accepting me, that it was worth any amount of poem-power.

However, *next* day the " impulse " came again, which

is by no means always the case when once interrupted ; and once fairly started, I have worked out what I *think* is perhaps the best poem I ever wrote, so far as I can judge.

But this is only one of constant instances which I could tell. I do so feel that every hour is distinctly and definitely guided by Him. I have taken Him at His word *in everything*, and He takes me at my word *in everything*. Oh, I *can* say now that Jesus *is* "to me a living bright Reality," and that He really and truly *is* "more dear, more intimately nigh, than e'en the sweetest earthly tie." No friendship could be what I find His to be. I have more now than a few months ago, even though I was so happy then ; for the joy of *giving* myself, and my will, and my all to Him seems as if it were succeeded, and even superseded, by the deeper joy of a conscious certainty that He has *taken* all that He led me to give ; and "I am persuaded that He is able to keep that which I have committed unto Him" : so, having entrusted my very trust to Him, I look forward ever so happily to the future (*if* there be yet much of earthly future for me) as "one vista of brightness and blessedness." Only I do so want everybody to "taste and see." Yesterday I somehow came to a good full stop in my writing much earlier than I expected, and asked what He would have me do next, go on or go out at once ? Just then a young lady came in ; "Had I just a few minutes to spare ?" So I went out with her at once. She had overheard a short chat I had had some days ago with another, didn't know *what*, but it had set her longing for something more than she had got. She had started out for a walk alone, thinking and praying, and the thought came to her to come straight to me, which she seemed to think an unaccountably bold step. Well, God seemed to give me exactly the right message for her, just as with Miss M. last week, the two cases starting from a very different level, but the result the same, a real turning-point. Don't conclude, however, from these that I am always seeing results, because I am not : but that I am entirely content about, just as He chooses it to be.

It has occurred to me that, as I profess to be "writing," you will expect a new book as the result, and will be disappointed ; so I tell you simply what I *have* written, and what I am going to write.

"Our Swiss Guide." Article for *Sunday Magazine*, on the spiritual analogies in all sorts of little details of mountaineering.

"For Charity." Song for Hutchings and Romer.

"Enough." Short sacred poem.

"How much for Jesus?" A sort of little true story for children ; for an American edition.*

"True Hearted." New Year's Address (in verse) for Young Women's Christian Association, for January, 1875.

"Tiny Tokens." A small poem for *Good Words*.

"Precious Things." A poem.

"A Suggestion." Short paper for *Home Words*.

"The Precious Blood of Jesus." A hymn.

"The Thoughts of God." The aforesaid poem.

"Shining for Jesus." Verses addressed to my nieces and nephews at Winterdyne.

---

* This manuscript we have no clue to ; any information concerning it would be acceptable.

"New Year's Wishes," by Caswell's request, for a very pretty card.

These are all written, and copied, and done with. Next week (D.V.) I set about what I have long wanted to do: "Little Pillows," thirty-one short papers as a little book for children of, say, twelve years old ; a short, easily-recollected text, to go to sleep upon, for each night of the month, with a page or two of simple, practical thoughts about it, such as a little girl might read every night while having her hair brushed. I think this will take me about a fortnight to write and arrange for press ; adding probably a verse or two of a hymn at the end of each of the little papers. There are lots of little monthly morning and evening books for grown-up people, but I don't know of one for children except those containing *only* texts. I dare say I shall get in somehow three other little poems that want writing (being on the simmer): "The Splendour of God's Will," "The Good Master," and (don't be startled at the transition) "Playthings"; also "Johann von Allmen," a little article for the *Dayspring*. I can clear off things easily here, especially through not having so many letters. If I could manage three months every year in a Swiss or Welsh valley, I should keep my printer going.

En route. September 29, 1874.

I don't know whether there will be enough of interest for a final circular, but when I am out I never feel inclined to do anything but write home. As I did not know your address, I had to write my last to Maria, at any rate part of my long letter to her was to do duty as circular.

I was nearly if not quite "the last rose of summer" at Ormont Dessus, the hotel shuts up on October 1. But the last week was the most perfect weather possible, and, without being unpleasantly hot, was warm enough for sitting out not merely in the sunshine, but in the moonlight. My last day, Sunday, was one of the most exquisite days imaginable, brilliantly clear, the autumn tints throwing in touches of crimson and gold in splendid contrast to the pine woods; and, what is so rare in Switzerland, the noon and afternoon were as glowing as the morning, everything vivid all day.

At the little French service I soon saw we had "somebody" in the pulpit, and it was M. de Pressensé, who is, I have been told, one of the first French orators. His sermon was both eloquent and good. Madame de Pressensé, the well-known writer, was almost close to me, a sweet and handsome-looking elderly lady. Their daughter has married M. Bernus, the very charming young pastor of the Eglise Libre at Ormont Dessus, a curious change for this rather elegant and distinguée-looking Parisienne to settle down in little wooden rooms over a little wooden chapel in this out-of-the-way valley! M. Bernus is cousin to Helen Trench that was! I found this out when I went to get books at the Church Library. The people sing beautifully; it was a downright treat, in German choral style as to music, slow, rich harmonies that bear dwelling on; one tune was Cassel, No. 190 in "Havergal's Psalmody." It was such sweet singing, every one keeping to *cres.* and *dim.*, neither instrument nor apparently any stated choir, but all the parts correctly sung by the peasant congregation.

I have finished not only "Little Pillows," but a companion to it for morning use, "Morning Bells"; both manuscripts are ready for the press. I do not think it is nearly so easy to write for children as for adults; constantly I refrained from what I would most like to say about the texts I had chosen, because it would not be simple enough for the little ones. I have purposely avoided any stories or anecdotes, lest children should skim the book through in search of them, instead of reading them morning and night steadily; at least I know that is what I should have done. I do so hope these books will be really helpful to some of Christ's little ones.

On Monday morning I left Ormont Dessus at eight on foot, sending my bag " by post." By-the-bye the oddest instance of the Swiss way of sending all things by post was when one day Madame Treina apologised for giving me only chicken for dinner "because the beef had not come by post"! Instead of going direct to Montreux by diligence and rail, I went for a three days' walking tour. Please, nobody is to be shocked at this, because I quite came to the conclusion that it was not incorrect at all, and I found other ladies doing it. Besides, who is any the wiser? If one is seen marching alone, one may have friends five minutes before or behind for aught any one knows! I have really had a good spell at writing, and I thought a three days' march would be a good thing to finish up with. It was a nice morning, and I walked till nearly twelve, and then "camped" till three in a mossy nook by a little stream, mended gloves, did my accounts, watched the water,

and so forth.   Then I walked on again and got to the
little town of Saanen at five.

After crossing the Col de Pillon, an easy two hours'
pass out of the Ormonts valley into the Saanen-thal, it
was all road, smooth and level, nothing exciting, but
just a very quietly pretty valley, what one would call
" peaceful "; the Ormonts always suggested the French
term *" riante "* to me.   The whole way was musical
with these pretty cow bells, as most of the herds have
been brought down from the high alps, and instead of
being from one hundred to five hundred large, they are
distributed among their owners for the winter.   A herd
on the mountains may belong to thirty or forty different
people.   The last fortnight my mountain rambles have
been all the more enjoyable for the descent of the
" bétail " from the " high alps," so that they were perfectly undisturbed.   The high pastures or " alps," for
the meaning is the same, where the cows are in summer,
range from 5,500 to 7.500 feet ; then in September they
come down to the " middle alps," where hay has already been twice made ; then in October they come
down to the valleys, where generally there have
been three crops of hay.   It is very systematic, and a
whole district acts simultaneously in these pastoral arrangements.   The middle alps are enclosed with rough
fencing, so I don't mind the beasts there ; it is when two
hundred or three hundred creatures are loose on the
high alps, with no fences or retreat whatever, that I object to meet them.

This Saanen-thal is more one's ideal of rural Swiss
life than almost anything I have seen ; no pensions, or
any signs of foreign tourists, but pure aboriginal.   No

one would believe who has not seen it, the difference between the Protestant and Romanist valleys. Here in the Saanen-thal the chalets are beautiful, as spruce and pretty as the carved things one sees, and look roomy and comfortable, averaging about fifteen windows in front! Nice little gardens are quite the rule, and in Ebuit, a small village, I saw several quite up to the mark of a "First Prize" at a Perry Barr flower show, which is saying a great deal ; dahlias seem the pet flower just now. One never sees any "gentlemen's houses "· the land is all in small properties, and there is no Swiss nobility. The only things answering to our country houses are quite near the larger towns. A Swiss country pastor's life must be peculiarly isolated, often a day's journey from any one except peasants and peasant farmers.

At Saanen I put up at a queer old-fashioned inn, very comfortable and very cheap, with a capital piano, which was quite a treat, as it is a good while since I have even seen one. Tuesday morning was gloomy and suspicious, so I started at a quarter past seven, but it did not rain till the afternoon. I reached Chateau D'Oex by half-past nine, and was disappointed with it ; it is pretty, but there are places ten times more so within reach ; yet heaps of English stay there. Towards eleven I got to the Gorge de la Tine, a lovely narrow deep cleft, with an almost emerald river at the bottom, broken with white foam ; I turned off and rested on moss nearly a foot thick, overlooking this beautiful gorge. Then I reckoned on some dinner at the village. At quite a large tidy-looking inn outside, I asked for some cold meat, and to be shown into the salon till it was ready.

Thereupon the very cheerful little waitress ushered me into their idea of a "salon," a room with one table covered with oilcloth on which I was to dine, and another of sticks nailed across like an arbour table, a bed in one corner, a big box with three puppies in another, and three chairs. The floor might have been washed last year or the year before! Then for the dinner, "they were sorry they had not what I asked for, but would do the best they could for madame." So in came a dish with four little squares of lukewarm lean bacon nearly black, and four ditto of fat. Another dish of two cold potatoes cut in half and dipped in some sort of brown juice, and *with these* half a dozen warm baked pears. Further, some very oily. salad ; however, I am not particular, fortunately! Meanwhile the mother of the puppies aforesaid showed a positive determination not to let me leave the place without having a piece out of me ; she watched every opportunity of the door being ajar to come in and make a rush at me ; twice it came to a regular fight with my alpenstock! Every time they shut her up she got loose, and came at me again.

I have none of the nervousness about dogs that I have about bulls, still when I found she really meant mischief, I thought, rain or no rain, I would push on to some more hospitable quarters. So I trudged on to Montbovon, rather out of my way ; but it began to rain, and I did not care to walk three miles in a pour to Allières, which is some way up the Col de Jaman. The Montbovon hotel folks, who were very pleasing, told me I should find accommodation in the auberge at Allières, not very luxurious, but I should be " very well " there.

This being evidently disinterested advice, I relied on it and departed. However, for the first and only time in Switzerland, I found a strange contrast to the usual civility and even kindness of the people. I got there about a quarter past six, and found it just a remove better than the Sennbütte, which you will remember we camped at on our way from Mürren.

A tall, bold, rough girl, of twenty-five or so, let me in. "Yes, you can have a room when it's ready, not before. Here, in here!" And she ushered me into a dark, dirty room with tables and benches, marched off, and shut the door. I did not like my quarters at all, but there was no help for it, as it would be impossible for me to cross the col or even get back to Montbovon in the dark. But of course I had been asking all along to be guided, so I was not uneasy, but expected I had been guided there for some good reason, perhaps some wandering sheep to be found. It got quite dark, and then five or six men came in, and she brought a candle, and they sat down at one of the tables and smoked. I hardly think they saw me. I asked if my room was ready. "No, you must wait!" and out she darted, slamming the door. So I waited, sitting on my bench in my dark corner for nearly an hour, she coming roughly in and out, talking noisily and bringing wine for the men. At last—"You can come upstairs now!" So I went, glad enough.

It was not quite so dirty as downstairs, but not brilliant. A jug and basin on the table was all the apparatus; the bed was barley straw, no pillow, but a pink cotton bolster. "Are you going to bed now?" she asked. I told her yes, very soon. About eight o'clock, just as I really was going to bed, came a sharp, angry rap at my door. I was glad it was locked, for before I could answer the handle was rattled violently.

"What is it?"

"Are you going to burn the candle all night? How soon are you going to put it out, I should like to know! burning it all away 'commę cela!'" I considered it advisable to answer very meekly, so I merely said it should be put out in a few minutes, whereupon she banged downstairs. It seemed to me that this was an "opportunity," so I asked God that when morning came He would shut her mouth and open mine.

Wednesday morning I was up at daybreak, having gone to bed so early. At first the whole sky was clouded, and I feared I had lost my excursion, for the beautiful Col de Jaman is just one of those which it is worse than useless to cross except in good weather. However, at sunrise the whole veil was withdrawn within a few minutes, and a more glorious morning could not be. I came down about half-past six. My friend was pottering over the fire with a big kettle. I asked her to get me some coffee. "Can't have coffee till it's made!" said she savagely. So I went and sat outside the door and waited patiently. In about half an hour she poked her head out. "Do you want anything besides coffee?" still in a tone as if I were a mortal enemy! I suggested bread and butter. "Butter!" (as if I had asked for turtle soup!) "there is none, but you can have a piece of bread if you like." So I had my coffee and a hunch of bread ; but I don't pity anybody who breakfasts on Swiss bread and milk.

Then it was my turn! I went close to her, looked

16

up into her wicked-looking eyes, and put my hand on
her arm and said (as gently as possible) : "You are not
happy ; I know you are not." She darted the oddest
look at me ; a sort of startled, half frightened look, as
if she thought I was a witch ! I saw I had touched the
right string and followed it up, telling her how I saw
last night she was unhappy, even when she was laughing and joking, and how I had prayed for her ; and
then, finding she was completely tamed, spoke to her
quite plainly and solemnly, and then about Jesus and
what He could do for her. She made a desperate effort not to cry. She listened in a way that I am sure
nothing but God's hand upon her could have made her
listen, and took "A Saviour for You" (in French),
promising to read it, and thanking me over and over
again. The remaining few minutes I was in the house
she was as respectful and quiet as one could wish. I
also got a talk with her old mother. So if God grants
this to be the checking of this poor girl in what I should
imagine to be a very downward path, was it not well
worth getting out of the groove of one's usual comforts
and civilities ?

Then I trudged on up the col, and as I heard the
bells of a large herd ahead I put myself under convoy
of a little group of peasants, a woman, two men, and a
lad ; they were bright and intelligent, and seemed
greatly to enjoy asking me questions about England,
and were immensely gratified at my admiration of their
own beautiful "patrie," so this made a nice opening for
further talk about the more beautiful country above, and
how to get there. I stayed some time on the top of the
col, which I reached in about an hour and a half ; the view

was singular and fine ; the lake of Geneva was hidden
under an expanse of smooth white cloud, out of which the
opposite mountains rose into an atmosphere as transparent as possible, while the farther heights above Lausanne loomed through a strange blue haze ; all the rest
of the view was vividly clear in splendid sunshine. It
is about three hours down to Montreux ; very pretty all
the way, till you come through uninteresting vineyards,
like the Rhine ones, three feet high, and not so pretty
as raspberry beds.

I got here (Montreux) about noon, and turned into a
hotel-pension conveniently close to the station.

A nice letter from Miss E. J. Whately, forwarded
from Ormont, was awaiting me ; she has been delayed
in England, and is now staying at Spa, and cannot get
here even if I waited a week for her, so we hope to meet
another time. They are chiefly English in this pension,
but not the sort who would care for me or I for them, I
fancy. I have been a stroll this afternoon, and am now
writing in my room before bedtime. I can't think how
I shall do with English hours, after my early ones here.
That reminds me several have asked me to say how I
am. Very well indeed, thank God. But I really do not
feel sure whether I have "laid in a stock of strength,"
i.e. whether I shall be able to do any more in England
than I have done, without getting so very tired. For
here I have been taking so much rest, and doing absolutely nothing to tire myself, and in every way setting
health first, that I have had the best possible chance.
Except at Sepey, where I had two or three bad nights, I
have been perfectly well the whole time, and now I
really do mean to try and be very prudent with the

health God has given me, only of course I do not mean
to be idle; I seek to gain strength that I may use it.
On the Col de Jaman I was greatly tempted to go up
the Dent de Jaman, a most inviting rocky peak, commanding a splendid panorama; but it would have been
two hours' extra exertion, and I thought I had better
eonomise strength, and not run even a remote risk to
finish up with.

Last Saturday week I was for a few minutes in (I believe) imminent danger, which I never was to my knowledge before. It was most utterly unexpected and un-
foreseen, or I should not of course have dreamt of putting
myself in such a fix. I was having a higher afternoon
scramble than usual, having waited for some time for
a clear day to ascend a certain point (not a summit)
on the great rocky mountain, Sex Rouge, from which I
expected a peculiarly fine view. In two hours and forty
minutes I reached my point, the edge of a shoulder over
which I saw right into the midst of the great glaciers,
and at the foot of a wall of great rocks which prevented
further progress. It was merely a cow-track up to the
highest alp most of the way, but beyond that came thirty-
five minutes of very steep slope, partly poor grass and
partly loose stones, but not so bad as to make me hesitate about climbing it. However, I found it more awkward coming down than I expected; so I scanned the
place carefully, and fancied I could make out a much
easier descent by making a certain angle farther down
the edge of the shoulder, and then striking across the
slope. I thought I had taken my bearings very accu-
rately, a thing I seldom fail to find myself exact in; but
somehow I lost them and trended too far to the left be-

fore ending the angle.   It had certainly promised to be
far easier than the other way, but after leaving the
shoulder I found it getting worse and worse ; still I
thought every minute a few steps more would end the
difficulty, so I crept on carefully across the small loose
stones until I found it so steep that it would be nearly
impossible to take any more steps without sliding down,
stones and all.   I had been so sure of my bearings that
I had been only looking at my footing till then ; but
on pulling up to take a wider view of things, I was
startled to see that instead of only a slope below me,
which one might have slid down with impunity, there
was a precipice not twenty feet below where I stood, a
sheer edge with nothing whatever to catch at, not a bush
or rock or boulder, nothing but the slipping stones
which threatened to give way under my feet every in
stant.   I believe that if I had felt the least confused or
nervous I should have been lost, for the smallest wrong
movement of foot or of balance would have been enough
to send me and the stones down what must have been
a fatal slope.   I stood quite still, while I committed it all deliberately to Him who could keep my feet
from falling, and then did what I could.   I found it
would be positively more dangerous to attempt to turn
round ; so the only thing was, as cautiously as possible,
to *work* foothold with my alpenstock, moving one foot
forward into it, and then working another, and so on.
In less than five minutes I had passed the worst, and in
about ten was beyond all danger.   I cannot understand
how I got there ; there was some peculiar ocular delusion about the slope which altogether misled me ; it
looked as if every step must land me on a less steep

slope, instead of which it was worse at every step. I have come across no parallel to it.

Connie and Elizabeth will recollect the steep shale slope where Abraham picked steps for us up the last part of the Dündengrat ; it was much steeper than that, sharp rocky little stones instead of shale, and the precipice just below ! Though God kept me perfectly calm and cool at the time, I could not think of it for days afterwards without shuddering, and it will certainly make me more cautious not only how I go, but where I go, if ever I have any more mountaineering. Yet this was apparently a most innocent little excursion ; not one I should ever have thought of taking a guide for, or expecting to find the least difficulty.

DIJON. *October* 2.

I left Montreux Thursday at noon. I determined to try the experiment of day instead of night travelling for a long journey. As one can only go first class by the night expresses, one actually saves by sleeping on the way, as two nights at hotels do not equal the difference between first and second class, and the second class carriages are quite equal to our first. I think the home journey will be less tiring this way, as it is cool weather ; if hot, then night is best. Besides, just now the homeward trains are all so very full that one could not have the least chance of room to lie down, and it would be intolerable to sit bolt upright all night. I can sleep anywhere if I can only lie down, but I can't do with sitting up.

So my Thursday's journey was only from Montreux

to Dôle, which I reached at nine P.M. I waited from three to four at Auvernier, a tiny junction station near Neuchatel ; the rest of the world goes on to Neuchatel and back again, getting the benefit of twenty minutes extra riding, and a great noisy station for hurried refreshments. But turning out at Auvernier I had an hour's quiet rest on a bench at a little table overlooking the lake, with a last view of the snow mountains gleaming among clouds. There were several countrywomen getting refreshment, café noir and vin du pays ; and tracts were quite a new idea to them ; they were uncommonly delighted, and wished me all manner of good things, nearly equal to Irish benedictions.

I had sunshine up to the last hour in Switzerland, but on entering the Jura heavy rain came on ; nothing could have been more delicious, for it laid all the dust, which is so extra horrible on the way to Paris.

I seem to have a way of getting into queer situations, and always coming out of them all right ; so at Pontarlier, where the train stops twenty minutes, I got out for some refreshment, and on coming back to what I felt sure was my carriage every vestige of my effects was gone, carpet-bag, alpenstock, and all. Then ensued a hunt for pretty nearly half an hour, the train for some unknown reason stopping forty instead of twenty minutes, just as if for my private convenience. Now fancy me scampering at the heels of a man with a red light, it being perfectly dark, and no gas outside the station, all over a labyrinth of rails and trucks and empty carriages and live engines, hunting for various carriages which had been detached from our train, as the officials would have it I was mistaken about the carriage. I could not help laughing at the position, dodging full tear in and out of sheds and across turning tables, behind the red lamp, as if it were a will o' the wisp. I was about giving it up as hopeless, and decided on staying the night at Pontarlier, when an official suddenly shouted to me from behind a pump, " Est-ce là vos effets, madame?" And sure enough it all was, though nobody ever knew how it got there. So I went comfortably back to my own carriage and had no further adventures.

In the compartment were two respectable men from West Bromwich, who had been to Lucerne for a three weeks' holiday with Cook's tickets; they applied to me to interpret something for them, and this led to a little talk, which speedily drifted as usual into better things, to which I found a decided response. I had alluded to Christ's work for us, and the one to whom I was talking said quickly : "Yes, Miss, it's a *transfer*, that's the word; the last three days I've had that word always in my mind; that's just what it is, a transfer. He takes our sins and makes over His righteousness to us." Then he told me that he had met on the Rigi an invalid Irish clergyman who seemed full of that one thing; "he began with the finished work and he ended with the finished work; and I never saw it so clearly before, though I have been, so to say, looking about for it this long time; it was worth all the journey there and back to get hold of this view." It seemed curious that such an excellent clergyman should be obliged to give up his living from ill health, and ordered abroad; but he was sowing the seed in fifty places instead of one. Yes, that great transfer, it is blessed ! Was not this a nice instance of the real use of such seed sowing?

At Dôle I omnibused to the Hotel de Genève, where I was extremely comfortable.

Friday, a lovely morning, my train left at 9.27 ; but I had an hour's stroll about the town and suburbs, which I had specially planned to do, thinking it an unusually good opportunity for tract distribution, being not at all a likely place for other sowers to have been at work ; so I finished up the rest of my supply.

It was not much more than an hour to Dijon, where I had to wait till 2.36 ; so, as I had only had one proper dinner since Sunday, I thought I had better come to this Hotel du Jura and have a long rest and a good meal at table d'hôte! I struck up with some lively English, who turn out to be relatives of Miss Weldon, of Kidder-minster.

Travelling in cool weather does make an enormous difference in fatigue. I got to Paris at 10.36 P.M. It had rained most of the way, so it was a nice, clean, cool journey. On arriving I drove in a tiny open carriage, which was most refreshing, to Cook's Hotel, thinking it a better plan to go where heaps of Swiss tourists go than to any other hotel. I had a most paternal driver, really such a nice fellow, who told me I was "trop jeune" to travel "toute seule"! and wondered I was not afraid. So this led to a small sermon on God's care and love, which he seemed to think interesting. I was very comfortable at the hotel ; and though I had a short night, it was a good one, for I "paid attention to it," as Mr. Dowling says he does when he goes to bed for only three hours.

In the train I had one of those curious musical visions, which very rarely visit me. I hear strange and very beautiful chords, generally full, slow and grand, succeeding each other in most interesting sequences. I do not invent them, I could not; they pass before my mind, and I only listen. Now and then my will seems aroused, when I see ahead how some fine resolution might follow, and I seem to *will* that certain chords should come, and then they do come; but then my will seems suspended again, and they go on quite independently. It is so interesting, the chords seem to fold over each other and die away down into music of infinite softness; and then they unfold, and open out as if great curtains were being withdrawn one after another, widening the view, till with a gathering power and intensity and fulness it seems as if the very skies were being opened out before me, and a sort of great blaze and glory of music, such as my outside ears never heard, gradually swells out in perfectly sublime splendour. This time there was an added feature: I seemed to hear depths and heights of sound beyond the scale which human ears can receive; keen, far-up octaves, like vividly twinkling starlight of music; and mighty, slow vibrations of gigantic strings, going down into grand thunders of depths, octaves below anything otherwise appreciable as musical notes. Then all at once it seemed as if my soul had got a new sense, and I could *see* this inner music as well as hear it; and then it was like gazing down into marvellous abysses of sound and up into dazzling regions of what to the eye would have been light and colour, but to this new sense was sound. Was it not odd? It lasted perhaps half an hour, but I don't know exactly, and it is very difficult to describe in words.

Saturday the people called me at 5.30 A.M., saying

the tidal train went at seven. So I was off at 6.35, and on reaching the station found the train that day was not till 9.10. However, it turned out for the best, of course. I went on to Boulogne by a 7.30 train, and thus had time for a two hours' rest and an unhurried meal, which I think was a better preparation for the crossing than a hurried scalding with soup or coffee and a rush to the boat. It was a bad look-out in any case, for the wind was tremendous, so that it was positively difficult to walk along the quays, which are supposed to be quite sheltered, and even in this harbour the boat swayed so that it was not easy to get on board. But for being Saturday I almost think I should have waited; but I made up my mind to endurance, and went. I shall never forget the first stride of the vessel out of the harbour, I never felt anything like it as she met the first wave, it was just a sheer leap and a plunge! Now I take it to be a proof that I really must be very much stronger, for although it was so rough I was not nearly so ill as usual. I had not that terrible sense of utter illness which one fancies must be like actual dying; and I felt most thankful for the comparative exemption and the sign of strength. I should think there were three hundred people to watch the unfortunates come on shore! it was regularly running a gauntlet.

I came on to London, feeling quite well, and went straight to Clapton Square; I had telegraphed to them from Folkestone, and got in about 8.30, the boat being an hour late from the head wind.

It was rather nice that I had an opportunity of a last bit of "holiday work" in the very last five minutes before coming to anchor at the H.'s. I was looking for a boy to carry my bag; two poor little chaps were so eager that I chartered them both; one was a matchbox boy, and the other selling papers; they trotted on each side of me, as I divided my small burdens between them, not liking to disappoint either; and after having told the "old, old story" so many times in German and French, it was uncommonly pleasant to give a little of its sweet music in English to these poor little London lads; they were so attentive and apparently interested.

I wish you had seen and heard the welcome I got here! it was so nice, and altogether I was so happy. Curious that you should have sent me Psalm ciii. 1-3; my mind was specially full of it, only adding verses 4 and 5. I have so very, very much to bless Him for, and the beautiful sequence of five blessings seemed to sum it all up: "forgiveth," "healeth," "redeemeth," "crowneth thee with lovingkindness and tender mercies," and "satisfieth thy mouth with good things." What a great deal it is! And really I may add, "so that thy youth is renewed like the eagle's," for I feel so mentally fresh and unweary, and the H.'s all say they never saw me looking anything like so well. So herewith ends the "circular" series of 1874!

GOLDEN LAND.

FAR from home, alone I wander
  Over mountain and pathless wave ;
But the fair land that shineth yonder
  Claimeth the love that erst it gave.
Golden Land, so far, so nearing !
  Land of those who wait for me !
Ever brighter the vision cheering,
  Golden Land, I haste to thee !
On my path a golden sunlight
  Softly falls where'er I roam.
And I know it is the one light
  Both of exile and of home.
Golden Land, so far, so near,
On my heart engraven clear,
Though I wander from strand to strand,
Dwells my heart in that Golden Land.

PENSION WENGEN, 15*th September*, 1876.

OUR SWISS GUIDE.

WRITTEN IN 1874.

(*Reprinted from the " Sunday Magazine."*)

NOT the least interesting part of mountaineering is the perpetual upspringing of lessons and illustrations and analogies. Sometimes an idea starts up which has, for one's self, all the delicious charm of. a quite new thought, though very likely it may have flashed upon the minds of scores of other travellers ; sometimes a very old and familiar one presents itself, and we have the pleasure of proving it, perhaps for the first time, by practical experience. · In noting one little group of illustrations among many, those which cluster round the idea of a " Guide," we shall not be careful to steer clear of such old ideas, though we may hope to add some freshness to them.

The application throughout will be so very obvious to any mind accustomed to take the least interest in analogies of spiritual life, that we prefer giving the points of illustration only, leaving the reader to supply the " heavenly meaning " which shall underlie each sentence.

Curiously enough, the name of our favourite Swiss guide, the one who inspired us with most confidence, and to whom we should most like to entrust ourselves in any future tour, at once gave the keynote of thought ; it was *Joseph*. While we instinctively trusted his sagacity and strength, it was additionally pleasant to find that our bright young guide was a believer in the Lord Jesus Christ, our true Joseph. He had remarked that his great physical strength and health was "the most splendid earthly Gift," but on our mention of the most glorious Gift of all, our Saviour Christ himself, he rejoined fervently, "Ah, one can never estimate the value of *that* gift ! "

But to proceed to our illustrations.

1. The first duty of a really first-rate guide, when arranging for a long snow or glacier excursion, is to see that we are properly provided with everything needful. He ascertains that you have snow spectacles, without which the glare of the snow is not simply inconvenient, but injurious ; and veils, without which you stand a fair chance of finding your face completely flayed, if it should be a sunny day. He examines the spike of your alpenstock and the nails of your boots, and inquires after your wraps, and often gives curiously practical advice as to other points in your outfit. He not only tells you what you must have as to provision, but, if the excursion involves a night in some mountain hut, he sends on the necessary fuel and food, and sometimes even bedding. In all these matters you do not need to trouble at all ; if you will only leave it altogether to him, he will think of everything, arrange everything, and provide everything ; and when the time comes you will find all in

order, your shoes fresh nailed, your alpenstock newly spiked, the porter sent on with provision, and the coil of strong rope and the ice-axe all ready for the difficult places which you do not yet know of.

But many travellers do not even know that the guide is thus willing and competent; they do not ask, or perhaps they even decline, his aid and advice. Instead of throwing it all upon his responsibility, they take all the trouble themselves, and then generally find something gone wrong or something overlooked.

2. Before you start, the guide has disposed of all those heavier matters which you could not possibly carry for yourself. Very often they are taken completely out of your sight. Encumbered with these, you could not even set out on your journey, much less progress quickly and pleasantly.

But there are always plenty of little affairs which seem mere nothings at first, but which are soon found to be real burdens. The guide is perfectly willing to relieve you of all these. They are no weight to him; he quite smiles at the idea of its being any trouble to him to carry them, but they make a serious difference to you. He offers to take them at first; and if you decline, though he may not perhaps offer again, he will cheerfully take them when, later on, you feel their weight, and hand them one by one to him, till the very last is given up, and you walk lightly and freely. A beginner says she "would rather carry her little knapsack, it is really no weight at all!" and thinks a parcel or two in her pocket "can't make any difference," and prefers wearing her waterproof, because "it isn't at all heavy." But she has not gone far before she is very glad, if a sensible girl, to give up her knapsack, tiny though it be ; and then she finds that a waterproof won't do for climbing, and she hands that over ; and presently she even empties her pocket, and the guide trudges away with it all. Then she is surprised to find what a difference it does make, and understands why her friend, who knew the guide's ways better and gave up every single thing to him at first, is getting along so cool and fresh and elastically. But mark that the weight of a burden is seldom realized till we really are going uphill and in a fair way to make progress. Indeed, this very sensitiveness to weight is a quick test of increased gradient. We think nothing about it as long as we are walking on a level or slightly downhill ; but as soon as we begin the real ascent the pull of the little burdens is felt at once, and the assistance, which before we did not crave, becomes very welcome. It is then that we feel we *must* "lay aside *every* weight."

3. One may almost certainly distinguish between a tyro and an old hand by watching for a few minutes the style of march. A novice will walk at an irregular pace according to the irregularities of the ground, making little "spurts" when she comes to an easy bit, and cither putting on steam or lagging behind for extra steep ones ; stopping to gather flowers and poke at curious boulders ; taking long or short steps according to circumstances, and never thinking of such a thing as noticing, much less imitating, the steady rhythm of the guide's walk. Probably she expresses her astonishment at his unexpectedly slow pace, and would prefer getting on a little faster ; very likely she dashes ahead or aside, and presently has to be recalled to the track, which is not so easy to keep as she supposed.

One with more experience is quite content to take the guide's pace, knowing certainly that it pays in the long run, and saves an enormous amount of fatigue, and therefore of time also. Very short steps, slowly, silently, and steadily placed, but as regular as martial music, never varying in beat, never broken by alternation of strides and pauses—this is the guide's example for up-hill work; and yet it is what one never believes in till one has learnt by experience that one gets through twice as much by it.

4. It is wonderful what a saving of fatigue it is if from the very beginning one obeys the guide implicitly and follows him exactly. You spy such a handy "short cut," you can see so precisely where you can join the path again, it will save you such a provoking long round, you can't think why the guide does not choose it! So away you go, exulting in your cleverness, straight up-hill, instead of that tiresome zigzag.

But it is rather steeper than you thought, and you get just a little out of breath; and you find an awkward little perpendicular rock right in the way, and you must go round it; and then you get into rhododendron bushes, which are thicker than you thought, and you get very wet; and then you see your companions reaching the point you are making for, and you scramble and hurry. And by the time you have done with your short cut you find you have not only gained no time, but that the few minutes away from the guide have heated you and taken more out of you than an hour's steady following. Later in the day you recollect your short cuts of the morning, and wish you had economised your breath.

5. The full value of exact following is not learned in the valleys or pastures. It is on the "high places" and on the unsullied snowfields that one discovers this.

It is when we are high away above the green slopes, seeing no track but our guide's own footsteps, that we learn its safety. He set his foot on that stone : there you must set yours, for the next is loose and would betray you ; he planted his alpenstock on that inch of rock : there you must plant yours, for an inch either way would give no firm hold ; he climbed by that jut of rock : so must you, for the other would be too hard a step ; he sprang but half way over that torrent, and you must do the same at cost of wetting your feet, for he knew that the slab of rock that you could have reached at one bound was treacherously slippery and dangerous.

It is here also that we get into the way of instant and unquestioning compliance with every word our guide utters. I was struck with the remark of a Swiss Alpine Clubbist in a description of his ascent of the Tödi. His guide suddenly shouted to him, " Turn sharp to the right ! " He saw no reason whatever for this, but obeyed instantly. The next moment an immense block of stone fell upon the spot where he would have been had he hesitated an instant or even looked round to satisfy himself. The quick and practised eye of the guide saw the trembling of the loosened mass which the traveller could not see. A query would have been fatal. He added, " In these high places one learns to obey one's guide without stopping to ask 'Why?'"

But when the snow slopes, so cool and pure and beautiful, are reached, another phase of following is learnt.

There is not the excitement and effort of the rock climbing, and at first it seems very quiet and easy work, with
a special exhilaration of its own, making one feel as if
one had started quite fresh, all the rest of the journey
counting for nothing. Once we set out on such a slope,
tracking after our guide in a general sort of way, rather
interested in making our own footprints, and hardly dis-
tinguishing his from those of our companions. If we
turned to look back, it was surprising what a number of
unconscious little curves our feet had made. But the
snow was rather soft, and we soon found it much harder
work than we expected. One of us was walking, as she
always did, close behind the guide, because she was not
quite so strong as the rest, and was therefore under his
especial care. Suddenly she called out, "Oh, do set
your feet *exactly* in the guide's footsteps, you can't think
how much easier it is!" So we tried it, and certainly
should not have believed what a difference it would
make. All the difficulty and effort seemed gone; the
fatiguing sinking and laborious lifting of our feet were
needless; we set them now exactly where the guide's
great foot had trodden, keeping his order of right and
left, and all was easy, a hundred steps less toil than
twenty before. But, to have the full benefit of this, one
needed to keep also very near to the guide, for the last
comers trod rather in their companions' footmarks, and
were often misled by some false or uncertain treading
of these, which marred the perfectness of the original
steps.

6. Thorough knowledge of the guide's language adds
both to the enjoyment and safety of our following. He
has much to tell us by the way, and is always ready to

answer questions and give information. One who does not easily understand loses a great deal. A companion may be very willing to translate, but may do so incorrectly, and in any case the freshness and point of many a remark is lost ; while it often happens that the usual interpreter of a party is not near enough for appeal or too tired to keep up the interchange. In sudden emergencies too it may be really important that each should personally understand, and thus be able instantly to obey, the guide's directions.

Moreover, it is very desirable not only thus to "know his voice," but to be able to speak to him for one's self. Once one of us slipped in a rather awkward place. She called out, "Stop a moment !" but the guide in advance knew no English, and therefore did not heed her, and but for the quick call in German of another who saw the slip, she might have been frightened and hurt.

7. When we come to really difficult places, or glaciers with hidden crevasses, we find the use of the coil of rope. This is fastened first round the guide himself and then round the rest of the party, allowing a length of eight or ten feet between each. Once I questioned the strength of the rope, upon which the guide untwisted it a little, and showed me a scarlet thread hidden among the strands. He told me that this was the mark that it was a real Alpine Club rope, manufactured expressly for the purpose, and to be depended upon in a matter of life and death. It is remarkable that this typical "line of scarlet thread" should have been selected as the guarantee of safety.

Once roped thus, you have a sense of security in passing what would otherwise be very dangerous places, especially concealed crevasses. And not only a sense but a reality of security. You feel the snow yield beneath your feet, you sink in, and you have neither hand nor foothold ; you get perhaps a glimpse of a fathomless blue depth below you. If you struggle you only break away the snow and enlarge the cavity. But you are in no real danger, and if you have confidence in your guide and the rope, you wait quietly, perhaps even smilingly, till you are hauled out of the hole, and landed on firm snow again. Why? Because you are firmly knotted to your guide, and also to all the rest of your party. You had not even time to call out ere he felt the sudden strain upon the rope, and instantly turned to help you, drawing you easily up to his side without hurt. Your friends felt the shock too, but they could not do much to help, only they watched and admired the guide, and found their own fears (if they had any) lessened, and their confidence in him and his rope greatly increased.

But it is the guide himself who bears the brunt of these difficulties. He goes first, carefully sounding the snow, avoiding many a crevasse which we should never have suspected, and sometimes getting a fall which would have been ours but for his trying the way for us. If we really follow his steps exactly and patiently, the probability is that we never go in at all, for the snow that has borne his weight never gives way under ours. But if we swerve even a few inches from his footmarks, we may soon find ourselves in the predicament described above.

8. Sometimes we come to a slope of frozen snow so steep that it looks absolutely impossible to climb it. And so it would be, but for our guide. Our impossibil-

ities only develop his resources. Now he unshoulders his ice-axe and with wonderful rapidity cuts steps by which we ascend even more easily than hitherto. And we' notice that these extra-difficult slopes are a positive advantage to us, because while he has all the hard work we have time to take breath. When the steep bit is passed, we have gained greatly in height, and yet we feel quite freshened for further ascent instead of fatigued.

9. The guide decides your rest as well as your progress, if you are wise enough to let him. . He very soon measures your powers, and not only knows precisely when a crevasse is just too wide for you to leap without help, or a rock just too awkward for you to climb, but he also seems to know precisely when you had better make longer or shorter halts. Sometimes you are unwilling to rest when he proposes it, and perhaps he lets you have your own way and go on, and then you are quite certain to be sorry for it. But more often he insists, and then you always find he was right, and that he had timed the halt better than you would have done. Then, without waiting to be asked, he unfastens your wraps, contrives a seat upon the snow, and folds a shawl round you. It is no use saying you do not feel cold, he is responsible for you, and knows what is safe, and will not let you risk getting chilled by the subtle glacier wind. Then he gives you the provision he has carried for you, meat, and bread, and wine, and leaves no little stone unturned towards making your halt as refreshing and pleasant as possible. There is no need for you to be calculating time, and fidgeting about going on ; he knows how much is yet before you, and he will tell you when it is time to be moving again.

10. I mentioned that the weakest of our party was specially cared for. Sometimes while the others had merely general orders, she had his strong arm, and thus escaped the slips which the more independent ones now and then made. Weakness or ailments proved his patience and care. On one occasion the "mountain sickness," which sometimes befalls travellers on great heights, suddenly attacked one not accustomed to fail in strength, and then nothing could exceed Joseph's kindness and attention. He made a wonderfully comfortable couch on the snow, told us what was the matter, administered advice and wine, and waited patiently and sympathetically till his patient, completely prostrate for an hour, felt able to stand. Then in a firm decided tone he said, "*Ich* übernehme die Kranke!" (*I* undertake the sick one!) and leaving the other guides to attend to all else, his powerful arm helped "die Kranke" down to a level where the less rarified air soon set all to rights.

11. It is understood that a true Swiss guide is literally "faithful unto death," that he does not hesitate to risk his own life for the sake of his charge, and that instances are known in which it has not only been risked, but actually sacrificed. We have never been in a position to prove this, but the undoubted fact completes the illustration. Yet this completion only shows the imperfection. For that poor faithful guide may perish *with* the traveller, and not *instead* of him; the sacrifice may be all in vain where the power and the will are not commensurate. In such illustrations we may learn as much by the contrasts as by the similarities; and how often, as in this instance, does the very failure of an earthly type bring out the glory and perfection of the Antitype.

Our glorious Guide, who has called us to the journey, and whose provision for it is "without money and without price," cannot fail in His undertaking. All who are in His covenant hands are "kept by the power of God through faith unto salvation," and "shall never perish." What He hath begun He will perform, for He "is able to keep you from falling, and to present you faultless before the presence of His glory with exceeding joy." He is not merely willing to lay down His life, but He hath laid it down for us, and now death cannot touch our Leader any more ; He hath "the power of an endless life," and we are united to that life by the strong cords of His eternal purpose and His everlasting love, which no friction can weaken and no stroke can sever. However tremendous the gulf beneath us, if thus united to Him, He will lead us on till our feet, no longer weary, stand far above the clouds upon the mountain of our God, never to repass the toils and dangers of the ascent, never to return to the valley, never to part from the strong and loving Guide who has led us to such a Hitherto of rest and wonder, and to such a Henceforth of joy and praise.

XII.

A SONG IN THE NIGHT.

WRITTEN IN SEVERE PAIN, SUNDAY AFTERNOON, OCTOBER 8th,
1876, AT THE PENSION WENGEN, ALPS.

I TAKE this pain, Lord Jesus,
  From Thine own hand ;
The strength to bear it bravely
  Thou wilt command.

I am too weak for effort,
  So let me rest,
In hush of sweet submission,
  On Thine own breast.

I take this pain, Lord Jesus,
  As proof indeed
That Thou art watching closely
  My truest need ;

That Thou my good Physician
  Art watching still ;
That all Thine own good pleasure
  Thou wilt fulfil.

I take this pain, Lord Jesus ;
  What Thou dost choose
The soul that really loves Thee
  Will not refuse.

(266)

It is not for the first time
   I trust to-day ;
For Thee my heart has never
   A trustless " Nay " !

I take this pain, Lord Jesus ;
   But what beside ?
'Tis no unmingled portion
   Thou dost provide.

In every hour of faintness
   My cup runs o'er
With faithfulness and mercy,
   And love's sweet store.

I take this pain, Lord Jesus,
   As Thine own gift ;
And true though tremulous praises
   I now uplift.

I am too weak to sing them,
   But Thou dost hear
The whisper from the pillow,—
   Thou art so near !

'Tis Thy dear hand, O Saviour,
   That presseth sore,
The hand that bears the nail-prints
   For evermore.

And now beneath its shadow,
   Hidden by Thee,
The pressure only tells me
   Thou lovest me !

XIII.

MEMORANDA OF

A SWISS TOUR WITH F. R. H.

BY HER SISTER M. V. G. H.

IT was on a calm evening in the beginning of July, 1876, that we crossed by steamer from Newhaven to Dieppe. Some Mildmay deaconesses were on board, and others, who were leaving their work for needful rest and change. Frances said: "Of course we shall have a delightful passage! I find these dear deconesses have been praying for it, and so have the dear boys at Newport." And so it was, and we landed at Dieppe before the usual time.

Frances walked with me along the quaint old quays, and it was curious to see one of my own names, that of my godmother, "Vernon," on an ancient stone building.

No need to describe the journey through Normandy and Paris to Lausanne, where we slept at the Falcon Hotel.

(268)

July 13.—By steamer on the lake of Geneva to Montreux, where Frances landed and took a mule to "Les Avants," to call on Miss E. J. Whately. I went on to the castle of Chillon to wait for Frances, and after exploring it I sat down by the lake. A poor Italian woman came with clothes to wash. She told me her husband was dead, and so she was alone, "alone always," and far from her own country. So I spoke of the one Friend and Saviour, ever near, ever loving, and who said, "I will never, never leave thee." She readily learnt a text, and then went on with her work. It was very hot. I took off my hat and rested on a bank ; presently two young women came running to see what was the matter : "O madame, nous croyions que vous etiez morte ! vous vous reposiez si tranquillement." I thanked them, and explained I was only tired and the washerwoman was within call. They sat down, and I gave them some biscuits, and they told me about their home and their fruit gatherings. Then I drew a little parable from their running so kindly to help a stranger ; how the Good Shepherd, Jesus, saw us really perishing ; how He pitied us, and came down close to us in our souls' sleep. That He would not leave us lying there, but would bring us to His own safe fold, if we were only willing to "follow Him." Let me not forget to pray for this kind Pauline and Adelaide.

Frances returned to me beaming ; saying, "Miss Whately is all and more than I expected. Only it was tantalizing to meet her, and yet see so little of her ; we only had time to find out how much there was to talk about. Anyhow she is no longer one of my unknown specials ! "

We went on to Vernayaz. It was late, but I went through the Gorge du Trient. Strange crypt-like aisles and ceaseless water music.

July 14.—Frances awoke me at four A.M., and we were ready before our guide and mule; and then Frances gave me my first lesson in Swiss slow paces, so unlike the Havergal speed.

The vivid colouring of the flowers was new to me; they seem always in Sunday dress here, bright and fresh. Halting at the Pension du Mont Blanc in the village of Finshauts, Frances was charmed with the utter quiet of the valley, and decided to stay a week. Valerie Longfat proved a most attentive waitress. We began our Swiss holiday by very early " rising and setting," as Frances wished me to get into good training before real expeditions came on. Our usual morning walk brought us in time to see the sunrise on Mont Blanc. Frances' favourite evening stroll was to a fairy glen of flowers and ferns, and few could arrange its spoils with so much taste. The little chalets around looked tempting to me, and one evening's visit led to many more. Two very aged women were sitting in their shady porch; one of them said she was " la vieillarde de Finshauts," and able to walk about with her " bon baton." I answered: " *One* good stick is enough, a dozen would only throw you down; now just as you lean on *one* stick, so do lean upon the one Saviour, the mighty One, the strong One. Some lean on a dozen angels and saints and mediators, but the Bible says, ' There is one God and one Mediator.' " She seemed to catch my meaning, and presently several of her neighbours joined us; so I proposed they should bring their chairs, and I read a chapter.   These little open air services are very pleasant.

Sunday, July 16.—A brilliant cloudless day.   Many peasants came by, going to early mass.   I sat down on some logs of wood, and made a seat for any one who would like to rest.   All returned my salutations, one and another chatting awhile, and taking tracts.   A woman asked me why I did not go with them to mass.   I told her I could not join in worshipping the host ; that Jesus Christ ascended into heaven ; that His glorified body was at the right hand of God ; that Stephen saw Him there ; so His body could not be in heaven and in a wafer too.   "But," she said, "I think you love Him." "Ah, yes ! and in England I do take bread and wine in remembrance of His great love to me."   She told me her name was Julie Zacharie, the familiar name of friends in Worcestershire ; and it seems her ancestors were English !

After mass she called and invited me to see her home, a curious old chalet : thick stone walls, and the windows so narrow that I could only dimly see the variety of images and pictures.   Julie showed me many of her old books.   Before leaving I asked if I should kneel down and pray for God's blessing, that He would teach both of us.

"No, no, dear lady ; I am just come from mass ; I have taken Jesus there.   Dear lady, you must believe our mass is a miracle ; God can give our priest power to change the sign into the real body of Jesus."

"Show me in your Bible where God promises to do this."

"Oh, it is in our 'Instructions'! Madame, do you know them?"

"Yes, I was reading them to-day. The Epistles, Gospels, and Psalms are God's word, but not the 'Instructions.' Give me your book, and we will read exactly what the Lord Jesus said. Luke xxii. 19: 'Do this in remembrance of Me.' *What* did they then do? Ate bread, drank wine. The apostles could not *then* have eaten the Lord's body, for He was sitting alive by them; hence, as it was a sign, a memorial then, it must be the same now. Besides, whatever goes in my mouth never reaches my spirit, my affections; so, while taking bread, the outward sign, in my mouth, in my heart I feed on Him by faith with thanksgiving."

Julie listened, and said: "Well, we do both love Him; will madame come with me this evening to my chalet by the river? I have cows there, and madame shall take cream."

I was resting upstairs in the evening, when a knock came at my door, and Julie appeared in my bedroom. We had a pleasant talk, and then she willingly knelt down with me. May the Spirit shine through all entangling webs!

Every day we found fresh walks, and the alpenrose blossomed where the snow was yet lingering. I tried crossing a snow slope, but gave it up, and watched Frances' agile steps, fearless and firm; now I can understand her glissades!

July 23.—Early this Sunday morning Frances wrote "Seulement pour Toi," and as our hostess and Valerie had often listened with pleasure to Frances' singing, we told them they might invite any neighbours to assemble at three o'clock, for singing and Bible reading. But by two o'clock arrivals began, charming maidens and all the old peasants we had chatted with in the week. I would not disturb Frances, so produced pens and paper and the new French hymn for any who would like to copy it ; this answered well. For the old women I proposed making some tea, but Valerie assured me no one ever cared for it ! Lemonade seemed a more welcome idea, and was duly appreciated. There was one sprightly girl, Katrine, whose mischievous laughter betrayed her dislike to our plans. But even Katrine was interested when I produced the photographs of my Indian orphans · in the Church Missionary school at Agurparah. The histories of little Daisy, Maria, and Monie (now called Frances, after Frances Ridley Havergal), and the novelty of some missionary information, awakened deep interest.

At three o'clock the room was full. Frances began by giving a free translation of her hymn, " Golden Harps," and singing it. Then came " Seulement pour Toi "; * with Frances' lively encouragement, this was soon sung *en masse*. Frances read, in French, verses from the third, fourth, and fifth chapters of Romans, giving a few sweet linkings of the same, and then asked me to speak to them. I found it quite easy to address in French, and many thanked me afterwards.

No one seemed willing to kneel for the concluding

---

* We give the words and music ; as published by Messrs. Nisbet & Co., in leaflet form. F. R. H. also arranged the same melody to " Precious Saviour, may I live," published by Hutchings & Romer.

Seulement pour Toi.

Words and Music by F. R. H.

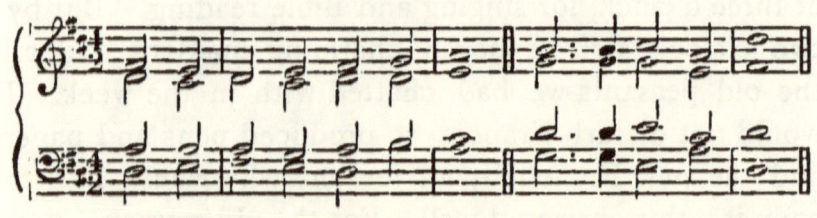

Que je sois, O cher Sau - veur, Seulement à Toi !

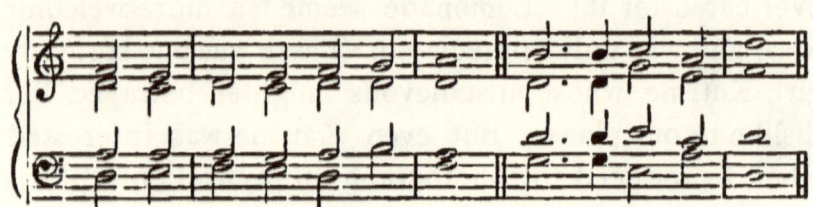

Soit l'amour de tout mon cœur Seulement pour Toi.

Je re - viens à mon Père, Seulement par Toi,

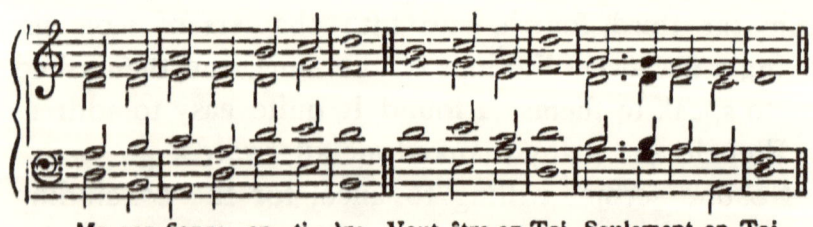

Ma con-fiance en - ti - ère Veut être en Toi, Seulement en Toi.

Le péché, Tu l'as porté
  Seul, seul pour moi ;
Et Ton sang Tu l'as versé
  Seul, seul pour moi.
Toute gloire, toute joie
  Sera pour Toi ;
Et 'espérance et la foi
  Seront en Toi,
    Seulement en Toi.

Aujourd'hui, mon cher Seigneur,
  Acceptes-moi !
To seul es mon grand Sauveur,
  Toi seul mon Roi.
Tous mes moments, tous mes jours
  Seront pour Toi !
Jésus, garde-moi toujours
  Seulement pour Toi,
    Seulement pour Toi.

Que je chante, et que je pleure,
  Seulement pour Toi !
Que je vive et que je meure
  Seulement pour Toi !
Jésus, qui m'as tant aimé
  Mourant pour moi,
Toute mon éternité   —
  Sera pour Toi,
    Seulement pour Toi !

July 23, 1876.

prayer. I would not begin while all were sitting, so Valerie's father set the example, vigorously saying, "Mettez-vous tous à genoux." A few stayed to talk to us afterwards.

We welcomed our tea, though the old women did not. Frances said she wished she had a French Bible that she might put references to "Seulement pour Toi." *M.*: "Then I will go and ask monsieur the curé to lend us one, and certainly I shall give him your hymn." *F.*: "Whatever will you think of next! Marie, do you mean it?" *M.*: "I do; besides the curé has been on my mind all the week." *F.* (laughing): "Then ask him to correct my hymn."

Away I went to the priest's house, and who should open the door but the mischievous Katrine, evidently amused to see me! Giving my compliments to the curé and a request for the loan of a Bible, he returned with Katrine, inviting me to his study. He brought the Bible in four large volumes, inquiring which I required. I told him we had only French Testaments with us, and that my sister wished to put references to a hymn she had written that morning; possibly he would kindly correct it. After reading "Seulement pour Toi," he inquired if the writer was French, as only one idiom was incorrect. He was extremely pleasant, and I told him of our little service, adding a few words on the preciousness of Christ and the Holy Scriptures. Then he called Katrine and bade her carry the volumes home for me.

The next morning we walked to Argentière. While we were resting under a tree, a lady, whom I had previously seen at our pension, and who wished to hear Frances sing, came by on her mule. She dismounted and

joined us, and at my request Frances sang to her, thus
ministering to one who seemed lonely and weary. I
should like to have known the name of this solitary
traveller. We stayed some days at Argentière ; Mont
Blanc was just opposite our windows. What variety of
rose and golden crowns descend on that kingly mountain !

July 31.—Frances walked with me part of the way to
La Flégère ; she returned to Argentière. No need for
a guide, she gives me such clear directions. Instead of
sunset on Mont Blanc, sheet lightning kept up illumina-
tion of its height, while the aiguilles flashed as if cased
in steel armour. A young lady from Denmark walked
with me up and down the terrace. I told her how we
all loved our beautiful Princess of Wales. She was interested to hear of the Bible, given her by the maidens
of England, and that led to her accepting one from me.
Her loyalty was as lively as mine.

The next morning was dense mist, but I went on to
the Bréven by breakfast time. Turning over the tourists' book I found my sister's entry, Aug. 2, 1871 : "F.
R. Havergal and Elizabeth Clay. Felt exceedingly triumphant over all the tourists at Chamouni, and especially over those who had been here in the heat of the
day. For from seven to eight P.M., while they were
in the dusk of the valley, and probably at table d'hôte
by candlelight, we were enjoying a glory of gold and
rose upon the whole chain of Mont Blanc, and watching
it die into that strange, pale, holy afterlight, which is
almost more thrillingly beautiful than any more glowing
effect. Furthermore at 4.30 A.M. we saw the first touch
of rose-fire on the crown of the monarch."

It was useless to wait in the clouds, so I went down to Chamouni ; suddenly, through the pine woods, Mont Blanc unveiled in silver. I walked on to Argentière, and Frances commended me for pushing bravely through the mist, and says I have the bump of locality.

August 3.—We left Argentière, walking part of the way with the Rev. J. H. and Mrs. Rogers, to the Tête Noire, where we lunched. I rested, but Frances, as usual, found ministering work. Then away to the Col de Forclaz, a satisfactory distance ! The next morning we walked to the Croix de Martigny, and then turned up the road towards St. Bernard, and slept at Lembranchier.

August 5.—By diligence to Orsière, interesting ride; all the travellers joined in singing "Seulement pour Toi," and even the driver tried to sing the bass, whereon Frances jumped up by him ; I do think she would make any one sing.

We reached the hospice of St. Bernard on Saturday, and were gracefully received by the good Father Hess.

Sunday, August 6.—Clear, cloudless sunshine. Sat under the rocks with Frances, reading Exod. xxxiii. 21, 22, of that rock and that clift in the rock, where the glory " passed by," connecting it with John xvii. 24, the glory which will not pass away, but which we shall behold forever.

When the chapel bells tolled for mass, Frances said that *for once* she should like to try joining in the service. I did not go, having tried it, and felt utterly wretched and the clearest conviction I was grieving God. In half an hour Frances returned distressed with the service, and expressed her grief that Protestant tourists often join in that form which involves downright error and idolatry. Nor did she find the music soothing or elevating, it was "just aggravating and monotonous." Just then five St. Bernard dogs came out; they barked at me, but immediately caressed Frances : instinctive discernment! There were many groups of peasants scattered about; they seem to make this a picnic pilgrimage, receiving food and lodging. We made sundry friends; even a large group of card-players put their cards away and thanked us for civil warnings. Leaflets and portions were gladly received. At four P.M. Frances, a traveller from Boston, and I enjoyed a service in the very hush of those rocky aisles and vast icy temples Frances chose Psalm xxii. 31 and Psalm xxiii., also Zephaniah iii.

After dinner Frances sang, by request of Father Hess, "Comfort ye," then "Seulement pour Toi," in which many joined. Being asked to sing her own music, she gave "Whom having not seen ye love."* It was evidently thrilling to all, and Signor Luigi and others expressed their admiration to me. They didn't know how Frances had prayed that her song might be a King's message.

August 8.—Walked back to Orsière. ~

9*th.*—Explored the Val de Feri. I will detail an in-

---

* Shortly to be published, by Hutchings & Romer.

cident illustrative of many others. I always carry a tiny kettle and tea, for our refreshment. The wind blew out my pine-cone fire, so we went to a chalet for boiling water. The little maiden put brown bread, which required chopping, and goat's cheese on the table. She had never tasted tea, and did not seem to like it at all.

I asked Constance* if there was any one ill in the village.

"Yes, little Aline; she used to lie alone all day long, till I asked her father to put the key under a stone, that I might get in. Aline has no mother."

I followed Constance up some dark stairs into a room like a hay-loft. A little tired face looked up from the rough bed:

"Oh, Marie! I am so ill; is father come? He went away so early."

Alone, alone, locked up in that cold loft, some greasy soup in a can, and a hard crust! Dear little Aline! I sat down by her and fed her with some jelly and biscuits, and sent Constance for some new milk. I took the thin hot hand and said in French:

"Dear Aline, there is One who loves you very much: the kind, good Jesus; do you know Him?"

Yes, she knew the name of Jesus, and that He died on the cross; but she did not seem to know it really was for her, in her stead. She seemed to drink in all that was said, and learnt this prayer: "Lord Jesus, wash me in Thy blood; take me in Thy arms."

---

* Marie Constance Jodant, in the village of Isere près d'Orsière.

I don't think Aline will be hungry again, for it was easy to arrange for a supply of milk. And Victorine, the daughter of our hotel-keeper at Orsière, promised to go often and take her nourishing food. Meanwhile Frances had been at work in a chalet ; I cannot recount half she does!

August 10.—Walked up to the Lac de Champé, and the next morning Frances found the way through the Gorge du Durnand ; we always enjoy unknown routes. Thence to Martigny, and by diligence to Champéry, where we remained till August 28th.

At Champéry the delightful ministrations of Mr. Rogers, the chaplain, new friendships, and Frances' incessant ministries, whether by song, or conversation, or Bible reading, filled up every day. One evening, after playing the Moonlight Sonata, an aged German lady assured me that it quite recalled Beethoven's own rendering of it.

After leaving Champéry, *viâ* Berne and Interlachen, we stayed at the Pension Schönfels. The pressure of letters seemed to follow Frances everywhere, and I remember how goodnaturedly she corrected roll after roll of poetical compositions by a stranger, although she was suffering extremely from the effects of being caught in a thunderstorm in an excursion from Champéry. While staying at the Pension Schönfels, the Baroness von Cramm and Miss Carmichael joined us from Champéry. Poor Frances could not join in any excursions, nor did she attempt writing any circular letters, as in former tours. She told me that in writing those circulars she rather avoided expressing either the

spiritual or the poetical ideas suggested ; so she wrote
" Holiday Work," and " Our Swiss Guide," as glimpses
of her practical work for Christ, and those celestial
revelations which Alpine scenery constantly unfolded
to her mind. It was at this time, however, that she
wrote the following sonnet to her friend the Baroness
Helga von Cramm :

TO HELGA.

COME down, and show the dwellers far below
 What God is painting in each mountain place !
 Show His fair colours, and His perfect grace,
Dowering each blossom born of sun and snow :
His tints, not thine ! Thou art God's copyist,
 O gifted Helga ! His thy golden height,
 Thy purple depth, thy rosy sunset light,
Thy blue snow-shadows, and thy weird white mist.
Reveal His works to many a distant land !
 Paint for His praise, oh paint for love of Him !
He is thy Master, let Him hold thy hand,
 So thy pure heart no cloud of self shall dim.
At His dear feet lay down thy laurel-store,
Which crimson proof of thy redemption bore.

 September 19*th*, 1876.

A letter has been sent to me, written about this time,
which may interest some.

PENSION SCHÖNFELS.

MY VERY DEAR MARGARET :

I can't tell you how your letter touched me. I never
thought He would let me give you a lift, who were
already so bright and devoted. I tried to help other
folks at Champéry, but I did not try with you, only just
said what came uppermost. Oh I am so glad you see

the "only for Jesus " in its special power. Having seen
it, one wants to live it out, simply and entirely, and we
can only go on trusting the Lord Jesus hour by hour to
show us how. I wonder what He is going to show us
next, dear M.! for He has so many things to say to us,
as we can bear them. We have been guided to a wonderfully quiet pension, off the usual beat. Seven Germans here, only one of whom can speak any English.
In answer to your query: well, I'll see about it; and
if I can get a chance of being decently photographed,
I will send you a copy; but I am sure you won't like
it, because the prevailing tone of my results under photo-
graphic torture is, " resignation under afflictive dispen-
sations!" which a cheerful friend suggested as the
most suitable inscription on my photos, of which she
declined to accept one! Query No. 3: "This is not
your rest " really does seem to be written on every attempt I make to find a quiet perch (as for a nest, I
don't dream of that). If one set of fatigues is done
with, another arises, personal or postal; but I really
stand as good a chance here as anywhere, I think, so
that will be a relief to your mind. And it has been
enforced the last two days, because I left Champéry
with a sharp sore throat, which developed into that sort
of cold that has made me totally stupefied yesterday and
to-day, and I have been in bed a good many extra
hours. It was such a pleasure to meet you and dear
Edith at C——; it is such a pleasure to recollect it,
and will be ditto if we can some fine day come over
and see you again. I think Maria is more likely to be
free to do so than I. I am not quite so freely situated
as she is, and have far more arrears to make up too, of

long promised visits, as my long invalidism has thrown me far behindhand in that respect; and being seldom strong enough for any winter travelling limits my time for getting through my visits.

Yours lovingly,

F. R. H.

When she was better we went to the village of Eizenflou, hoping for a fine sunrise on the Jungfrau. A feverish cold detained me there. Frances went to the village schoolmaster and secured the use of his schoolroom for a service the next evening, as her spirit was stirred up by finding no pastor ever came near these villages, and they were five miles from church. The evening was wet, and I wanted Frances not to go; but she said, "I may never come here again; and no man cares for these scattered sheep." The room was quite full. Frances addressed them in German from 1 John i. 7, and also led the hymns from their chorale book. Our hostess' report was: "Never, no never, had any one told them what the dear young lady did; it was wonderful! They never could forget her words; and surely she must be a born German!"

From Schönfels we went to the Pension Wengen, above Lauterbrunnen, for several weeks.

October 1.—Unclouded sunshine. The Jungfrau and Silberhorn were radiant. Frances remarked, "It will be one of the new delights of heaven to be able to express all one's thoughts." The next day we took horses to the Scheideck Hotel. After resting, we rode up the Lauberhorn, with Hans Lauener for our guide. He seemed such a nice fellow, and sang some French hymns with Frances, on the top of the mountain.

I had the audacity to sketch the Silberhorn for Mary Fay. In the evening Frances called me to watch the singular effect of the moon rising behind sharp jutting rocks; the silver rays of an invisible but coming presence were most striking.

Another day we went to the Mettlen Alp, which Frances thinks the finest view in Switzerland, through pine woods, and then I stood with her on the silver steps of the Jungfrau's throne. What then? Avalanches and our silent Alleluias! Here it may be of interest to quote copy of the entry in the visitors' book, at Pension Wengen :

Summer returned; cloudless sky. Thermometer from 90° to 100° during our stay. Obliging attentions, honest charges, and tried truthfulness. The Mettlen Alp stands out in picturesque beauty. "All thy works praise *Thee*." Avalanche Alleluias will long echo in English homes.

MARIA V. G. HAVERGAL.
FRANCES RIDLEY HAVERGAL.

Sept. 23rd till Oct. 16th, 1876.

This was Frances' last excursion ; her health entirely failed.

October 8.—Frances in acute pain all day, and could not get up at all. She wrote the hymn,—" I take this pain, Lord Jesus." They brought lukewarm water for fomentations, so I dived into the kitchen and secured a saucepan, gathered pine cones and wood, and got leave to use the salon stove night and day.

October 9 *and* 10.—Frances moaning all day, but so wonderfully patient, even in sleepless nights. I could not say "Thy will be done," till she spoke so sweetly of texts that hush and gladden her. She verily exults in that declaration, "I love, I love my Master!" (Exod. xxi. 5), connecting it with Rev. xxii. 6, " shall serve Him for ever."

October 12.—Tried camomile fomentations, at midnight, and darling Frances so grateful ; I never nursed any one so uncomplaining. Reading to her, "Let Thy judgments help me," I asked her what it meant. She said, " I think God's judgments prove our faith, forcing us to trust more, to lean more. 'Help,' because He comes so very close, helps us when no one else can."

Madame Lauener, the mother of our host, often came up to Frances' room. She is intensely fond of Frances, and repeats Scripture in German, and prays most soothingly by her.

October 13.—Mrs. Simpson (English Pension) came all the way from Interlachen, bringing remedies, fruit and jelly for Frances ; so extremely kind, as we are comparative strangers.

Frances sent for me to hear Madame Lauener repeat from memory the seventh chapter of the Revelation. Such a picture ! through the window the glisten of the snowy Silberhorn,* on the pillow dear Frances and her golden curls ; by her side the aged woman, who with beaming eye and waving hand emphasized those wonderful words ; truly it brought a glimpse of

---

* See Frontispiece.

" When robed in white before Thee,
    Without one stain or tear,
    Shall all Thy saints adore Thee,
    'Midst wonder, love, and fear."

                    (*Rev. W. H. H.*)

Sunday, October 15.—Frances was decidedly better, and able to take a few steps in the sunshine. Her comment on " For His mercy endureth for ever," was, " that is, every day." It seemed uncertain if we could leave next day, but it is impossible to fidget about anything when with Frances. She playfully said, " Now, Marie, can't you leave me entirely to our Father ! " Another time I was anxious, and she put her hand on mine: " Marie dear, just trust ! Jesus *is* with us, all must come right."

October 16.—Frances better, and able to leave in a chaise à porteur to Lauterbrunnen, from whence she enjoyed the drive to Interlachen. From the lake of Thun the snowy mountains of the Bernese Oberland brightened into sunset glory, and we saw them no more.•

October 18.—Left Basle through Alsace ; the Vosges mountains were dimly outlined, and then we went through a pancake country with straight roads and fields, and straight poplars, to Strasbourg.

October 19.—Frances was too tired to go out, so I raced round Strasbourg. I was extremely interested in the flower market, and had sundry talks with the women. I took a diligence to get a sight of the Rhine, and, walking back by a short cut, got into the fortifica-

tions. The captain was most polite, and allowed me to
speak to a few soldiers, giving them a rapid outline of
what the Captain of our salvation did, and does.

The cathedral is magnificent, but it is so intensely
grievous to see the shrines. One lady kept lighting little tapers at the Virgin's shrine, and another young girl
seemed quite faint with kneeling ; she came and sat by
me, and I had an interesting talk with her.

We then left for Brussels, and arrived in England
October 20th. The 21st from London to Winterdyne
viâ Oxford. Just after leaving Oxford Frances startled
me with : " Marie ! I see it all ; I can write a little book,
' My King ! ' "

That herald light was in her eye, which ever betokens
some direct communication from her King. And the
following letter to M. A. C. shows how prayerfully she
afterwards wrote it, trusting for every word to be given
her.

November 1, 1876. OAKHAMPTON.

I REALLY cannot let this be " gratis," though the next
shall be. I am so delighted and thankful to hear that
you really are going to give the whole winter to God's
work, and that Miss de K. has joined you, and that you
will be strengthening the hands of dear Miss Leigh, in
Paris. Altogether, your letter has made me very happy
and very grateful.

I am better now, but was far worse after you left us
at Schönfels. Two attacks in succession, the second
causing nearly a week of terribly prostrating pain. This
day three weeks I could not even stand alone ! So the

only thing seemed to be to seize the very first day of being anyhow able to begin the journey from Pension Wengen, and get at least a stage or two nearer home, which we did ; and though we had to take a week about it, and I was very ill on the way, we were brought safely to England. I am now at my eldest sister's, getting up my strength delightfully, and able for walks in the garden. Maria is quite renovated, and sleeps and eats properly, in spite of the really heavy strain upon her to have had to nurse me night and day while really very ill. Maria is not going to take to herself another wife at all ! (since E. Clay's departure to India), so, after all, you won't have the pain of being superseded. She is going to live at Winterdyne for some time, and this is an immense satisfaction to us all.

Do you ever have time to pray for other people's work, now that you have so much before you ? Because, if so, will you ask that He would give me special help in a little book which I want to write, as He may give me strength. The title will be simply " My King," and it will be little daily thoughts for a month, (uniform with the " Bells " and " Pillows," only for grown-up folk,) on thirty-one texts, all from the Old Testament, about our King. It is such a delicious subject, and I have so enjoyed the mere looking out of the texts about it, while not yet strong enough for serious writing ; but I am not sufficient for these things, and never felt more deeply my own insufficiency. Only the idea of the book came so *very* forcibly to my mind that I could not but think He had sent it me ; and so I have done what I never did before, shelved the little work I already had on hand, to do this first. I will send you one of the

19

texts, because possibly you might not have thought of it, and it seems so nice for use. 2 Sam. xix. 20 : the knowledge that Shimei had sinned being the very reason, not for keeping away, but for coming the first of all to meet the king. I took it as the text for a little talk with the servants here, and never found a more telling one. The 2d Book of Samuel is full of exquisite typical texts. The headings of the little daily portions will be such as " The Friendship of the King," " Decision for the King," " The Business of the King," " The Banquet of the King," " Speaking to the King."

It is so utterly bumptious of me to think of writing for grown-ups at all, much more on such a theme, that I feel more entirely shut up to asking and trusting for every word of it, than I ever did before.

Please give my love to dear Miss Leigh. I owe her ever such a debt of gratitude for her kindness, and most helpful influence, with one of my dear nieces.

Good-bye, dearest Margaret ; Paris is not " among plants and hedges," but may you there dwell with the King, for His work. Love to dear Edith when you write.

Yours ever,

F. R. H.

Two years passed away, and I again visited the Pension Wengen, in 1878, with Mrs. Usborne and Miss Cowan. Knowing how much my sister F. R. H. was loved there, I took care, when writing for rooms, to say she was not coming, lest they should be disappointed. But they did not notice it, and so the grandmother eagerly expected her beloved Fraulein Fannie. When I arrived, there she stood, smiling a welcome, but pointed up, saying, "O mein Hans!" Then she went to meet the other horses, searching for F., till seeing she was not come, her wail was quite touching : "O my beloved, my Fraulein Fannie, where are you? why are you not come to comfort me?" Her countenance was still beautiful, but there was now a far-off look in her eyes, sorrow for some one gone. And so it was; her son Hans, our bright young guide to the Mettlen Alp and the Lauberhorn, had met with an accident and died. His mother and brother gave me the following particulars.

All the winter Hans had been most active in relieving the peasants and going to their scattered chalets with soup and food, often through deep snow. There is a society here for that purpose, and Hans was its most useful member.

Some of the mountain land and pine woods, adjoining the Pension Wengen, belonged to him and his brother Ulrich. These pines are thinned, cut down, and taken into the valley beneath, and there sawn into planks. After the branches are cut off, the pines are brought to the glissade, which is formed by the freezing of some mountain stream, over which lies a deep bed of frozen snow. On the morning of March 5th, 1878, Hans, his brother Ulrich, and twenty men were thus at work. It requires great skill to steer the pine and keep it steadily in its torrent slide. Hans was ever the first, enjoying the dash of power requisite to guide the giant pine down that icy path. But in a moment the pine swayed out of its course, Hans was struck down, the whole weight of the pine crushing his side and leg. A mattress and pillows were brought, his brother wisely taking him at once to Lauterbrunnen, where he would be nearer a doctor than at home. Skilfully was he carried to the Hotel Staubbach, and a telegram soon brought doctors from Interlachen. But nothing could be done, the loss of blood was too great to allow of amputation. Hans was calm and patient, though in agony. He told them that "he had his passport all ready, that he saw the path of life before him, and he was quite sure he was in it."

He lived three days, during which the pastor, who was rationalistic, visited Hans, and the words of the dying guide spoke of a better hope. Hans told him, that no works, no merit, no good and noble life, gave him any comfort now, but it was the sacrifice of Jesus on the cross, and the precious blood there shed to put away sin, that was his "passport."

"It is believing in Jesus Christ brings me this joy. Without the blood that atones for sin, I could not stand accepted before the throne."

The pastor heard and believed; this testimony brought new light and life to him, and a crown to the dying Hans. (Since then his sermons are quite evangelistic). His only sorrow was to leave his mother and brother, but even then he comforted them : "God has prepared a place also for you, my brother. Mother, my mother, there is only a short course for you to run." Hans spoke of F. R. H., and more than once sang the hymn in which they had joined on the heights of the Lauberhorn.

"Vers le ciel, vers le ciel,
   J'entends, Jésus, Ton appel,
O mon cœur, vers toi s'élance
Dans la joyeuse espérance
   De se voir, Emmanuel !"

And then with the ancient passport of "the blood," the young guide passed upward, and entered in "through the gates into the city." He died March 8th, 1878.

It is now October, 1881, and in F. R. H.'s study there lies her motto card, "My own text," identical with the dying guide's "passport," "The blood of Jesus Christ His Son cleans*eth* us from all sin" (1 John i. 7).

XIV

THE VOICE OF MANY WATERS.

FAR away I heard it,
    Stealing through the pines,
Like a whisper saintly,
Falling dimly, faintly,
    Through the terraced vines.

Freshening breezes bore it
    Down the mountain slope ;
So I turned and listened,
While the sunlight glistened
    On the snowy cope.

Far away and dreamy
    Was the voice I heard ;
Yet it pierced and found me,
Through the voices round me—
    Song without a word.

All the life and turmoil,
    All the busy cheer,
Melted in the flowing
Of that murmur, growing,
    Claiming all my ear.

What the mountain-message
    I could never tell ;
Such Æolian fluting
Hath no language suiting
    What we write and spell.

Rather did it enter
    Where no words can win,
Touching and unsealing
Springs of hidden feeling,
    Slumbering deep within.

Voice of many waters
    Only heard afar !
Hushing, luring slowly,
With an influence holy,
    Like the orient star.

————

Follow where it leadeth,
    Till we stand below
While the noble thunder
Wins the hush of wonder,
    Silent in its glow.

Light and sound triumphant
    Fill the eye and ear ;
Every pulse is beating
Quick, unconscious greeting
    To the vision near.

Rainbow flames are wreathing
    In the dazzling foam,
Fancy far transcending,
Power and beauty blending
    In their radiant home.

All the dreamy longing
 Passes out of sight,
In a swift surrender
To the joyous splendour
 Of this song of might.

Self is lost and hidden
 As it peals along ;
Fevered introspection,
Paler-browed reflection
 Vanish in the song.

For the spirit, lifted
 From the dulling mists,
Takes a stronger moulding,
As the sound, unfolding,
 Bears it where it lists.

Voice of many waters !
 Must we turn away
From the crystal chorus
Now resounding o'er us,
 Through the flashing spray ?

Far away we hear it,
 Floating from the sky
Mystic echo, falling
Through the stars, and calling
 From the thrones on high.

There are voices round us,
 Busy, quick, and loud ;
All day long we hear them,
We are still so near them,
 Still among the crowd.

Yet athwart the clamour
    Falls it, faint and sweet,
Like the softest harp-tone,
Passing every sharp tone
    Down the noisy street.

To the soul-recesses
    Cleaving then its way,
Waking hidden yearning,
Unwilled impulse turning
    To the far away.

Far away and viewless,
    Yet not all unknown ;
In the murmur tracing
Soft notes interlacing
    With familiar tone.

So we start and listen !
    While the murmur low
Falleth ever clearer,
Swelleth fuller, nearer,
    In melodious flow.

Voice of many waters*
    From the height above,
Hushing, luring slowly,
With its influence holy,
    With its song of love !

Following where it leadeth,
    Pilgrim feet shall stand
Where the holy millions
Throng the fair pavilions
    In the Glorious land.

Where the sevenfold " Worthy ! '
　　Hails the King of kings,
Blent with golden clashing
Of the crowns, and flashing
　　Of cherubic wings ;

Rolls the Amen Chorus,
　　Old, yet ever new ;
Seal of blest allegiance,
Pledge of bright obedience,
　　Seal that God is true.

Through the solemn glory
　　Alleluias rise,
Mightiest exultation,
Holiest adoration,
　　Infinite surprise.

There immortal powers
　　Meet immortal song ;
Heavenly image bearing,
Angel-essence sharing,
　　Excellent and strong.

Strong to bear the glory
　　And the veil-less sight,
Strong to swell the thunders
And to know the wonders
　　Of the home of light.

Voice of many waters !
　　Everlasting laud !
Hark ! it rushes nearer,
Every moment clearer,
　　From the throne of God !

www.ingramcontent.com/pod-product-compliance
Lightning Source LLC
Chambersburg PA
CBHW020853020726
47497CB00005B/1382